DESPERATE CREED

Prairie Wind Publishing
Omaha, Nebraska

DESPERATE CREED

Attention: Permissions Coordinator
Prairie Wind Publishing
15418 Weir Street
Box 207
Omaha, NE 68137

This is a work of fiction. Names, characters, places, and incidents are a product of the author's imagination. Locales and public names are sometimes used for atmospheric purposes. Any resemblance to actual people, living or dead, or to businesses, companies, events, institutions, or locales is completely coincidental.

Ordering Information:
Quantity sales. Special discounts are available on quantity purchases by corporations, associations, and libraries. For information, please email the Sales Department at sales@pwindpub.com

Interior design and formatting: Prairie Wind Publishing
Book cover design: Prairie Wind Publishing
Jacket photograph: Zivica Kerkez, Shutterstock

FIRST EDITION

ISBN: 978-1-7320064-9-2 Hardcover
ISBN: 978-1-7320064-1-6 eBook
ISBN: 978-1-7320064-2-3 Paperback:

Printed in the United States of America
10 9 8 7 6 5 4 3 2 1

ALSO BY ALEX KAVA

RYDER CREED SERIES

Breaking Creed
Silent Creed
Reckless Creed
Lost Creed
Desperate Creed

MAGGIE O'DELL SERIES

A Perfect Evil
Split Second
The Soul Catcher
At The Stroke of Madness
A Necessary Evil
Exposed
Black Friday
Damaged
Hotwire
Fireproof
Stranded
Before Evil

THE STAND-ALONE NOVELS

Whitewash
One False Move

NOVELLA ORIGINALS WITH
ERICA SPINDLER AND J. T. ELLISON

Slices of Night
Storm Season

SHORT STORY COLLECTION

Off the Grid

DEDICATION

This book is dedicated to all the dogs
and their handlers
who put their lives at risk after natural disasters
in order to rescue our loved ones and recover
those not quite as fortunate.

AND

In Memory of my boy, Scout,
(March 1998 to May 2014)
who is the *true inspiration* for this series.

Scout

DESPERATE
CREED

When you come out of the storm,
you won't be the same person who walked in.
That's what this storm is all about.
—Haruki Murakami

DAY 1

Friday, March 8

1

Chicago

Frankie Russo's head was already throbbing when her cell phone started blaring salsa music. At five o'clock in the morning she immediately regretted the new ringtone. She tried to tamp down the dread in the pit of her stomach as she stumbled out of the bathroom.

Nobody called at five in the morning with good news.

Her hand swiped along the wall, searching for a light switch in unfamiliar territory. Where had she left her phone? She stumbled just as her fingers found the switch. The unpacked boxes in her new apartment made her dance through a maze. She was dripping wet, adjusting towels, and deep down she caught herself hoping she'd miss the call.

Please just let it go to voicemail.

If it had something to do with her father, she'd rather the news be filtered. A recording didn't wait to hear your reaction.

Finally, Frankie saw her phone on the kitchen counter. Before she touched it, she could see who the caller was and relief washed over her. She was relieved, but at the same time, she was pissed off at the request for a video-chat. She adjusted the towel tighter around her body then answered the phone.

"It's not funny, Tyler," Frankie said to the smiling face. She pushed at the second towel on top of her head, and it almost threw her off balance.

"You know I hate when you want to video-chat with me at home."

"I've been hoping to catch you in a towel." The boyish grin only broadened without a hint of apology.

Frankie was too old for Tyler. Fourteen years older. Yes, she had already done the math. And yet, his inappropriate comment made her blush just a little. Instead of scowling at her co-worker she pretended it was no big deal. She tilted her phone giving him only a headshot and a whole lot of her kitchen ceiling.

The two of them had become comfortable with each other. Probably too comfortable. For almost a year their teamwork on different advertising campaigns had spilled over into their personal lives. Frankie blamed herself for not putting up any boundaries. She was the older and wiser one, the so-called seasoned professional assigned to work with the hotshot new kid, fresh out of college. But suddenly, she and Tyler became the envy of McGavin Holt. Paul McGavin, the managing partner of the advertising firm, had put the two together time after time, highlighting their successes as if it were because of his brilliant decision to make them a team. Frankie didn't care if he bragged or took credit. What mattered more was the much-needed boost to her career. And the timing helped take her mind off the recent failures in her personal life, like the reason for this new apartment.

"You won't believe what Deacon and I discovered," Tyler was saying. "It changes everything."

She took a closer look at him and noticed his beard stubble and tousled hair. He hadn't shaved yet, and he was out walking. She could see streetlamps, brick buildings and slices of empty streets. His eyes were bright and wild, most likely from too little sleep and too much caffeine. If she didn't know him better she'd say he was drunk, but Tyler and his friends didn't drink alcohol. Red Bull and Monster were their addictions.

"Where in the world are you?" she asked. She glanced at the digital clock on the microwave. "It's five-fifteen in the morning."

"I just left Deacon's place. Remember I told you about my friend,

Deke? Deacon Kaye? You said he sounded like a rapper. He loved that, by the way." He was rambling.

"Why are you calling me, Tyler?"

"Remember I said I was going to have him use one of their labs to do a chemical breakdown of those organic breakfast bars?"

"And remember *I told you* we don't get paid to do chemical breakdowns. Tyler, we're supposed to be creating a marketing campaign."

"What about honesty, Frankie? There's nothing organic about this product."

"Honesty?" She laughed while she put down the phone to pour herself a cup of coffee. At least she had unpacked and set up the coffeemaker. The aroma filled the kitchen, contributing a small semblance to her upside down life. "We work for an advertising and marketing agency, Tyler." She readjusted the towel on her head and tucked the one around her body a bit tighter before picking up the phone again. "That energy drink we worked on last month doesn't really give anyone super powers."

"No, but it also won't give you cancer."

She frowned at him. His smile was gone, but he was still wound up.

"Glyphosate showed up in all the samples. And that's not all, Frankie, the levels are pretty high, beyond the limits of safe. Glyphosate's an herbicide. It's found in weed killers. The World Health Organization considers it a carcinogen that can cause cancer in anybody who works around it on a regular basis. It's not supposed to show up in food. Carson Foods has been hiding it in their research. They know about it, Frankie. If glyphosate can cause cancer from handling it, can you imagine what it does if you eat it?" He brought the phone closer and said, "And how bout if you eat it every morning for breakfast?"

He said all this with too much bravado, reminding Frankie that he was still just a kid. He also sounded a bit out of breath but continued to walk.

"Look, Tyler, maybe you should ask Mr. McGavin to take you off the project."

"Cancer, Frankie."

She rolled her eyes and took a sip of coffee.

"Did you just roll your eyes at me?"

"Do you know how many things supposedly cause cancer?" She held up her mug. "Depending on what latest survey you read, coffee causes cancer. Being out in the sun causes cancer. Doesn't mean I'm going to stop drinking coffee or spend the rest of my life indoors."

"The breakfast bars aren't the only things. I gave Deke samples from some of their other products. My little brother eats these cereals every morning. Sometimes a bowl after school. Regulations call for employees handling glyphosate to wear gloves, so they don't get it on their skin, but Carson Foods has no problem with it being on our food. And the worst part, the executives at the top not only know it's showing up in their food, but that the levels are too high. They're manipulating the data."

Frankie held back another eye roll. She appreciated Tyler's enthusiasm and the way he threw himself into their assignments. Everything was new and exciting to him. Fresh out of college, he really believed he could change the world. She vaguely remembered that feeling. But sometimes, being around him was simply exhausting.

"So why isn't anybody suing them?"

She watched as he held the phone up closer as if he didn't want the empty streets to hear what he was about to share. Even his voice was now just above a whisper.

"There is a lawsuit pending. But just a few days ago the guy got hit by a car."

He paused like he was waiting for his revelation to sink in, but Frankie shook her head. "Tyler—"

"Last week, Deke and I hacked into their CEO's emails. He's talking to a senator about some huge global deal for their products. I've got copies downloaded on my laptop. I sent you a copy. Listen to me, Frankie, they know. They know this stuff is bad. They're hiding it, and they're doing everything they can to keep it from coming out."

"Hacked?" She banged her coffee mug down on the counter before she spilled it. "Are you crazy? You could get arrested. And don't get me involved by sending me anything."

"Actually, I offered to show the emails to a police detective, and he told me to forget about it."

"Tyler, he's right."

"I know the cops aren't interested. We need to go higher to the federal level. You told me you know someone at the FBI."

"I told you I know someone who knows someone at the FBI. You really do need to forget about this."

"This is serious stuff, Frankie."

"Maybe we should talk to Mr. McGavin about reassigning you to a different campaign."

"I already talked to him. But not about being reassigned. I told him about the levels of glyphosate and that maybe we shouldn't be marketing this stuff."

"You what? And when did you do this?"

"On Monday."

Frankie had taken the week off to move. One week! Why the hell hadn't he told her first? They were supposed to be a team. But instead of asking any of that, she wanted to know, "What did he say?"

"He told me he'd look into it. But I could tell he wasn't going to."

"Why do you say that?"

"Just the way he said it. Hold on, there's a couple of guys here. They look lost."

Tyler dropped his hand to his side giving Frankie a view of the sidewalk and a slice of Tyler's legs. Beyond him she could see someone else from the knees down. Nice shiny, polished shoes unlike Tyler's scuffed and dusty tennis shoes. She kept telling him how much shoes defined a person, especially in their business. If a marketing account rep didn't pay attention to his own appearance, how could he convince a CEO that he could be entrusted with an entire company's image?

"What's up?" she heard Tyler ask, his voice muffled but calm.

She picked up her coffee mug waiting for him while she processed how much trouble he'd caused. She wondered if Mr. McGavin thought she was in lock step with Tyler. She'd put a lot of time and energy into this project. She didn't want to get thrown off. What kind of reputation would this get her?

She could barely hear the other men, but Tyler's tone suddenly changed from calm to guarded. The phone bobbed up, and she caught a glance at the two men. Both of them were white. One huge, one average. Jogging suits.

The discussion started to get heated, but their words were muffled.

Tyler's pitch rose. Something was wrong. He raised his hand with the phone as if he were bracing for a blow.

"Tyler, what's going on?"

She heard a pop-pop, like a car backfiring. But it wasn't a car. The street was empty. Tyler sea-sawed in and out of her view. She got a glance at his face. His eyes were wide.

Was that blood on his forehead?

Then the hand fell away, and all she could see was the sidewalk as the phone's screen slapped against the concrete.

"Tyler?" Frankie shouted into her own phone. "What the hell's going on?"

Did he trip? But she knew he hadn't. Had one of the men punched him? Was it really blood she had seen on his face?

She needed to dial 911, but she didn't want to break the connection.

"Tyler? Are you okay? Answer me."

Seconds passed. Finally a sliver of light returned then she saw the sidewalk. The phone started rising, and her view pulled back up. She heard a muffled voice. But it wasn't Tyler's.

"He was on his phone." A man said, his voice deep and not happy.

The sidewalk flipped away, and a face filled the screen. Dark eyes squinted at her. A beak-like nose like a hawk and thick black eyebrows on a huge forehead. He pulled away and turned his head. He mouthed something to the other man. The movement was enough to reveal an ugly scar peeking out from under his shirt collar.

Frankie's coffee mug crashed to the floor, and his eyes darted back to the screen. She held the phone at arm's length while she squeezed and punched buttons. She needed to end the call. Finally, the screen went blank then returned to her screensaver. She slid the phone onto the countertop.

She couldn't breathe. She was shaking and wrapped the damp towel tighter around her body. Her mind raced. She needed to do something.

The sound of salsa music vibrated against granite, and she jumped. Her phone came to life. The screen pulsed with Tyler's number. Was it possible he was okay?

Without picking it up, Frankie reached over making sure she was out of the camera's sight. She tapped the button and the screen came to life. But it wasn't Tyler's face.

A dark sky filled most of the screen with the glare of a lamppost. She could still see a slice of the man who held the phone at arm's length. His silence told her that he had called back to get a better look at her. This time Frankie could see something smeared on the bottom screen. Dark red. Not just a smear but droplets. A splatter.

Oh god, was it blood?

Staying out of sight, she eased her hand across the counter and tapped the END CALL button. When she was certain the call had been disconnected, she grabbed the phone. Holding it as if it were a snake threatening to bite, she started to squeeze and click buttons until the screen went black, and until she was sure the phone was completely shut off. Not just on vibrate. Not just airplane mode, but off. Then she slid the contraption on the counter again, this time sending it away from her with such force it crashed against the stovetop.

Still, she stared at it almost expecting the salsa music to blare again. She was cold and trembling. Her heart pounded against her chest. She had been holding her breath, and now her breathing came in short gasps.

She needed to tell someone. She needed to dial 911. And yet, she didn't dare turn the phone back on.

What the hell just happened?

2

Florida Panhandle

Ryder Creed could feel her watching.

Water lapped around him as he held his arms under the big dog. Despite the life vest that kept the dog afloat—and even with the security of Creed's hands cradling him—the dog's ears were pinned back and his eyes were wide.

"It's okay. You're doing great," Creed reassured him using a low, soothing tone that had worked before to calm the dog. But that was in a small rehab tank. Maybe it was a mistake to move to the Olympic-size swimming pool. Perhaps it was too soon.

The dog was a new arrival to the K-9 training facility. Creed and his business partner, Hannah Washington had agreed to take him after his experimental surgery. Knight was a two-year-old, black-muzzled Belgium shepherd. He'd had lost most of his front right leg while serving in Afghanistan. His prosthetic was a marvel of science and medical technology. It still amazed Creed how well the dog had adjusted to his new artificial limb. Being submerged in the large body of water wasn't only about adjusting to and using the new leg. It was also about trusting his new handler.

"I'm not going to let anything happen to you," Creed was saying when he noticed the dog's nose sniffing the air. Knight could smell her. He knew there was an intruder. "It's okay," Creed told him, bringing one of his hands up out of the water to pet him. "Everything's okay."

From the corner of his eye Creed could see her tucked into the shadows of the fieldhouse. His sister, Brodie looked and acted more like a young girl. In many ways she was exactly as he remembered. For sixteen years he imagined her as that same eleven-year-old girl he'd watched skipping in the rain, crossing the parking lot and into a rest stop bathroom, only to disappear into thin air.

It was less than five months since they'd been reunited. Only two months since she'd come to live with him and Hannah.

Not unlike the Belgium shepherd, Brodie came with her own injuries that needed healing. So even now, he let her watch from the shadows when he really wanted to tell her she was spooking the dog. But acknowledging her presence might *spook her*. He knew she tried to hide even that. She was doing her best to be brave when everything around her was new and difficult.

She had gotten used to shoving her emotions aside during her captivity when there were other daily needs she had to deal with, like being hungry or cold or left in the dark. But despite her attempt at pretending she was doing okay, Creed could see the truth in her eyes. Just like the shepherd, Creed could sense her discomfort.

When Brodie first came to live with them, she followed him around as if she was afraid to let him leave her sight. Creed felt like he had a ghost silently stalking him from behind trees and around corners. She had been gone from him—gone from the world, really—for longer than she'd been with him. She was still gauging her freedom, testing and pushing the limits, reaching and feeling for the boundaries.

Now he could see her edging closer.

To the shepherd, Creed said, "Don't be afraid. You're okay," but this time he said it louder, hoping to include Brodie.

She had admitted she was afraid of dogs. Early on, she told Creed that her captor, a woman named Iris Malone, had sent a dog to attack Brodie once when she tried to escape. Creed had seen the scar on her ankle. The bite must have been bone-deep. There was nothing he could say to make her trust another dog. But Grace, Creed's scrappy, little Jack Russell terrier, had come a long way in convincing Brodie that not all dogs would attack her. Creed knew this was a lesson Brodie would need to learn directly from a dog if she intended to make a home here.

The fifty-acre property was a training facility for K9 scent dogs. The kennel—with dog runs and acres of fenced-in yard—was home to dozens of dogs of all sizes and breeds. They came here from shelters; some had been dropped off at the end of their long driveway. Hannah liked to say they rescued abandoned and discarded dogs and turned them into heroes. When she told Brodie this, it seemed to make an impression. The idea of being abandoned was something she could understand.

Now suddenly, Brodie was at the edge of the swimming pool. Creed hadn't even heard her. She had learned to be quiet all those years she'd spent trying to make herself invisible. Perhaps there was a future for her in some clandestine profession, because he hadn't seen her approach the pool. He barely saw her now, but the dog told him she was there. His nose sniffed the air, and he was paddling to turn himself around, trying to get a good look at her. He wasn't panicked. He was excited.

Creed kept his attention on the dog as he guided Knight to the shallow end.

"What happened to his leg?" Brodie asked as if it was perfectly normal for her to sneak out of the shadows then engage in a casual conversation.

One of the first things she had asked of her brother was to tell her the truth, always. No matter how painful he thought it might be. And, she told him she didn't want it "sugarcoated."

"He was a bomb sniffing dog in Afghanistan."

"Like Rufus?"

He'd shared with Brodie how he and Rufus had worked as a team finding IEDs and clearing a path to protect units of Marines in Afghanistan. Until one day a young boy from the village brought a bomb into their camp. A bomb strapped and hidden on his small body.

Rufus had alerted, but by the time Creed made the connection, it was too late.

Creed was sent home, but Rufus' injuries weren't severe enough. After they patched him up, the dog was returned to service with another Marine handler. It cost Creed a favor to a man he didn't respect, along with a vow of silence, but he got to bring Rufus back and the two were reunited. The dog still slept at the foot of Creed's bed.

"Yes, like Rufus," Creed told Brodie.

"But the bomb went off? He missed it?" She looked confused.

"No," Creed corrected her. "His handler missed it."

"Did his handler lose a leg, too?"

"His handler was killed."

He checked her face. Her eyes were on the dog, but there was no emotion. It was one of the hardest things for Creed to accept about his sister. She displayed few feelings. Turning off her emotions had allowed Brodie to survive. But she was twenty-seven years old and after spending all of those years in isolation, he couldn't help wondering if she'd ever be able to turn that mechanism on again.

The dog started swimming toward Brodie, anxious to meet her. Creed expected her to bolt. Or at least, move away.

To his surprise, Brodie lowered herself to the side of the pool then sat, dangling her legs over the edge. She had no fear of water and was still a good swimmer. At least there were a few things Iris Malone hadn't stolen from her.

The dog was so anxious he'd forgotten his earlier dependency on Creed. He was paddling on his own, leaving Creed to follow. But it was obvious he was exhausted, and Brodie seemed to sense it. Almost instinctively, she slid into the pool—shoes, shorts and T-shirt. The water came to her waist. She didn't seem to notice or care. She grabbed for the handle on the dog's vest, and he bumped into her, grateful and ready to be helped out of the water.

Creed swam up beside them just as the dog licked Brodie's face and was rewarded with a rare smile. He was impressed that she didn't wince or pull back.

She noticed his surprise but instead of addressing it, she asked, "Can he walk on his own?"

"Yes, but I need to help him out of the pool. I don't want him to slip on the steps."

She allowed Creed to take over, relinquishing the fact that she didn't have the upper body strength to help the dog.

"Swimming will help him build back his muscles without putting pressure on his shoulder," he explained as he hugged the dog close to his body and walked up the stairs.

She climbed out of the pool and stood beside them. Creed handed her a towel. But he noticed Brodie kept her distance from the dog. She didn't reach down to pet him. Instead, she awkwardly wiped her arms and legs, but didn't wrap the towel around herself.

He looked up to the windows that ran the length of the fieldhouse. Just like in the kennel, he'd purposely designed them to be above eye-level so the dogs couldn't see out and wouldn't be distracted while they were training. But Creed could see the morning sunshine was being replaced by dark storm clouds. He saw a flash of lightning. Brodie noticed, too, but rather than triggering concern, it simply reminded her of something.

"Oh, I forgot to tell you," she said. "Hannah sent me to tell you there are storms coming, and you need to get out of the pool."

3

The rumble of thunder that followed was still in the distance. Creed smiled to himself. Evidently, thunder and lightning didn't bother or impress Brodie.

"Maybe I could swim with you guys sometime."

She was still focused on the dog. Another streak of lightning lit up the sky, and Brodie barely glanced at it. Creed looked up at her as he towel-dried the dog. In the last several months, he'd seen her flinch at the sight of a syringe and jump at the sound of a knock on the front door. But she seemed unaffected by the approaching storm.

There had to have been plenty of severe weather in Nebraska. That's where they had finally found her, locked inside an abandoned farmhouse in the middle of nowhere.

"Thunder and lightning doesn't bother you?" he asked, curiosity finally getting the best of him.

Her eyes darted to the windows. In that brief moment Creed caught a glimpse of the little girl he remembered. Her once long hair was cut so short it spiked up in places. She insisted it be short, sometimes taking scissors and cutting it herself. Though taller now, her adult figure was skinny, straight-hipped and flat-chested, the result of malnutrition. She looked more like a young teenager than a woman in her late twenties. And now she seemed almost embarrassed that she hadn't given the storm proper attention. She glanced at him and shrugged.

"I was usually in the basement," she said casually as though it was as simple as that—a basement, not a prison. "It was the one place safe from the storms," she added.

Her eyes flicked up to the windows again and back to Creed. "Do we need to get to the basement?"

He looked up and gave the slice of darkening sky careful consideration. If Hannah had sent Brodie to bring him in she must be watching the weather forecast. He waited for the next flash of lightning then counted to himself—one one-thousand, two one-thousand, three one-thousand, four one-thousand—then came the rumble of thunder.

"The storm's still a few miles away," he finally answered Brodie. "I need to get Knight settled back in the kennel and check on the other dogs. But you can head back to the house if you want."

As they approached the glass door to the outside, Brodie's eyes darted in the direction of the kennel. From the outside, the building looked like a contemporary warehouse that had been renovated into condominiums. In fact, his loft apartment took up the second story. Brodie had been up to his living quarters through the outside access, but she'd rarely ventured into the kennel.

Lately, she seemed less afraid of the dogs. Even the way she handled Knight gave Creed hope. But he also understood the kennel could be overwhelming for her just because of the sheer number of dogs. He'd seen her walk the long way around to avoid getting too close to the fence line when the dogs were running and playing in the yard.

He was about to tell her that he'd meet her back at the house when she surprised him, again, by saying, "Maybe I can help you check on them."

"You sure?"

He watched her eyes as she nodded. Nothing seemed to get by her. Her eyes scanned, flickered, examined everything and then started all over.

Creed opened the door and a blast of air hit him in the face. The breeze was filled with moisture—salty and warm as if the Gulf of Mexico was on the other side of the woods. It made him look up and study the clouds overhead, dark and swollen, moving slowly but not rotating. The low rumble of thunder suggested they had only a few more minutes, if that.

As they walked the short distance to the kennels he glanced at Brodie. He followed her eyes to the back door where Jason was hauling in a new delivery of dog food.

Jason Seaver was their only dog trainer and handler who lived on the property. His double-wide trailer was a stone's throw away from the main house and the kennels. He had come to them almost two years ago, a veteran sent home from Afghanistan after an IED explosion. The first time Creed met him Jason had a chip on his shoulder, ready to wrangle anyone who raised an eyebrow at his empty sleeve where his left arm was missing. He was belligerent, sullen and even suicidal, but Hannah had insisted Jason reminded her of Creed when she'd first met him. She had offered Jason a job along with an apprenticeship.

Jason and Creed had butted heads at times, and Creed shook his head wondering what Hannah had been thinking. But just as she never questioned him when he brought another dog home, no matter how skinny and mangy the dog looked, Creed didn't question Hannah's wisdom. Despite their differences, Creed conceded that he and Jason did have something in common. Both of them had come home from Afghanistan angry and broken. Creed finally offered the kid the two things that had ultimately saved him...a dog and a purpose.

Creed looked over at Brodie as they came in the same door that Jason had gone in. Jason glanced up at them, not missing a beat as he stacked and unloaded. He didn't seem to think it strange at all that Brodie was entering the one place she had been avoiding since she arrived. Another look, and now, Creed saw what may have changed her mind. She was watching Jason with a fascination on her face that Creed hadn't seen before.

Was this new? Or had he simply missed it? How could he miss it? Jason was here every day. He was a permanent fixture of their daily lives. A part of their little family. At their dinner table almost every night.

"Everybody's been fed," Jason said. "They're down and secure."

"What about Molly?" Creed asked. "She was fidgety last time." They hadn't had thunder and lightning since October. Creed had rescued the mixed breed almost a year ago. The dog was the only one of her family to survive a mudslide in North Carolina. Creed's disaster scent dog, Bolo, had pawed the ground insisting there was something underfoot when the rescuers could see only a sheet of metal buried in the ground. The metal ended up being the chassis of a vehicle.

"She's good," Jason said. "She's cuddled up next to Bolo. Those two are pretty tight." He grinned at Brodie. "Bolo sort of rescued her. Did I tell you that story?"

She nodded. "Yes, I remember. I like that one."

Creed looked from Brodie to Jason and back. Something on his face must have alerted Jason, because suddenly, the grin disappeared.

"I've been telling Brodie about the dogs, so she can get to know them."

Jason misunderstood Creed's look of surprise as disapproval and went on to explain, "You know, so she's not so afraid of them."

He hadn't noticed that the two of them were spending time together. How had he not noticed that?

"Jason makes the dogs sound like characters in a book," Brodie explained.

She loved to read. Called it her daily therapy. It made sense, and he wondered why he hadn't thought of it.

"That's a great idea," Creed told Jason.

It was a great idea. And yet, he couldn't figure out why it bothered him that the two of them were spending time together. Maybe he was just being too protective. Probably. And yet, there was a knot of concern in his stomach.

4

Chicago

August Braxton had gained a reputation for taking care of messes. He had planned thoroughly for this operation, trailing both targets for days. In The District he was known for his attention to detail and his ability to eliminate any risk factors. How could he have missed seeing that Tyler Gates was on his phone? Not just on his phone, but video-chatting.

He couldn't even blame Rex for this one. Although the big lug shouldn't have picked up the phone and shown himself. His curiosity too often led to mistakes. As a result, they now had another mess to clean up.

Fortunately, Gates paid attention to detail as well. Not only did he have a photo of Francine Russo in his contacts alongside her phone number, but also, her email address and the connection to her Facebook page. A good thing, because Rex said the woman had a towel on her head. Even when he took a close look at the thumbnail photo of her, he shook his head and shrugged.

It didn't matter. Within seconds, Braxton had HQ track down the home address of Francine Russo. It was still early. They'd be able to pay her a visit before she left for work. They'd get this minor inconvenience taken care of and be done.

Now, as they approached Russo's apartment building, Braxton kept his eyes scanning for cops. Surely, she called 911. But would they have already come to take her statement? At the most, they'd send a black and white.

Chicago was not Braxton's town, but he knew enough to believe the cops had more to concern themselves with than to drive on over and take a hysterical woman's statement. Maybe she could describe Rex, but there was no way to ID him. And if she knew exactly where Gates was when he called her, the cops would send a unit to the street location. A possible murder scene would be their priority.

By the time Braxton and Rex made their way through the lobby and to the elevator, HQ had provided Braxton with a second photo of Francine Russo. It was a professional headshot, taken from the advertising agency's website, confirming that she and Tyler Gates worked together.

Interesting, he thought. Do co-workers video-chat with each other at five o'clock in the morning? She had to be more than a co-worker. She had to know something. The fact that Gates called her almost immediately after leaving his friend's place, led Braxton to presume Russo knew what Gates and Kaye were up to. Perhaps she was a part of it. Again, he wondered how he'd missed her as a piece of this puzzle.

Her apartment building was nice, but as a senior account rep—that's how she was listed on the agency's website—she evidently didn't make enough money to afford a place with a doorman or a secured entry. The elevator was easily accessible. No floor was off limits.

Braxton straightened his tie and gestured for Rex to do the same. They had peeled off the jogging suits and already discarded them along with any blood from either victim. All the while he kept thinking this would be easy. He hated to have a hitch in his plans, but they would simply take care of it. And that would be that.

They stepped off the elevator, and he was pleased to see there were only four units per floor. He gestured for Rex to stand aside and out of sight when Braxton knocked on the door. Russo had, most likely, seen Rex, but Braxton was certain she hadn't seen him.

He turned his head, giving the peephole his best profile. Long ago, he had perfected the appearance of someone in authority. It was all about attitude. Usually he was so successful people didn't ask for an I.D. Even then, they rarely gave a second look at the credentials he flipped at them.

But when the door opened, Braxton had to hold back his surprise. Instead of Francine Russo, a sleepy-eyed man stood in front of him. He was middle-aged with tousled dark hair. His T-shirt showed he was in good shape. A bristled jaw and a coffee cup in one hand, suggested he'd been up for only a short time.

"Yeah, what?"

A tough guy. Or so he thought.

Braxton flicked his eyes to the number on the door though he doubted he'd gotten this wrong.

"I need to talk to Francine Russo," he told the man.

"She doesn't live here anymore."

"Are you sure about that? I have this as her address."

"Yeah, well, she moved out at the beginning of the week."

"I still need to talk to her. What's her new address?"

"Beats me."

"Excuse me? I don't think you understand how important it is that I speak with her."

"Who did you say you were?" Now the man's eyes flicked to the side and he saw Rex. "Is she in some kind of trouble?"

So the man still had feelings for Russo, despite what caused her to move out.

"She won't be if I talk to her soon. How about giving me her new address."

"I don't have it." When he saw that Braxton didn't believe him, he volunteered, "We broke up, okay. I'm not allowed to have her new address. They probably have it at her work. If you're for real, you already know where she works."

Then he shut the door.

Braxton could have shoved his foot in to stop it. He could have easily grabbed the guy by the throat and lifted him a foot off the ground until he promised to give them the new address. That seemed to be exactly what Rex wanted to do, but Braxton put his hand up to stop him.

Brute force wouldn't get them what they wanted here. They'd already made one mistake. It would take just a bit more patience.

5

Frankie Russo let out a frustrated sigh. Tyler could be bleeding on a sidewalk somewhere, and this police officer was treating her more like a criminal than a witness.

"What is your relationship to the alleged victim?"

She'd already told him when she first came in. The 911 dispatcher had recommended she file a report when Frankie realized she had no idea where Tyler was.

"You want to report an assault, but you can't say where it happened?" The dispatcher's voice had been so calm it only made Frankie more hysterical.

In those few minutes, Frankie discovered how little she knew about Tyler. She sort of knew where he lived but she couldn't tell the dispatcher his address. Nor could she tell the woman where Tyler's friend Deacon lived. She didn't even know if K was a middle initial, the beginning of his last name or part of a nickname.

The dispatcher had finally given Frankie directions where to go to file a report.

"We work together at McGavin Holt," she now told the police officer for the second time.

"Nothing more than co-workers?" The detective raised a suspicious eyebrow betraying his monotone voice.

"Nothing more."

"You don't go out after work for drinks?"

"Tyler doesn't drink."

"Meet for coffee?"

"He doesn't drink coffee either."

"But you talked on the phone?"

"Yes."

"Even video-chat? Outside of work."

"It's always about work."

"At five o'clock in the morning?"

Frankie released another sigh and sat back in the metal folding chair. So that part he'd heard.

"Yes."

She wasn't going to explain that when they were working on a campaign sometimes they talked at all kinds of odd hours of the day. They loved their job. She quickly added, "Can you just please check to see if he's okay?"

"But you don't know where the assault took place?"

"No."

"Because you weren't there?"

"I was in my apartment. We were talking on the phone."

"Tell me, again, why you think he was assaulted."

"He said there was a couple of guys. He thought they looked lost, and he dropped the phone. You know, by his side. I could hear him talking to them."

"What did they say?"

"I couldn't really hear what they said to Tyler, but his voice started getting sort of agitated. He put up his hand like he was protecting himself. That's when I heard a pop-pop."

"Pop-pop?"

"It sounded like a car backfiring but it didn't look like there was any traffic on the street."

"What happened after the pop-pop?"

"I saw just a glimpse of Tyler's face then I think he must have fallen. The phone fell. I could see it falling. I could see the sidewalk."

"You never saw the men?"

"Just a sliver of one of them."

"What did he look like?"

"Dark eyes. That's mostly what I saw. Sort of a hawkish nose."

"Black, white, old, young?"

"White." Frankie closed her eyes and struggled to remember. "I was looking at him from an odd angle. From down below, looking up."

The police officer was nodding, waiting.

"Oh, there was a scar. On his neck." Frankie's fingers went to her own, outlining the area. "About two inches, maybe three. Part of it was all knotted, almost like a rope."

Thankfully, he was writing this down. Everything else on his notepad looked like scratches and doodles.

"You didn't see any street signs? Nothing familiar in the background?"

"No. There wasn't anything I recognized." She didn't tell him that she hadn't paid much attention. She was pissed at Tyler for calling that early. She also left out that he'd caught her getting out of the shower and wearing only a towel.

"Your friend, Tyler didn't say where he was coming from?"

"Just that he had left his friend's place."

"What's his friend's name?" The detective's pen hung over the notepad, ready.

"Deacon. Tyler calls him Deacon K. I don't know if K is his middle initial or the beginning of his last name."

Frankie saw the detective glance at his wristwatch as he added "Deacon K" to the notepad. There was no urgency.

Or was it possible he just didn't believe her?

He pulled out a business card and scribbled a phone number on the backside. He handed it across the table to Frankie and said, "If you remember anything else, give me a call."

"That's it?" Frankie asked. "Can't you check if someone reported a man shot?"

"Shot? This is Chicago. Chances are more than one person was shot in the last twenty-four hours."

"What about checking hospitals or his apartment?"

"You said you don't know where his apartment is."

"No, but…you're the police. Aren't you able to look it up?"

He looked at her over the top of his eyeglasses, and she realized how foolish she sounded. Even if she called the advertising agency she wouldn't be allowed Tyler's personal information, including his address. How many Tyler Gates would Google find in the Chicago area?

"If you remember anything else," he said and pointed to the business card in her fingers. "Call me."

6

Frankie drove home. Frustrated. Angry. Only four hours after talking to Tyler, and already she was starting to second-guess what she'd heard and seen. Maybe it wasn't gunfire. But she swore she'd seen blood on his face.

He could have been punched. Maybe the men simply mugged him. Still, he had to be hurt or he would have called her. Was it possible that he was unconscious? Maybe confused and in an emergency room? After his attacker had called her back, Frankie turned her phone off. She'd only turned it back on to quickly dial 911.

What if Tyler had been trying to call her?

She pulled off the busy route and took side streets that led her into a residential area. With her move came a new and unfamiliar neighborhood. More upscale than she was used to seeing. She took a right into the parking lot of a church. At this time on a Friday it was empty except for a van at the back door.

Frankie drove to the far corner, away from any windows. She backed the car into a slot, pointing the nose toward the nearest exit. Suddenly, for the first time in her life she was grateful her father had instilled in her a bit of his quirky paranoia.

She left the engine running. Double-checked that all the doors were locked. She kept the radio on a local news station in case there was anything about Tyler. She dug the cell phone out from the bottom of her handbag, but instead of turning it on right away, she held it in front of her, staring at it.

The incident—whatever it was—that Frankie had witnessed, had unnerved her. She hadn't just kept the phone off because she worried the man who attacked Tyler would call her again. It was beyond that. She was afraid he could track her. He had to have seen her face. He knew her phone number. Depending on how Tyler identified her, the guy might have her entire name. Maybe even a better photo sitting beside that name and number on Tyler's contact list. All that information could help him track her down.

Her eyes darted around the parking lot and across the street. The houses were small but quaint and the yards and lawns were well-kept. In the distance she could hear a dog barking, asking to be let inside. The hum of traffic was muffled by towering maple trees and evergreens. No cars were parked on the streets. No walkers. No runners. In the next block she could see a repair van in the driveway. A quiet neighborhood on a quiet Friday morning.

It had to have been a mugging, Frankie told herself. That early in the morning? What else could it be? And why would a petty thief bother to track her down? She had no way of identifying him. Or turning him in.

She was being ridiculous. Still, she took a deep breath, and she turned the cell phone on. Her pulse started to race as the screen blinked to life. Seven text messages. Two missed calls. One of them might be from Tyler.

The missed calls were unfamiliar numbers. She scrolled the text messages. Most of them were from Angela, her new personal assistant. Frankie was supposed to have the entire week off to move and unpack. Mr. McGavin had approved it. Actually, he had insisted she take the full week. But Frankie had already gotten restless and told Angela yesterday that she'd drop by the office for a few hours. She really wanted to check in and see how her new assistant was doing. Just a glimpse at the texts and Frankie was reminded how much she missed her long-time assistant, Holly. Breaking in a new assistant while moving into a new apartment was not a good idea.

She started to scroll through the messages. All of them were from Angela. In a matter of minutes they appeared to go from curious to urgent.

JUST CHECKING ON YOU?

WHEN WILL YOU BE IN?

CALL ME AS SOON AS YOU CAN.

The last thing Frankie needed was Mr. McGavin getting upset with her, especially if Tyler made it sound like she was a part of his crazy cereal protest.

She glanced at her watch. Scanned the surrounding neighborhood, again. No one had followed her. No one was tracking her.

"Get a hold of yourself, Francine," she said out loud. "You're being ridiculous."

She called Angela and waited. She reached for the radio to turn down the weather report and decided to turn it up instead. She didn't want to miss anything on Tyler.

"McGavin Holt," Angela answered.

"Hi Angela. It's Frankie. What's going on?"

"Oh hey. When will you be here? I've been looking at your schedule, and I don't see any meetings at all for today."

"That's right. Remember, I'm officially gone all this week."

"Oh sure. No, I remember that, but," Angela paused and Frankie could hear shuffling. When she continued, her voice was almost a whisper. "There are a couple of guys here. They said they needed to talk to you. Since you said you were stopping by today I thought maybe you were expecting them?"

"I didn't make any appointments. Are they new clients? Maybe take their names and contact information. I can call them when I get in. Or schedule something for next week."

"No, I don't think they're new clients." There was a muffled sound. This time her voice was so low, Frankie barely heard her. "They said it was an official matter."

Frankie felt sweat trickle down her back, and yet, it was chilly inside the car. She pulled her jacket tighter across her body.

"Official? You mean like law enforcement?" Was it possible the police had already sent a couple of detectives to check up on Tyler? "Did they say what it's about?"

"No. I told them you might not be coming in until later. They insisted on waiting."

Before Frankie could ask anything else, Angela whispered, "Just between you and me, the one guy looks a little rough."

"What do you mean?"

"I don't mean to get all judgy, but he's got this ugly scar on his neck. It's like right under his shirt collar, but I still could see it."

Frankie's eyes darted around the parking lot. Panic kicked her into escape mode while her brain screamed at her, *Oh my God, it's him!*

She swallowed hard and steadied her hands.

"Tell them I should be there in about an hour. Maybe forty-five minutes. Thanks Angela. I gotta go." And she ended the call before Angela could hear her heart pounding or the panic in her voice.

She pressed her body against the seat and ran a hand across her face as her mind raced.

Was it possible they simply had information about Tyler? Was she being crazy?

She closed her eyes, trying to think over the banging of her heart in her ears. She could still hear the urgency in Tyler's voice. She could see his hand going up as if he were bracing for a blow. The muffled sounds were emblazoned on her memory. Tyler's eyes wide with surprise. Blood on his face.

Then instead of Tyler's face, those dark eyes stared right at her like a hawk inspecting its next prey. He'd tracked her, just as she feared. Now, he was waiting for her.

Should she call the police? What would she tell them? She wasn't sure they believed her the first time.

Frankie glanced at her watch, again. She had an hour to figure it out. What could they do to her in a public place like McGavin Holt?

The weather forecast was finishing up. Another blast of chilly air would replace the premature spring temperatures. As she reached to shift into gear, the local news began with a report about a young man who had been murdered. It had happened in the early morning hours. Frankie punched the volume up.

"Authorities have finally released the name of the victim."

She was holding her breath, her hands white-knuckled on the steering wheel. Her foot stayed on the brake pedal.

"Chicago police say it appears to be a pre-dawn home invasion that turned deadly. Twenty-five-year-old Deacon Kaye was shot twice…"

It wasn't Tyler. She could breathe. But only for a second or two until the name hit her. *Deacon…Deacon Kaye.* Tyler's friend.

7

Florida Panhandle

Ryder and Brodie had settled Knight in the kennel with the other dogs. By the time they got to the house it was pouring down rain. Hannah stood at the back door, holding it open. She handed each of them a towel. A rumble of thunder rattled the kitchen windows.

"Lord have mercy, you two took your time." Hannah slammed the door shut.

Creed knew she hated thunderstorms. Sometimes she'd pace from window to window watching the clouds while keeping an eye on the small television under the kitchen cabinet. Usually the TV was reserved for her cooking shows, but this morning a meteorologist walked in front of a map glowing with patches of orange and red. Hannah had turned down the volume, but her eyes darted back to that map behind the weatherman.

The Florida Panhandle had more lightning strikes per year than anywhere else in the country. Because of that, Creed had made sure their facility had enough backup generator power to get through any electrical outage. But that still didn't comfort Hannah.

She pointed to the dark sky outside the kitchen window. Her eyes caught Creed's. He knew she didn't want to panic Brodie, but she couldn't hide her own concern from Creed. With only a glance between the curtains he saw what worried Hannah.

The north side of their property was a thick pine forest, but this window's view included a clearing that allowed a good look at the horizon. He could see a greenish-yellow tint lighting up the sky just below the black storm clouds. Usually that meant the storm was severe enough to produce tornadoes. But those clouds were moving to the east and hopefully would stay to the north of them. Despite that, the sky continued to darken. A rumble of thunder vibrated through the walls, and Hannah shot him another concerned look.

"Brodie's not scared of thunderstorms," Creed said as he took his towel and playfully rubbed it over Brodie's short, wet hair. She actually smiled wide enough he thought he might get a laugh from her, too.

"Really?" Hannah asked Brodie. Then she placed her hand on her ample hip and said, "Sweet Pea, you're a better woman than I am, because they scare the bejesus out of me."

"Do we need to go to the basement?" Brodie asked. She had folded up and placed aside her own towel and was suddenly stroking the kitten in her arms.

Creed hadn't even noticed the cat coming into the kitchen. The two were inseparable. Only in the last several days had Brodie ventured outside the house without taking the kitten along. When she first arrived, Creed wasn't sure how a cat would fit in with a houseful and a kennel full of dogs, but the kitten didn't appear scared of anything. It took only a couple of swats and the dogs quickly learned to keep their distance.

He felt Hunter bump his leg, and Creed reached down to scratch the black spot behind the yellow Lab's ear. The Border collie named Lady shifted back and forth in the doorway to the living room. Hannah was making all of them a bit skittish.

"No, no," Hannah told Brodie, her eyes darting back to the television screen. "Willis Dean says our area will mostly get a lot of thunder and lightning. It looks like the dangerous storms are staying to the north of us."

Very dangerous, Creed suspected but he kept it to himself. A tornado may have already touched down. A flash of lightening and a quick clap of thunder made the entire kitchen vibrate. Hannah jumped despite her best effort not to.

"I wish I had kept the boys home from school today," she said. "But it's only the beginning of March. Good Lord!"

Creed knew they were in for a weekend of wicked weather. All the warm, damp air from the Gulf was set to collide with colder air coming down from the middle of the country. He didn't watch as closely as Hannah, but he checked the forecasts regularly to help prepare and take care of their dogs. Unfortunately, several of the dogs didn't tolerate the thunder and lightning. Dogs could smell the changes in the atmosphere.

During the first storms of the season, Creed kept a close eye on how the newest members of their kennel did. Some preferred the safety of a crate. Others looked to and huddled with the alphas in the pack.

All of their dogs came to them after being abandoned. Many of them came from the street or from alongside roads and highways. Some came from shelters, others through well-meaning owners dumping their dogs at the end of Creed and Hannah's long driveway. Hannah called them "well meaning" owners, changing their minds for one reason or another and at least attempting to give them a second chance. Creed considered them cowards.

It wasn't that long ago he'd caught a man off-loading a new mother. If Creed hadn't seen the man and confronted him, the gunny-sack full of the dog's puppies would have been thrown in the nearest river. It took every ounce of self-discipline Creed had, to keep from pounding the guy into the mud. Instead, he told Bolo to stand guard and watch—and yes, intimidate the hell out of the guy—while Creed grabbed the wiggling bag out of the back of the vehicle and took it, along with the mother dog to safety.

All the puppies and the mother survived. One of those puppies, a smart and funny jackass, was now one of their best scent dogs. And Creed knew for a fact, that puppy named Scout had rescued his new owner and handler, Jason Seaver. Sometimes it still surprised Creed how quickly the two of them had become invaluable members of their team.

Even last night, Jason had worked alongside him checking generators, securing gates and fence lines and adding crates and bedding. The kid genuinely cared about the welfare of the dogs. He'd learned from Creed what each dog needed and catered to them. Taking care of the dogs was second nature to Creed, but he realized he had no idea what he could do to help settle Hannah's nerves.

"I'll go pick the boys up, if you want," Creed volunteered. He'd do anything if it would bring a shred of peace to her. She was usually the one calming everyone else down. Her kitchen, with her comfort food and words of wisdom, was a sanctuary to anyone who came into Hannah's care.

"You know just as well as I do, the worst place to be during a tornado is a vehicle," she said this without looking up at him. Instead, her eyes turned back to the small television screen. Both hands were on her hips. Lines of worry didn't leave her brow, but Creed could see a hint of relief. The angry patches of red on the map appeared to be staying to the north of them in southern Alabama even as the rain started to pound against the glass. Lightning flickered but the thunder took a beat longer.

"Thanks for the offer, Rye." She finally looked over at him, but her eyes were studying Brodie. She glanced back at Creed as if to say she couldn't believe the storm didn't scare the young woman.

Brodie sat by the table, petting the kitten stretched out on her lap. She was staring out at the dark sky. Creed didn't think she looked afraid at all, but she did seem far away. She'd been living with them for only two months and already he'd caught her staring off like this at least a dozen times. He wondered what she saw, what memories in particular still haunted her. And he wished he could wipe them all away.

Her therapist had told him Brodie was suffering from PTSD (post traumatic stress disorder), and that it would likely get worse as things settled down around her. PTSD was something Creed was familiar with.

He'd been a Marine, a part of a K9 unit in Afghanistan when an IED sent him home early.

Everyone dealt with PTSD differently. He understood that, but it was still difficult for him to watch Brodie stare off into the black clouds and not know what she saw or thought or feared. Because he knew from experience that despite her insistence that she wasn't afraid of thunderstorms, there were a whole lot of internal storms. Some that could rip a person apart from the inside out.

The phone rang and everyone in the kitchen—including the dogs and kitten—startled at the sound.

Hannah grabbed the phone off the counter. One glance at the caller's I.D. and her face relaxed. She was smiling when she answered.

"Girl, we are in the middle of a thunderstorm. Can I call you back?"

But the caller's response made Hannah's eyes go wide and wiped the smile from her face.

"Slow down," Hannah said. "You best start from the beginning."

8

Birmingham, Alabama

Willis Dean had been on his feet for the last six hours, most of them in front of a green screen with a camera pointed at him. A phone call from the weather desk had awakened him around 2:00 a.m. Truth was, it hadn't really wakened him. He couldn't get comfortable in his youngest son's bedroom. Off to college for nearly three years now, the room was still decorated with the sports paraphernalia of a teenaged boy. Plus, how could he expect to sleep after the bombshell his wife had hit him with over dinner.

The truth was, Willis knew it was going to be a bad day even before it became a very bad day.

What was worse, he was relieved to leave the house. He was relieved to be thrown into the thick of things at the studio, juggling the National Weather Service alerts, social media posts, video cam feeds and live updates from storm spotters. Violent weather made the adrenaline surge through his veins. It made him feel alive, and it always had since he was ten.

Forty-eight years later, his hair had turned gray, his voice had grown deeper and his waistline a bit thicker, but his excitement hadn't diminished one bit. He had always been able to sense a storm coming. Obviously his ability to sense his wife's discontent was not as sharp.

But this early spring storm had caught Willis off guard. He had expected volatile weather for the weekend, but this batch had sneaked up on everyone. A prelude, a sneak peek that even the National Weather Service office hadn't forecasted. What had gathered in the dark hours of pre-dawn was now battering southern Alabama and the Florida Panhandle.

Willis barely noticed the personnel changes happening around him in the television studio. About two hours ago, storms started blooming on the radar so quickly it was difficult to keep up. The daily morning show anchors and crew pitched in assisting Willis and his staff. It was nothing less than a small army that worked around him. Another dozen or so crews were out on the roads helping to gather information directly from watching the sky. They risked their lives to be invaluable human warning systems.

Willis had taken off his suit jacket and tossed it aside. He'd heard long ago that viewers knew when the weather was seriously bad because Willis Dean not only took off his jacket, but he also rolled up his sleeves. The red suspenders were his latest signature trademark as were his Sperry deck shoes, though the latter were rarely shown on camera.

Now those cameras switched to the radar while Willis and his assistant, Mia Long exchanged places. She had gestured to him from the window of the weather desk. From what he could see, she was pointing to one of the iPads set up amongst the monitors and the video feeds. Willis simply nodded. He shut off his microphone as she turned hers on. Seamlessly, she took over, picking up where he left off, continuing to break down the weather alerts for viewers and listeners.

Willis bent over in front of the iPads. The screen was filled with black storm clouds. In the upper corner was a small box where he could barely make out the face of one of his storm chasers, Gary Fletcher.

Willis pushed his glasses up and moved in closer.

"Gary, it's Willis. Where are you?"

When the audio flicked on, Willis immediately heard the rush of wind.

Gary's gaze remained upward focusing on the sky as he shouted, "About eight miles west of Smith Crossings. This thing is huge. It was wrapped in rain up until a few seconds ago."

Willis looked over to a radar map on one of the monitors, searching for the small town. There it was, smack-dab in the middle of the blooming sea of red. And sure enough, an angry comma was forming right before his eyes. Radar wasn't able to confirm a tornado, but the radar beam bouncing off items formed what meteorologists called the debris ball. And Willis could see it taking shape, the dot punctuating the comma.

"Good job, Gary. Now go get somewhere safe."

"We thought we were." Gary's voice rasped through the sound of a tunnel. "But we're gonna move. I don't trust this one."

His storm chasers took great precaution to stay out of the path. That Gary was nervous made Willis nervous. In Alabama, getting out of the path wasn't an easy task. Escape routes were few with too many winding backroads that spaghettied out in directions that could take you away only to turn and send you straight back into the storm.

Willis heard the metal pings before he saw the hail.

"Get out of there now, Gary," he told the man as he watched him dive into the passenger seat of the vehicle. The driver accelerated even while the doors were still slamming.

To his tech, Willis pointed to the radar map and said, "We have ground truth on this one. Call it in and get it to Mia." He glanced back to the iPad, hoping to get a glimpse of the storm chasers, but the screen had already gone black.

"God help them," he said to himself as he hurried back to the cameras. He had to believe the crew would get to safety, whatever it took. He'd never be able to do his job if he worried about them.

Willis understood all to well the adrenaline rush, the excitement. It was awe-inspiring to be that close to such an intense and powerful storm. He'd started out as a chaser. Still to this day he kept an iPad mounted to the console of his SUV. His wife hated it. If they went anywhere together she always insisted they take her car.

Maybe she had hoped and expected his fascination would diminish after this many years. Instead of diminishing, it had only grown stronger. It wasn't just what he did for a living, it had become a part of who he was. He took the obligation and responsibility seriously. Almost too seriously. Because every spring, every storm, Willis Dean found himself cringing and wondering, *how many would die this time?* And although people respected and listened to him, Alabamans were used to hearing spring tornado sirens.

The National Weather Service insisted that sirens blast in the entire county even if only a small corner of that county was affected. Which sometimes resulted in too many false alarms for the rest of a large county. As a result, at the sound of a siren, many people were more likely to go outside and look up at the sky, rather than hurry and take shelter. So it was Willis' job to convince them that the threat was serious. And right now residents of Smith Crossings were hearing their sirens.

Mia saw him headed back, and as was their routine, she started talking to him on air before he arrived in front of the cameras.

"Willis, we have a tornado warning issued for Smith Crossings and the surrounding area. What can you tell us?"

They made a good tag-team, but now, she stepped aside as he took his place in front of the green screen. She relinquished her spot to the voice of authority. He took that responsibility seriously. His wife told him he should enjoy the celebrity status. She laughed about him having more Twitter followers than some of her favorite Hollywood actors.

He thought that was one of the things she enjoyed about his job. The fact that they could get seated at a restaurant first when there was a line. That other local celebrities greeted them those rare times that they went to a concert or a play. But after last night, Willis realized it wasn't enough. Truthfully, he wasn't sure he knew her anymore. To Willis, the so-called celebrity status often felt like a weight, a burden, especially when he saw the aftermath of a storm.

Several years ago, he'd asked a county coroner to share his autopsy reports on storm victims after a particularly brutal tornado had claimed fourteen lives. Willis hadn't told anyone about the photos he'd seen: skin sandblasted off, bodies impaled by debris from their own home. Then there were those sucked up and spit out. Those images haunted him. And ever since, it drove him to get information out earlier even if it meant breaking protocol and announcing warnings seconds before the National Weather Service.

He'd done that just now. He switched on his microphone.

"That's right. Our storm chasers confirmed a tornado on the ground."

He pointed to the area on the radar. He had learned to keep his voice calm but intense and urgent. Yet, as he looked at the red and yellow spreading, he couldn't believe how well defined the debris ball had grown in just a few seconds. This storm was starting to explode and widen.

"Right now, the tornado is five to six miles west of Smith Crossings in Butler County." He clicked and enlarged the map. "Smith Crossings, you should be hearing your sirens going off. But even if you don't hear them, you need to get to your safe place. If that's not underground, go to the smallest room on the lowest floor. An interior closet, a bathroom in the center of your house. Get away from windows. It's moving to the north, northeast. It's getting ready to cross over Interstate 65. If you're driving on the interstate anywhere south of Montgomery, highway 10, US 31, get off. Get off immediately. Take the nearest exit. Head to a convenience store or a rest area. If you can, get inside. "

He talked directly to the camera, having trained himself to imagine he was speaking to those watching or listening. The ongoing challenge was to persuade his audience without making them panic.

"Don't park under a bridge or overpass," he continued. "Again, this is a very dangerous tornado that is now on the ground. In minutes it will start to pass over the interstate and is headed directly toward Smith Crossings. Also on the other side of the path, you should be taking cover, too. Anyone in Midway, Honoraville, Black Rock and Ruthledge."

Out of the corner of his eye he could see Mia. She had a piece of paper in one hand and with her other, gestured toward the radar screen. He invited her to join him.

"The National Weather Service has now issued a tornado warning," Mia announced "for Butler County and also Crenshaw County."

Willis found it on the screen and pointed it out, highlighting the area.

Mia continued, "Golf ball sized hail was reported by one of our storm chasers who is at the interstate rest area close to the Highway 10 junction. Along with strong winds and heavy rains. Be on the look out for flooding across roads."

As Mia described the conditions, Willis couldn't help noticing the storm on the radar had just swallowed up that same area where Interstate 65 met Highway 10. At this time of morning, that was a busy junction. A knot twisted in his stomach. It was the worst part of his job, knowing that dozens of people would be injured. And despite his best efforts, there would be deaths.

9

Chicago

Frankie left her car in the parking garage of her new apartment building. The morning was chilly and she'd grabbed a lightweight jacket. Most of her clothes were still packed along with seventy-five percent of everything she owned.

Now she felt like she was sleepwalking as she scurried from room to room. The stacked boxes only added to her disorientation. She found her red backpack, the one she used for work every day. While her colleagues showed off trendy leather messenger bags or fashionable totes, Frankie found comfort in the soft, well-worn canvas that easily conformed to whatever contents she stuffed inside. She wandered around her bedroom and bathroom, filling the bag with items she might need. At the last minute, she slid her laptop down the middle, cushioned between underwear and running shoes.

In the back of her mind she kept playing her friend's instructions. "Just come on home," Hannah had told her, slipping easily into her role of big sister from their childhood. The summers Frankie had stayed with Hannah and her grandparents were some of her best and most cherished memories.

From her dresser top Frankie grabbed a raggedy Teddy bear, another childhood treasure that was almost as old as Frankie. She considered stuffing it into the backpack. But that was silly. She was acting like she'd never be coming back. With careful fingers, she undid the stitching on the bear's bottom until there was a three-inch opening. She poked up around the stuffing and pinched the solid item, pulling it out carefully so she didn't rip the loose threads of the bear.

The wad of cash was fatter than Frankie remembered. And for the second time in a single day, she found herself grateful for her father's lifelong paranoia. She unrolled the bills, split the bundle in two then turned them into two tightly rolled wads. She put one into a zippered pocket inside the backpack. The other wad she zipped into the interior of her handbag.

Her father would be scowling at her. She could hear him in the back of her mind, "You lose your bags you'll lose all that cash."

"It's the best I can do, Daddy," she said out loud as she checked her watch. Tapping the faceplate, she noticed that she already had 4,575 steps for the day. It had to be all of her pacing.

She pulled the backpack over her shoulder along with her handbag, just like she did every day when she left for work. Neither felt heavier, and a bit of panic kicked in her stomach. She really hadn't packed well. Before she closed and locked the apartment door, she took one last look around at the sum of her life: boxes on top of boxes and her few bits of furniture. Last night she thought her life had become unmanageable with all the changes: the move, the new assistant. And she was alone, again, for the first time in years. But now, all those worries seemed small.

Maybe she was overreacting. Maybe Tyler would show up at an emergency room, injured but safe. Maybe the men waiting for her at McGavin Holt simply wanted information.

Frankie walked three blocks to catch the train.

Walked, not rushed.

One of the things she loved about her new neighborhood was that it would cut her commute. No more crawling through Chicago traffic to get downtown every day. Instead of driving, she could take the train. She glanced at the schedules and kept an eye on the other people waiting on the platform. No one seemed to pay attention to her.

She turned on her cell phone, ignored the messages and typed one quick text to Angela:

IN TRAFFIC. BUT ON MY WAY. ARE THEY STILL WAITING?

Almost immediately came the reply:

YES. I GOT THEM COFFEE.

Frankie realized she needed to sound as normal as possible. And because they had been working so closely together, she decided to ask:

IS TYLER IN?

She held her breath, waiting, hoping that one question didn't backfire. That Angela wouldn't come back and ask if Frankie knew why he wasn't at work yet. She glanced around as the platform began to fill. It seemed like she waited forever before the response came:

HE TEXTED EARLY THIS MORNING THAT HE WOUILDN'T BE
IN TODAY.

Frankie stared at the phone. How was that possible? Why wouldn't he have texted her? The second part from Angela came, and Frankie felt as if ice had been injected into her veins.

I THINK SYLVIA SAID THERE WAS A DEATH IN HIS FAMILY.

Frankie shut the phone off, closed her eyes and took a deep breath. The men waiting for her had Tyler's phone. Her stomach churned as she dropped her phone into the handbag. Then she tightened her grip on the shoulder straps of both bags and stood up straight.

Shake it off. Focus. You cannot think about what happened to Tyler. Not right now.

But the radio news alert about his friend, Deacon still played in her head. "A home invasion turned deadly. Shot twice."

In a matter of minutes, Frankie boarded the train. But instead of taking the downtown one, she chose another. This one was headed to O'Hare International Airport.

10

Florida Panhandle

Creed noticed the sky had lightened but the rain continued. It didn't lighten Hannah's anxiety. She had taken the phone down the hallway and into the next room. Something was wrong, but from what he could hear—a whole lot of quiet—Hannah was mostly listening.

"Do you think the storms are over?" Brodie asked.

"Hard to tell, but I think so. For us anyway."

He pointed to the television where the meteorologist still gestured at a map full of red splotches. A banner raced across the bottom of the screen with a list of counties under tornado watches and warnings. From what Creed could see, the worst of the storms were hitting southern Alabama, just to the north of them.

"Would it be okay if I go write in my journal or read?"

It pained him that she still asked permission no matter how many times he told her she didn't need to ask.

"Sure. What are you reading now?"

"*Robinson Crusoe.* Jason said it's one of his favorites."

"Are you enjoying it?"

"I just started. It's one that Gram gave you. Do you remember it?"

"Actually, I do. He's shipwrecked during a storm."

"I like seeing Gram's handwriting," Brodie said as she left the room with her cat trailing close behind.

The fact that she still enjoyed reading gave him a sense of comfort. She had already gone through an entire shelf from the bookcases in his loft. He still remembered the day he showed her his apartment above the kennel. The open floor plan allowed her to see the floor-to-ceiling built-ins as soon as she walked in the door. She must have stood in front of the wall of books for an hour, her head tilted and reading the titles. Even though he told her she could take them out and check out the descriptions, she didn't dare touch them for that first hour.

As kids, both Creed and Brodie had loved to read, encouraged by their grandmother. Gram had bought them brand new books for birthdays and holidays and sometimes just because. She selected specific ones for each of them, carefully writing inside the cover the date and their name along with: "love, Gram." And now those make-believe worlds of adventure and mystery were helping Brodie cope not only with what she had survived but her re-entry into a normal world.

All those years, a decade and a half that she was gone, Creed didn't know whether she was dead or alive. His mind had conjured up imaginable scenarios of what had happened to her. Torture, mutilation, sexual assault and her body buried or discarded deep in a woods for nature and wildlife to savage even further.

As horrible and incredible her story was, she had been spared many of the horrors he had imagined. Truthfully, he never expected to bring her home in one piece, let alone alive. It was the reason he started K9 CrimeScents. With every search of a girl or young woman he hoped to bring back the remains of his sister and finally lay her to rest.

Then last fall, Maggie O'Dell found an old Polaroid. The photo was one of dozens pinned up on a killer's pegboard. A man suspected of human trafficking. In the photo were a teenaged boy and a young girl. Written along the white edges of the Polaroid was a date along with the names: Ryder and Brodie. The names alone told Maggie it couldn't be a coincidence. The fact that Creed had a Polaroid that was almost an exact copy—taken seconds apart—revealed the painful truth. This madman named Eli Dunn had something to do with Brodie's disappearance.

It had taken a scavenger hunt across the farmlands of Nebraska to find the truth. Still, Creed had expected to find Brodie's grave. Dunn had promised as much.

Now, Brodie liked to say that Creed had rescued her. She gave him too much credit. Fact was, if it wasn't for an Omaha detective named Tommy Pakula they might never have found her. Pakula was the one who put the puzzle pieces together that led them to an abandoned farmhouse. Dunn's sister—Iris Malone—and her son, Aaron, had held Brodie captive for all those years. With her brother's help, Iris had hoped to replace her deceased daughter, Charlotte. And she had been doing it for decades, over and over again. She discarded the rejects, handing them back to Eli Dunn, allowing him to do whatever he wanted with them.

In a disturbing way, Creed knew Brodie had been one of the lucky Charlottes. They now knew that Dunn sexually assaulted, trafficked and sometimes murdered many young women. Some of them were Iris' rejects. But Iris had grown tired of Brodie's attempts to escape and had casted her out. Maggie and local law enforcement had arrested Eli Dunn the week before. Creed didn't like to think about how close he had come to losing her for good.

11

My name is Brodie Creed.

She started each entry the same way. Her therapist, Dr. Rockwood, had suggested Brodie write it at the top of her daily entry.

"I know that sounds strange," the woman had said, "but you spent the last sixteen years being called Charlotte. It may take some getting used to hearing Brodie."

It wasn't strange at all. There were still times when someone called for Brodie and it took a second call before it registered in her mind. The more difficult part was trying to embrace that name. In her mind, Brodie was the little girl who disobeyed her parents and climbed into that RV at the rest area.

Iris Malone had told Brodie how naughty she was. So naughty her parents didn't want her anymore. She said they told Iris to keep her, to never bring her back. Brodie was the scared, little girl who cried herself to sleep. Brodie missed her family and wanted to go home. Brodie was weak, a big baby.

But Charlotte…Charlotte was the brave one.

Now, everyone was expecting her to be Brodie, again, but she wasn't sure how to do that. She hadn't told this to anyone, not even the kind and all-knowing therapist. She didn't dare, but she also knew it wasn't right that secretly she felt like a piece of her was still Charlotte.

How was that possible?

She'd never even met the real Charlotte. The little girl had died long before Brodie was taken to replace her.

But none of this matter right now. The storm had triggered a memory, and she wanted to write it down before it left her. The memories were coming more often just in the last several days. Dr. Rockwood had warned her that it might happen.

"Don't be surprised if the memories come flooding back. Don't be afraid of them. They can't hurt you. Write them down. It'll help you feel like you have control over them."

"But why," Brodie asked, "am I remembering all the bad stuff now when I'm safe? When I'm finally free?"

"You've gone through such trauma," the woman had told her. "You were drugged, dehydrated and malnourished. Your mind and body were in survival mode. There was no energy for anything else. Post-traumatic stress disorder works that way sometimes. When things calm down, when you're feeling safe is when your mind feels safe to remember the things that may have been too painful when you were vulnerable."

"It's not a setback?" Brodie wanted to know.

"Not at all. It's a good thing."

"But it doesn't feel like a good thing," she admitted to the therapist.

"Write it down. Control it. Own it. Then set it aside and move on with living."

Brodie had been faithful about keeping the journal ever since she'd left Omaha. But only recently had the memories come flooding back—more like nightmares than memories. The morning storm had triggered another.

She hadn't lied to Ryder. She wasn't scared of thunderstorms. But as they made their way from the kennel to the house under the dark sky, Brodie had started to hear voices carried by the fierce wind.

In the back of her mind, she could still hear Iris at the top of the basement stairs. She was calling for Aaron. There was urgency in her voice. Urgency on the verge of panic.

Brodie remembered feeling the rumble of thunder. The beams that held up the house seemed to tremble. Iris must have felt it, too, because suddenly, she was yelling for Aaron to hurry.

"What's happening?" Brodie had asked when Iris came clomping down the basement steps, the flashlight stream leading her way in the dark.

She shot the beam directly into Brodie's eyes. Even now Brodie blinked, remembering the sharp pain of the sudden brightness. She had no idea how many days before, Iris had taken away the lone light bulb. Nor did Brodie remember what she had done to deserve the punishment of total darkness. It hadn't been the first time.

But that day, with the storm descending upon them, Iris Malone stomped around like a madwoman. She searched through bare cupboards and cursed Brodie—actually, Charlotte—as if she was the reason there were no emergency supplies. Not even a single light bulb.

Brodie recalled a brief and fleeting impulse to race up those stairs to the unlocked door. Of escaping into the storm. Iris wouldn't dare follow. Her fear of lightning would hold her back. But the idea had quickly been tamped down. Not out of fear of the storm, but because she was too weak and sick to even move. Stomach cramps had kept her curled up on her mattress clutching the threadbare blanket. Iris made sure that Brodie had very little food, keeping her weak. What rations she was given often came with drugs hidden inside, further ensuring that she couldn't escape.

"It's your own fault," Iris had told her once. "I told you if you behaved I wouldn't need to punish you."

But it wasn't just escaping that warranted punishment. There was always something. An illicit piece of fruit she'd managed to steal. The furnace manual she kept hidden for something to read. Even a pink ribbon she'd found to tie back her long, greasy hair.

But that night, Brodie didn't attempt—couldn't attempt—escape. So she simply closed her eyes against the flashlight's laser beams. She remembered biting back the bile and curling tighter against the stomach spasms. But she also remembered the wicked pleasure in listening to Iris' gasps and Aaron's quick breaths each and every time the thunder crashed.

The wind made the house above them groan and sent the walls creaking. It seemed to last for a long time, and it sounded like the structure would give way and collapse on top of them.

But for once, Brodie's captors were more frightened than she was.

12

Creed was sitting alone with a cup of coffee when Hannah came back. Without a word, she marched to the counter, poured herself a cup and sat down at the table across from him.

"You remember my friend, Francine Russo?"

He nodded and waited. The woman had visited a couple of times, but it had been at least two or three years ago. Of course he remembered her. She was attractive: olive skin; hazel eyes; thick, dark hair. A bit high-strung though. She and Hannah would stay up late into the night talking, laughing, catching up, but by the third day, Frankie seemed restless.

Hannah always ribbed her about being a city girl, that she missed her Starbucks not being within walking distance. Frankie usually admitted it was too quiet in the middle of nowhere. But Creed knew the two women still called and kept in touch. Something in their childhood had bonded them together. He'd never asked. He'd never pry. He figured if Hannah wanted him to know, she would tell him.

He listened now without interrupting.

"Frankie and I have known each other since we were girls. I've never heard her so frightened.

"They hacked into a corporation's computer system?"

She shook her head even as she said, "Yes, that's what her co-worker,

Tyler, told her."

"And she knows for sure that this Tyler, that his friend has been shot dead. What about Tyler?"

"It only just happened early this morning. I think she's hoping he'll show up in an ER somewhere. If the men who attacked him took his wallet, the hospital might not be able to identify him."

"How does she know it's the same men waiting for her at her office?" Creed asked.

"She said she recognized the man's scar. Look, I know it all sounds crazy, but I know Frankie. She's not one to jump to conclusions. She's also not easily spooked." She paused with her elbows on the table, her coffee cup wrapped in her hands. "She sounded so scared, Rye."

"Is she driving down or flying?"

Hannah stared at him then her face broke into a smile of relief. She reached across the table, grabbed his arm and gave it a squeeze. "You and me are two peas in a pod. She's headed to the airport."

She laced her fingers back around her coffee mug. There was something else. Creed saw her bracing to tell him, as if this next part was more contentious than any of the rest. "Frankie asked if there was any way I could ask my FBI friend to check on this."

"Maggie?" He tried not to react, but he swallowed too hard.

"Yes."

"Do you think this is an FBI matter?"

"Probably not," Hannah admitted. "Actually, I hope it's not. But Maggie would have resources available to her. She could find out what the Chicago police might know. If these young men did hack into a computer system, that is a federal offense."

"You should call her."

"You won't mind?"

"Me? Why would I mind? Besides, it shouldn't matter what I think? You and Maggie are friends."

"It's just that…well, ever since last fall, anytime I mention Maggie you've been like a long-tailed cat in a roomful of rocking chairs."

"Really?" He laughed. "Is that a real thing?"

"My granny used to say it all the time." Her expression got serious again. "Don't change the subject. Something happened in Nebraska between you two. It wasn't just about finding Brodie."

He got up from the table, took his coffee cup to the sink and started rinsing it out. The task gave him an excuse to give her his back without being too rude.

"I know it's none of my business, Rye," Hannah continued. "I haven't said anything, because we all have been busy and concerned about Brodie. But now that I have your attention, I will say this. I hope you're not going to throw away a friendship."

"Me and Maggie *are* friends," he told her, turning around to face her.

"It's just that every time I mention her name you get all funky."

"Funky? You mean like a long-tailed cat in a roomful of rocking chairs?"

She waved her hand at him and smiled.

"Don't worry about Maggie and me," he told her. Even as he said it, his fingers twisted at the leather strap of his watch. His new GPS watch. A gift from Maggie. "I hope she's able to help Frankie."

Hannah was still examining him, waiting for more. Expecting more. He didn't want to talk about it. How could he? He wasn't sure what his own feelings were, let alone pretend to know Maggie O'Dell's.

"Speaking of friends," he said, wanting to move on, "Did you know that Jason and Brodie were spending a lot of time together?"

"He's been including her in his training sessions with Scout. They just started doing it a couple of weeks ago. He thought it might help her not be so afraid of dogs. Looks like it's working."

Creed wondered how he had missed it. He hadn't taken an assignment since Brodie arrived, making sure he was around if she needed him. They received K9 requests from across the country. Sometimes he'd be gone for days, maybe weeks. Brodie's therapist had told Creed that for now, he seemed to be Brodie's anchor. She made it sound like it was important for him to stay close. But Brodie seemed to be doing well, and of course, there were always errands, picking up supplies, picking up new dogs. He'd driven to Maryland to personally bring Knight to their facility. Now he wondered if he'd been gone more than he should have been.

"It's good for her to connect to others," Hannah said. When he didn't respond, she added, "You can't protect her 24/7."

Sunlight streamed in through the kitchen window, but raindrops still tapped the glass. He knew she was right. He'd spent so many years wondering, imagining what had happened to Brodie. All those emotions— anxiety, fear, sadness, helplessness, dread. They had wound so tightly and firmly into his psyche. He shouldn't be surprised that they hadn't dissolved after finding her. Not just finding her, but able to bring her home alive. But that was part of the problem. He hadn't been able to bring her home right away.

They had found her in Nebraska, imprisoned in that deserted old farmhouse. Her initial medical care started in Omaha. So Creed had spent weeks traveling back and forth. Brodie hadn't suffered only from PTSD but also from malnutrition and dehydration. Her captors not only kept Brodie locked up, but at times, had also starved and drugged her.

Iris was now in prison. Aaron was dead. Brodie had killed him. His death had been ruled self-defense, but there was that trauma to add to Brodie's mental injuries. He didn't know how to help her. It frustrated him. All those years he thought he'd lost her, and now, here she was, and he didn't have a clue how to get to know her.

In her wisdom, Hannah had told him to be patient. She reminded him that even Brodie didn't know who she was.

In all the years he'd searched for her, dreamed about her, he always imagined her as that eleven-year-old girl. The little sister he could still see skipping through the rain puddles.

"Rye?"

Hannah was standing beside him, her hand on his arm and a look of concern that she usually reserved for others.

"Maybe it's time for you to get back out in the field," she said.

But this weekend was Brodie's first scheduled visit with their mother. Olivia was driving all the way down from Atlanta. Hannah told Creed that it might be better if he wasn't around for either woman to depend on him.

Less than a half hour later when he received the phone call from the Butler County Sheriff in Alabama, Hannah told Creed it was a sign validating her instinct. She'd been right so many other times, he didn't dare argue with her.

But he still wanted to check with Brodie.

"You don't need to babysit me," Brodie told him. "Besides, you sucked at babysitting."

"No, I didn't," he answered, sounding exactly like a teenaged boy who sucked at babysitting.

"You always burned the pizza."

"That's true," he said, and he left it at that, not wanting to let on how much he enjoyed that it still made her smile.

13

Chicago O'Hare International Airport

While riding the train, Frankie bought the last seat on the next flight to Atlanta using her phone. But almost immediately she received an email telling her she'd still need to check in at the ticket counter.

Now, she waited. The ticket agent raised an eyebrow at her computer monitor, and Frankie's heart skipped a beat. She'd never purchased an airline ticket three hours before the flight. Maybe there were rules. She'd switched connecting flights with less time, but that was probably different. Should she ask the ticket agent what the problem was? Or would it only draw more attention to her and how paranoid she was at this very moment.

Then without warning, the woman looked up, handed Frankie her boarding pass and told her the gate number.

"Enjoy your flight."

Frankie tried to be casual and not show her relief. Her mind was already running over what Hannah had told her, so much so that she almost collided with the woman waiting in the ticket line behind her. Hannah had offered her a safe haven, but Frankie worried she might be putting her friend—along with her children—in danger. Hannah promised she'd arrange a meeting for Frankie with her FBI friend.

"Just get down here," Hannah had said.

She made it through security and found her gate, but continued walking, not stopping until she was two gates down. In the last three years Frankie had traveled for the agency, meeting clients all over the country, so she was familiar with O'Hare, especially this terminal. She found a seat with her back to a wall and a view of everyone coming from the security checkpoint, making the turn and down the ramp to the gates. A television monitor was close enough for her to read the news alert crawl at the bottom of the screen. Satisfied that no one was paying attention to her, she pulled out her cell phone and turned it on.

New messages started pinging. With only a glance, Frankie could see none of them were from Hannah. All were from Angela, and she was getting impatient.

WHERE ARE YOU?

STILL STUCK IN TRAFFIC?

HOW MUCH LONGER DO YOU THINK YOU'LL BE?

The last message was twenty-seven minutes ago.

She sat back, shook her head and released a heavy sigh. She missed Holly. Angela was no Holly.

In her mind Frankie had gone over exactly what she'd tell her new, young assistant. They barely knew each other, which meant she didn't owe Frankie any loyalty or favors. Her old assistant had worked with Frankie for five years, and with Frankie's help had recently been promoted to project manager. Holly would have been quick to help come up with ways to delay and distract the men without Frankie needing to prompt her. But on the other hand, Holly knew her too well for Frankie to have ever gotten away with the excuse she was getting ready to use. Holly would have seen right through it and would have wanted to know what was going on.

Frankie tapped:

FEELING SICK. MUST HAVE EATEN SOMETHING BAD AT

THAT NEW DELI. HEADING BACK HOME. PLEASE TAKE

CARE OF THINGS.

She shut off her phone before Angela responded. The woman would either freak out or recognize this as an opportunity to show off her skills.

One good thing, Mr. McGavin didn't expect her back until next week. Even if Tyler had set Mr. McGavin on edge with his cereal protest, she knew her boss wouldn't interrupt her time off. He was a true proponent of working hard but refilling the creative well with time off.

Reluctantly she left her spot to buy snacks, a couple bottles of water and two pre-paid phones, all of which finally made her backpack heavier. And yet, when she returned to her favorite seat she still had an hour and twenty minutes before her flight boarded. All the urgency, all the rush, and now, she had to sit and wait. She tried to relax and sipped from one of the bottles of water, her back to the wall, her eyes watching and observing.

That's when she saw him.

It wasn't possible.

It had to be a different man.

He was supposed to be waiting downtown outside her office. But of course, he could have left when Angela didn't hear from her. Or after Frankie sent the last message. How long ago was that? She glanced at her watch. Tapped the faceplate.

Damn it!

She didn't need to know how many steps. Just the time.

A little over an hour. Plenty of time to get here. But how did he know she was at the airport?

Maybe it wasn't him.

And yet, Frankie knew she'd never forget those eyes, that hawk nose, that massive forehead. From thirty feet away she saw him tug at his shirt collar like a man not used to wearing a necktie. When his fingers came away she saw just enough of that ugly scar to know it was the same man.

And yes, he was here! Never mind how.

He hadn't seen her...yet. He was trying to blend in, but his head rotated like a square block on thick shoulders. He was checking out the passengers waiting at Gate 2.

Her gate!

She needed to get out. Her heart began to pound. Her pulse started racing, and she felt like a trapped animal sitting against the wall. The man was less than thirty feet away. What was worse—he blocked her path. There was no way to leave the terminal without walking by him.

Frankie shouldered her backpack and handbag, keeping both high enough that she could slouch, half her face hidden behind the bundle. She got up, startled to find her knees wobbly.

Stay calm. Don't look at him.

A sudden swell of passengers separated Frankie from the man. She knew how to slide into a moving crowd without making anyone slow down or take notice, allowing the wave to swallow her. But the crowd was walking in the wrong direction. Away from the terminal's entrance, toward more gates and deeper into a trap. Somewhere down this way was a women's restroom. She knew it was close.

Heart still pounding, she eased her way to the other side of the crowd. She moved with the flow and waited until she was exactly at the doorway then she pivoted and ducked inside. She almost collided with an abandoned janitor cart tucked in at the elbow of the entrance.

Frankie found an empty stall, a prized corner unit with extra room to breathe. As she fastened the lock she noticed her fingers were shaking.

What was she going to do? Could she stay here until they called her flight? He wouldn't be able to follow her on board. Or would he convince the airline attendants that he had some sort of authority? He'd obviously convinced Angela.

The fact that he was here—that he even knew she was here—dispelled any chance this man only wanted to talk to her. That he only wanted to give her information about Tyler. And being in a public place didn't seem to discourage him. She could still see his eyes looking at her through the screen of her phone, eyes filled with anger when he realized there was an unexpected witness to his crime.

She needed to think. She needed to focus. Be creative. Come up with a solution. She got paid to play out scenarios all the time. What was important to one demographic didn't matter to another. It was her job to make people see and believe exactly what the advertising campaign wanted them to see and believe.

The man on the phone had gotten a look at her face, but her hair had been up in a towel. Who was she fooling? Tyler probably had a photo of her in his contacts alongside her phone number. Still, he had no idea how tall she was, how she walked or what she was wearing.

She looked down at her clothes. What if she'd been followed from her apartment? Had there been someone on the train platform with her? Is that how they knew she was at the airport? But how would they know what airline? And even the gate number? Was there someone else tracking her that she hadn't noticed?

Almost immediately, she took off her jacket and started peeling off her clothes, hanging them on the hook on the back of the door. Out of her backpack, she pulled out jeans and a black T-shirt. She exchanged her leather flats for running shoes. At the bottom of the bag her fingers found a hairband. She tied her hair in a ponytail and weaved it through the back opening of a black baseball cap. She folded and rolled her clothes and shoved them into the bag as she silently prayed, "Please let it still be there. Please let it still be there."

Several deep breaths later and she exited the safety of the bathroom stall. She took time to wash her hands and seeing the slight tremor almost unnerved her. She met her eyes in the mirror and pulled the bill of the cap down low while she took an extra minute to listen. A couple of the stalls were occupied, but no one else was using the sinks. She would have seconds, not minutes to pull this off.

As she rounded the corner she almost gasped with relief.

Thank God!

The janitor cart was still there. She dropped her bags into the yellow vinyl trash container, not paying attention to the garbage they landed on top of. She grasped the handholds and backed the cart out of the entrance. The mop and bucket rattled. The castors squealed, and she kept from wincing at the noise they made all the way from the tile of the bathroom entrance until they hit the industrial carpet.

Frankie pulled the bill of her cap even lower. She curved her shoulders inward as if she did this everyday and off she went. She didn't dare look around.

14

"She's here. She's in this terminal."

"I don't see her."

They talked using earbuds, a small white button with an inch long stem that was hardly noticeable. It was almost identical to the one Tyler Gates was using. If August Braxton had noticed that one small detail, they wouldn't be in this mess.

Usually technological advancements made his job easier. He probably should care how they all worked. Years ago, he might have cared. But now? He was getting too old for this crap. He left the technical stuff to the experts. He counted that as one of his strengths, that he depended on people smarter than him. Smarter in certain things. No one had better instincts than him. That's why he was still on the payroll.

Ironic. All the technological advances and artificial intelligence that money could buy, and they still needed his old world, old school instincts.

Braxton brought up the woman's photo again on his cell phone screen. His fingers pinched and pulled it larger. It was a headshot that didn't look anything like Francine Russo's driver's license photo. In this one, she wore full makeup. In the other, her face was scrubbed clean and she wore her hair a bit short. She looked years younger.

His eyes scanned the crowded area. More and more passengers flooded the gates as boarding calls were made. He rubbed his jaw trying to brush away the exhaustion.

So which image are you today, Francine Russo?

Braxton swiped away her photo and replaced it with the map. Was it possible he missed something? And yet, there was the red light, beating like a heart, stationary as if she was sitting somewhere close by. Somewhere within reach.

The system wasn't advanced enough to show him the exact location. Just the area. Any movement came in tiny increments, jerky and delayed by a second or two. Maybe if HQ's experts were in Chicago instead of the District, the surveillance equipment would run smoother. Yet, they were able to direct him to Gate 2. They even gave him the airline, flight number, departure time, and seat number. He didn't ask how they managed to accomplish all that. He supposed they'd gotten the information the same way they'd gotten the information that Deacon Kaye had hacked into a corporate server.

Talk about irony. He couldn't help but smile. The same company that depended on Braxton's boss to hack into computers and tell him exactly where Russo was and where she was headed—that same company had been surprised and offended to find their own system so easily exploited. And by two guys barely out of college. The corporation, along with Braxton's boss, had gotten too big, too ballsy. They all thought they were infallible. Just like the Titanic.

He smiled to himself. He liked reading historical books. The Titanic was his latest fascination. Not just the event, but the ramifications the sinking of the unsinkable had on an entire era. The ripple effect.

His stomach growled reminding him that coffee and a protein bar had been too many hours ago. Hunger pangs only added to his frustration. Maybe this job would be his last. He had enough stashed away to take a long vacation. A cabin in the mountains. He could hike, read, fix himself gourmet meals and sip some of the expensive wines he'd collected.

He glanced across the noisy, bustling crowd. Rex's head and eyes continued to pivot on massive shoulders. Everyone discounted the man as a dim-witted brute. That caveman forehead didn't help. But those beady eyes missed very little. He reminded Braxton of a huge lizard of dinosaur proportions. He'd never tell the man to his face how he'd come up with the nickname. Rex, short for T-Rex. Although, he suspected Rex might actually appreciate the dinosaur comparison. Maybe not the lizard.

Bottom line, the man followed orders and was loyal to a fault. In this business those two traits were invaluable and had saved him more times than he liked to admit.

On his phone's screen the red dot pulsed, moving but very little. She was still here...somewhere. He stretched his neck to see above and in between the crowd. He needed to quiet his stomach.

He tapped the earbud and told Rex, "I'm gonna grab a quick sandwich. You want anything?"

"I'm good."

Of course, he was good. He'd downed three fast-food breakfast sandwiches between hits. The man could wolf down food no matter the circumstances.

Braxton saw a vendor on the other side. The line didn't look long. He wasn't thrilled about a plastic-wrapped pre-made sandwich, but it'd have to do. He waited for a janitor and cart to pass then he weaved his way through traffic.

15

In the back her mind Frankie kept telling herself, just be exactly what people expect to see.

Walk with purpose. But not too fast.

Get to the next bathroom. But again, not too fast.

Remember, you don't enjoy cleaning toilets so much that you're in a rush. Keep it slow.

People stepped aside for the moving cart, but no one really took time to look at her. In a matter of seconds she was steering the cart right by Gate 2, the mop handle bouncing around in front of her. A broom was slid into the left side of the cart with its bristles obscuring her vision, but it also would partly obscure her face.

Still, when she saw the man with the scar, every nerve ending came alert. He was looking up the ramp, watching for new passengers coming to the gates from the security checkpoint. She would be in his line of vision the entire trip. Would he notice something different about the woman pushing the cart?

Her heart already pounded in her ears. Would she even hear if the real janitor started yelling at her?

Passengers engulfed her on both sides, going both ways. She stayed close to the right, plodding along with a steady pace. She didn't stop for anyone, didn't weave around. A straight line.

Boarding calls blared around her. People talked on cell phones. Families scurried to keep up. Passengers bumped each other's roller cases without slowing and without apology. And Frankie just kept moving, pushing the cart, hoping to not meet up with another janitor pushing another cart.

The whole time she could feel the presence of the man with the scar. He was now behind her, his eyes on her back. Only a bit farther and she'd turn a corner to an open concourse with several paths to other gates. She tried to picture exactly where the escalator was. He wouldn't be able to see her once she turned that corner.

Unless he was walking up and down the ramp looking for her. He might be right behind her, right now. She didn't dare glance back.

She hugged the wall.

Almost there.

She turned right. Ten feet away was another women's restroom. Frankie guided the janitor cart into the entrance and waited for a group of women to exit. She did a quick scan to make sure no one could see her then she dug her bags out from deep inside the trash container. She didn't even care that her backpack now had something disgusting hanging from it. She simply brushed it off, shouldered both bags and left.

This time her eyes darted around searching for the man while she headed for the escalators. Walking briskly.

Don't run.

Once she hit the bottom it was an effort to keep from breaking out in a sprint.

Just keep walking. Blend in.

She glanced up at signs directing passengers, but Frankie really didn't need them. She knew exactly where to go. While other passengers moved toward baggage claim, she rushed to the exit. As soon as she walked out the door she gulped in the blast of fresh air. It didn't matter that it was filled with the fumes of gasoline and diesel. It was one step closer to escaping.

A shuttle started to leave, and she raised her hand, getting the driver's attention. He stopped. The side door slid open, and Frankie bounded up the steps. The door slid shut, and they were moving again, almost knocking her off her feet. She purposely by-passed several open seats. Her eyes darted out the windows. She wanted to see if the man with the scar had followed her outside. She tried to watch while she teetered down the aisle.

Very few passengers dared to look up at her and away from their phone screens. Most of the time it annoyed Frankie how glued people were to their electronic devices. Today, she was grateful for those same obsessions. She didn't want anyone to see the panic and urgency on her face, in her gestures. She made her way to the back, an empty bench all to herself. Only now did she realize she was out of breath.

No time to rest. She dug out her cell phone. She turned it on and ignored the messages pinging and lighting up. Instead, she brought up the rental car service still bookmarked. Not the one McGavin Holt always had her use. The one her boyfriend—ex-boyfriend—had a membership with. The one Gordon had asked her to use when she arranged their weekend getaway before Christmas. Before she knew the lying bastard was banging his fitness trainer. The fitness trainer who used to be Frankie's friend. In a single swoop, she'd lost her two closest friends.

Forget about it, she told herself. She couldn't think about that right now.

What impressed her was how his rental car membership made it so easy and convenient. She brought up the website. She still remembered his gold card membership number, his user name and password. She even remembered his VISA number. Details, numbers—she had a knack. Call it payback. The best part, even though she was listed as a secondary driver, no one could track the rental car to her. It would be in his name.

In a matter of seconds she had an SUV reserved. A few minutes later, her watch vibrated letting her know she had a new email. She logged into her account and there waiting was the confirmation number along with the parking stall number. The keys would be in the vehicle, and it would be ready to go when she arrived in the next ten to fifteen minutes.

Okay, so this would just take her longer. She should have thought of it sooner. She could have saved herself the cost of a flight and the near confrontation with Tyler's attacker. She shut down her phone. Tossed it into her bag and told herself she'd need to use the pre-paid phones from here on out. And as soon as she got outside of the Chicago area, she would call Hannah, again.

She leaned her head against the back of the seat. She could relax if even for a short time. And yet, her heart still pounded in her ears. Without glancing down, she knew her hands were still shaking.

She'd be okay. She just needed to get away from Chicago. Lose these guys. Whatever was going on, Hannah would help her figure out what to do.

16

Old Ebbitt Grill
Washington, D.C.

Maggie O'Dell arrived late. But she had a good excuse. This was the third time in less than a month that her boss had called her into his office for an unscheduled meeting. Twice before, the impromptu summons seemed like a waste of time to Maggie. Checking and double-checking on reports that had already been submitted. In hindsight, Maggie now wondered if those two call-ins were simply practice runs for today. Because today's meeting was a doozy.

She waved to the host who was busy with a couple of politicians she recognized. Poor Ermelo was getting an earful, but he nodded for her to go ahead and gestured toward the back. She found her friend, Gwen Patterson in their favorite corner, sipping a glass of wine.

"Sorry," Maggie said as she slid in on the opposite side of the booth. She'd already texted an explanation earlier.

A waiter appeared with a bottle of Sam Adams and a frosted pilsner. When he left, Maggie raised an eyebrow at her friend and said, "A beer for lunch?"

"It's Friday. I put in our food order already, too. I'm starving."

Maggie was glad to hear that. Chemo had stolen her friend's appetite for too long. It wasn't bad enough that it had also replaced Gwen's beautiful, strawberry-blond hair with a steel gray. She used to wear it chin-length but now kept it clipped short, almost a pixie-style that actually made her look younger, despite the gray.

"Everything okay?" Gwen asked.

Maggie smiled as she poured the beer.

"What?"

"All you've been through, and you're always worried about me."

"Someone has to," Gwen said, matter-of-fact and sipped her wine.

Gwen was fifteen years older than Maggie. She'd been a mentor to her when Maggie was a newbie, just getting started as a criminal profiler. Gwen was a consultant to the FBI's Behavioral Science Unit, and the two had worked together to apprehend some of the deadliest and most dangerous killers.

"A.D. Kunze wanted to let me know that the director was impressed with the way I handled the human trafficking case in Nebraska."

Gwen raised her glass, "Congratulations."

"That was last fall. Why would he take four months to tell me that?"

"The director or Raymond?"

Maggie held back a grimace. Sometimes she hated that Gwen was on a first name basis with her boss, but her friend's question only confirmed what Maggie was already thinking. When had the director told Kunze that he was impressed with her? Maybe it didn't matter.

Their food arrived, and Maggie sat back. The waiter had also brought a second glass of wine for Gwen. He asked if Maggie would like a second beer, but she had barely taken a drink and shook her head. She was surprised to see that he had two platters with burgers. Gwen was a gourmet cook and lately chose one of the seafood entrees from the menu, only to pick at it, eating very little.

She glanced at Gwen preparing her sandwich, adding salt and pepper then carefully placing—from the side garnish—pickles, jalapenos, onion and lettuce. It was the most interest she'd seen Gwen give food in a long time. Maggie fussed over her own sandwich, pretending that her friend's sudden appetite wasn't a big deal.

"Go on," Gwen said as she sliced her creation in half. Her fingers expertly picked up the first half, keeping everything together. She stopped before bringing it to her lips. "So tell me," she coaxed. "Why was he finally telling you what the director said?"

"Because the director is creating a new special unit to assist local law enforcement in solving violent crimes. They just invested millions to upgrade ViCap and our crime lab. Maybe he's looking to justify the expense."

ViCap was the Violent Criminal Apprehension Program, a unit of the bureau that analyzed and collected data on violent and sexual crimes.

"Actually that's a great idea," Gwen said. "Getting back to solving crimes instead of getting mixed up in politics."

"Do you really believe that's possible for Kunze? He seems to thrive on having all those connections."

Gwen shrugged. "Sounds like he might not have a choice if Director Bowman has something else in mind."

The new FBI director had been on the job less than a year and had already made it clear he wanted no part of letting the agency be used for political football. Maggie couldn't help wondering how that set with her boss, Assistant Director Kunze who had made a career by exchanging favors with politicians. Too many times he'd sent her on wild goose chases to check on political pet projects of various members of congress. Once, he even ordered Maggie to retrieve a senator's family along with their houseboat from the middle of the Gulf of Mexico during a severe thunderstorm. And he usually equipped her with less information than he had available, willing to put her in danger for the sake of keeping his contacts from a media firestorm or scandal.

"So this new unit," Gwen said using her fork to punctuate the word *unit*. "It sounds interesting. And it sounds like perhaps Bowman wants you to be a part of it?"

Maggie nodded while she chewed, holding up a finger for Gwen to give her a second or two. She was still processing her conversation with Kunze. It seemed a bit surreal. Finally she swallowed, wiped her mouth with the cloth napkin and said, "He wants me to be the head of it."

Her friend's face lit up. "Oh Maggie, that's fantastic. The director must have been very impressed."

"A.D. Kunze said I can pick my team, but of course, he already presented me with names he *highly* recommends I consider. Your name is on his list."

"Mine?"

Gwen had remained a consultant to the FBI despite having her own successful psychiatrist practice. When she found out she had breast cancer two years ago she scaled back, seeing fewer clients, turning down speaking engagements. Maggie still remembered being stunned and a bit scared that her mentor, her rock, seemed to shrink away from her normal everyday life to adjust to her new reality. Gwen Patterson was one of the strongest women Maggie knew, and she hated seeing her friend so filled with doubts and fears that it had almost crippled her.

"You said you could use a break from listening to the meltdowns of DC's political class." Gwen's clients ranged from congressional staffers to senators' spouses and even a four-star general.

"That's quite the choice," Gwen laughed. "Listening to politico meltdowns or chasing criminals?"

In her role as consultant, Maggie knew Gwen had helped with some of their strangest and most dangerous cases. She was an expert in criminal behavior, having penned numerous articles and several books. Not only had she interviewed killers but several times she had also been caught up in their sick mind games. Maggie would be lucky to have her be a part of this unit and a part of her team.

"You have so many talented FBI agents you could choose from," Gwen said.

"But none that I trust like I trust you."

Gwen nodded. "Let me think about it, okay?"

"Sure. No problem," but Maggie could hear her own disappointment in her voice before she tried to stash it away. And Gwen noticed.

"It's just that, maybe I should talk to R.J. about it first."

FBI agent R.J. Tully was Gwen's significant other and Maggie's sometimes partner.

"Are you worried you might not be able to work together?"

"You're asking R.J. to be a part of your team?"

"Of course," Maggie said. She hadn't even considered that he might not agree.

"Then I should definitely talk to him about it."

"You've worked together dozens of times before."

"Not since the cancer. He's been a bit overprotective of me."

"I get that. He doesn't want to lose you."

"It's not like I'm in the line of fire like you two." Gwen finished the last bite of her hamburger. Maggie was glad none of this conversation had taken away her appetite. "You and Ben have worked together, and it hasn't always gone well."

"It's not quite the same thing." Maggie sipped her beer. "Ben and I aren't...well, you know. We're not in a relationship."

"Does he know that?"

"Of course, he does. It was his choice, remember?"

Dr. Benjamin Platt was the director of USAMRIID (United States Army Medical Research Institute of Infectious Diseases). They had grown close while Maggie was under Ben's care after being exposed to the Ebola virus. There was a time when she believed they might become more than friends, but Ben had made it clear he wanted to have more children. His only daughter had died of complications of the flu while Ben was deployed to Afghanistan. As an officer and a medical doctor it seemed a cruel irony that he would be saving the lives of soldiers and unable to help save his only child seven thousand miles away.

"So what about Ryder Creed? Do you think the two of you will have any problems working together now that you've…you know, been together?"

This wasn't a subject Maggie wanted to talk about.

"Ryder and I agreed to not talk about it." She took a gulp of her beer. "Besides he's younger than me. He just turned thirty."

"You know you get nowhere with that excuse. R.J. is younger than me. By the way, what did you get him for his birthday?"

She knew Gwen was right. Age was a stupid excuse. Ryder was an old soul. Sometimes he seemed wiser and more mature than she was.

"A GPS watch," she finally answered when she realized Gwen was waiting for her response.

"Those are nice." Gwen's eyes were watching her, studying her. "Expensive. Sort of a relationship worthy gift."

"Oh no. Do you think so? I don't want him to get the wrong idea."

"I think the sex might have already done that."

Maggie winced, and it only made Gwen laugh.

"Why does this make you so uncomfortable? It seems so obvious that you both care deeply for each other. You've been through some crazy, difficult situations. Mudslides, an explosion, the bird flu. What else will it take to make you realize what this guy means to you?"

"Maybe I just don't know how to do relationships. Maybe it's the relationship part that scares me."

"Scares you? Bullshit! That's a cop-out."

Maggie raised her eyebrows. She rarely heard Gwen swear. This conversation had taken too serious of a turn.

"Hey, come on now," she said with a smile. "Contrary to popular belief, I do have feelings."

"Yes, you do. And you are braver and stronger than anyone I know. I've seen you stand face-to-face with killers. You can be fearless. And yet, you're a big ole scaredy-cat when it comes to getting close to someone. Trusting someone."

"Yes."

"Why?"

"Because it's the one thing I know can hurt me beyond repair. And I can't control it. I have no defense against it."

"Oh sweetie. We all have those fears to some degree. You know after the mastectomy I convinced myself that R.J. would leave me."

"Seriously? He's crazy about you."

"I knew it was more about me, my fears of not feeling whole. It had little to do with him. At the same time it made me realize how much I want him in my life. How much I *need* him in my life."

Gwen pushed her plate away and pulled her wine glass closer all the while never taking her eyes off Maggie.

"It's easier to rely on just myself," Maggie finally said. "Any time I've counted on someone else I've been disappointed—present company excluded, of course." When Gwen didn't answer, Maggie filled the silence. "Is that so awful?"

"I just worry that you're missing out on some incredible happiness while you're protecting yourself. In the meantime, what about Ryder? He appears to be someone who's been through his own personal fires. I'd venture to guess that he has his own issues with trust and commitment. Are you being fair to him? Not trusting him after all you two have been through?"

"I do trust him. He's saved my ass a couple of times. So obviously I trust him with my ass."

Gwen smiled and said, "Your ass and the rest of your body." Then as if that wasn't enough damage, she followed with, "But not your heart."

When Maggie's phone started ringing the sound was muffled inside her jacket pocket. She tugged it out as quickly as possible but not before other diners scowled at her.

"I'm sorry," she told Gwen. "I should have shut it off."

"Take it. I really don't mind."

When Maggie glanced at the caller's I.D., her first thought was that somehow the person on the other line had read her mind.

"Hi Hannah. How are you?"

17

Southern Alabama

(50 miles south of Montgomery)

For the last several miles Ryder Creed had to swerve around pieces of debris in the road. He first noticed trees stripped of their leaves, and in some instances, stripped of their bark, too. In two spots he had to stop and remove fallen branches, once pulling out his chainsaw. Electrical poles leaned, wires dangled and swung in the breeze. Then he started seeing not just branches, but whole trees, shoved onto their sides exposing tentacles of roots. It looked like a giant had plucked them out of the ground and flung them aside.

From the road, Creed saw pine trees snapped in two. Rows and rows of them. An entire forest gone. He could see the horizon that was normally blocked. This area of southern Alabama was thick with pine, pecan and century-old oaks. Sometimes the kudzu grew so thick it netted the trees together. He'd seen the invasive vine take over and swallow abandoned sheds and rusted old tractors, covering them like a blanket of green. But all of that was gone now, sucked up and leaving broken stumps in puddles of muddy water.

He came around a curve and slammed on the brakes. The asphalt buckled in front of him. Huge swatches were gone, puzzle pieces chiseled out, leaving behind crumbs. The ditches ran full and in places overflowed across the highway filling the deep gouges.

Creed looked up in the rearview mirror. He'd insisted Grace stay in her crate instead of sitting in her regular spot on the folded bench behind him. The hard-shell was placed in the middle with the door facing forward, so she could still look over the Jeep's center console and get air from the vents.

"What do you think, Grace?"

She was standing, staring out the windshield. She glanced at him and sniffed the air. She was ready to get to work. That the landscape looked like an explosion had ripped through the area wouldn't bother her. Creed had worked after hurricanes and mudslides, but this...this reminded him of Afghanistan.

Creed kept the Jeep idling and the A/C blasting. The clouds had disappeared. The rain had washed the sky blue, but now the sun added even more heat and moisture. He kept the radio tuned to a local news station, listening for updates along with weather forecasts, not deceived by the sudden lack of clouds. When he used the chainsaw earlier, he could taste the salt and humidity in the air. The storms weren't over. This was only the calm in between.

He checked his vehicle's GPS. A portion of Interstate 65 was still closed, so he'd taken this alternative. Highway 31 ran parallel. He was surprised no one else had been through then he remembered that most of the first responders would be coming from the other direction, down from Montgomery.

He knew this area well enough to know that there were only a few straight routes. The unpaved back roads twisted, curved and looped adding extra miles. Most of them were dirt and gravel surface, sometimes more clay than dirt. If the tornado had chewed up and spit out asphalt, it had probably made a rutted mess of the others.

"Hang on, girl," he told Grace as he backed up a short ways and scanned the highway beyond this buckle. There was more debris up ahead, but after this section at least the asphalt looked smooth again. Finally, he decided the Jeep could handle it.

The next five miles included two more stops to clear sheet metal and to cut more branches. As he got closer to the Interstate 65 junction he started seeing more debris, bigger pieces he could identify. He almost wished he couldn't. A car door, a twisted bumper, sections of chain-link fence, chunks of roof, scattered bricks.

Further along, instead of pieces there were piles: shredded metal, a billboard stuck in a tree, a six-story cell tower bent in half. Then he started seeing the vehicles: toppled, smashed and ripped apart.

Creed had seen traffic accidents. Pile-ups on the interstate. Vehicles rolled and upside down in the ditch. But the scene around him now looked like nothing he'd seen before.

In the field to his right, a stock trailer had been tossed and now laid on its side. Cows were being coaxed out of the wreckage. Except for a few stumbles, they looked fine. He checked his rearview mirror and saw Grace watching the cattle.

"They seem to be okay," he told the dog. "How is that possible?"

The cab wasn't there, and Creed's eyes scanned the field, the toppled trees, and debris. Pink cotton candy clung to the leafless branches of a giant oak that managed to remain standing, the tree a beacon in the now stripped horizon. A large piece of metal wrapped around the trunk, and Creed felt his stomach twist when he recognized what was once a chrome grille and bumper.

He shook his head. Mother Nature's cruel irony—the cattle walked away unscathed, but the driver of the rig? Creed couldn't imagine anyone inside that cab had survived.

He glanced back at Grace. Her nose bobbed, sniffing and watching. There would be too much scent. Blood and death dragged, scattered and flung. He'd worked a couple hurricanes and a mudslide. It was difficult in natural disasters like this where rescues quickly turned into recoveries. As a multi-scent dog Grace had been trained to find the lost as well as the dead.

She could also sniff out cocaine and meth, C. diff and the bird flu. Two years ago, Creed and Grace had made national headlines when a search for drugs on a commercial fishing boat turned up a drug cartel's second cargo. Grace had made the discovery under a hull filled with mahi-mahi. Instead of cocaine, she'd alerted to five children stashed under the floorboards. The cartel had kidnapped them and were planning on trafficking them.

Even Creed had been amazed with his dog and the fact that she could smell the children under the big fish that were stacked three-feet-deep. Ironically, the word "fish" was the search term he and Grace used for drugs. Asking her to find fish in a crowded airport drew less attention and panic.

But now, as Creed pulled the Jeep to a stop, he was overwhelmed by the devastation in front of him. He realized how difficult this task would be. Grace would need his help. He'd need to give her direction without hampering her.

Survival time after a disaster like this would be a narrow window. Yet, he couldn't ask Grace to ignore the dead for the sake of finding the living, because there wouldn't be much distinction in the scent. This soon after the tornado, blood was still blood. And it could have been dragged or flung far away from where the body might have ended up. More than ever, Creed would need to follow the number one piece of advice he gave all of his handlers. He needed to trust his dog.

First, he checked to see if he had cell phone reception. He promised to text Hannah when he arrived. But more than that, he needed to ask her to send Jason and Scout. In the distance, he could see the glint off metal and glass. Vehicles were flung in every direction. It looked like a giant had tossed his entire collection of matchbox cars. There was no way Creed and Grace would be able to do this alone.

18

Birmingham, Alabama

Willis Dean glanced up to see Mia Long standing in front of his desk. He'd retreated to his messy office just a few minutes ago. They'd gone off the air after the last watch and warning expired, but Willis couldn't stop looking at the photos coming in. He'd been concerned about Smiths Crossings and grateful none of the area schools had been hit. But he hadn't considered the interstate.

Crumpled vehicles had been tossed and scattered over the fields. Debris littered the area, pieces strung from the few trees that were still standing. At the interstate junction, piles of brick and boards, glittering glass and more smashed trucks and cars were all that remained from what was once a gas station, fast food restaurant and convenience store. From the aerial drone photos, he wondered how in the world anyone had survived.

"Four dead," he said, shaking his head.

"It's a wonder there weren't more," Mia told him.

This time when he looked up he noticed that she had a takeout container in one hand and a coffee mug in the other. She gestured for him to clear a spot so she could set them down.

"You're bringing me food?"

"You haven't eaten since you got here. Paul ordered sandwiches. I grabbed a ham and cheese for you."

"Thanks."

Instead of making a spot for her to set the container down, Willis took it and the mug then did a half-circle, suddenly overwhelmed with the mess that surrounded him. A mess that usually didn't bother him. Finally, he decided a pile on the credenza behind him looked sturdy enough for the food container. He sat back down and sipped the coffee. It was still hot with just the right amount of cream, no sugar. Mia always remembered exactly how he liked it.

"We heard from Gary."

"And?" His eyebrow lifted at the same time that his stomach clenched and prepared him for the worst.

"His crew's okay. A few scrapes and cuts. They're still a bit shaken up."

"How close were they?"

"Too close. He said it whipped their vehicle around. Broke every window."

Willis took off his glasses and rubbed his eyes. He was exhausted, but he immediately felt a tension in his shoulders break loose. When the damage reports started coming in, he realized where the tornado had hit. No matter how many precautions a storm chaser took, there was always a risk.

He glanced at the monitor on his desk as the screen refreshed. The new reports were already coming in from the National Weather Service.

"How do you want to handle the schedule?" Mia asked.

The first outbreak of the season. Everyone would be on-call, but of course, his entire crew would want to be in on it. They were all weather geeks. Even if they weren't in the studio they'd be on their phones and iPads checking the radar, watching the sky.

"Why don't you go home and get some rest," he told her. "I'm doing the radio interviews this afternoon. I just as well stay."

"Okay, I'll see you later."

She turned to leave, and Willis was relieved that she hadn't seen through his excuse. He could easily do the radio interviews from home. He'd done that many times before. When Mia stopped in the doorway, he felt his heart skip a beat.

He was practically holding his breath when she glanced over her shoulder and pointed her chin at his credenza.

"Don't forget to eat."

"Oh yeah. Thanks again."

His desk phone started ringing. She gave him one last wave and was gone.

"Willis Dean," he answered.

"Dad, I tried to call you, but you must still have your cell phone off."

"Robbie, are you okay?" He grabbed at the jacket he'd left draped over his chair. He dug the cell phone out of his pocket.

"What's going on? Mom said you guys are getting a divorce."

Willis slouched back in his chair and slid the phone across his desk. That was just like Beth. She kept everything secret, but when she made the decision to tell, she told everyone.

He'd never lied to his boys, and he wouldn't start now.

"I guess we are."

"So it was a surprise to you, too?"

Willis couldn't help but smile. It appeared his oldest knew his parents well.

"Yes, it was."

His wife's unhappiness was a complete surprise to him. He knew that he spent too many hours consumed by his job. How many family events had he walked in the door late or missed entirely? But he loved his boys. He loved his wife. He'd never questioned either.

It was at that moment it occurred to Willis, his three sons would be just fine. All of them were off building lives of their own. Beth would be fine, too. She had said as much. Willis would be the only one displaced from his home of thirty years, the rose garden he'd curated, the magnolia trees and crepe myrtles he had planted along with the bird feeders he'd built and placed.

It was clear to him now that he spent too much time in his backyard and literally with his head in the clouds.

"Dad," his son's voice brought him back. "Maybe it'll all blow over, just like the storms. You know mom. Tomorrow she might change her mind and redecorate a different room."

That made Willis smile, but a bit of sadness poked at him. Maybe that was the problem, Willis realized. Maybe he really didn't know his wife. He didn't seem to know her at all.

19

Southern Alabama

(50 miles south of Montgomery)

Sheriff Krenshaw took a look at Grace then took a step back as if to get a better view of the handler and dog.

"Search dogs I've worked with before are usually bigger. Labs, shepherds. What the hell is this?"

"Jack Russell terrier. Her name's Grace."

"Where you from, son?"

Creed was used to this. He didn't take offense. Instead, he simply said, "Florida Panhandle. Just outside of Pensacola."

"Look son, no disrespect intended but…"

Creed relaxed his stance even as he braced himself for the insult, because usually when people prefaced a remark with, "no disrespect intended," it was right before they said something insulting.

"This is only the beginning," the sheriff said as he waved his arm in a wide circle as if to emphasize the enormity of the disaster. "We have more storms coming. That means we don't have much time to find survivors. They're saying this weekend could be as bad as 2011. Now again, no disrespect, son, but you probably were off surfing at Pensacola Beach in 2011 and don't even remember that massive outbreak."

"You're right I don't remember. I was in Afghanistan."

The man blinked several times, and Creed could see his jawline tighten like he'd just bitten down on something bitter.

"Army?" he asked.

"Marines." Creed waited a beat and added, "I was a K9 handler."

Now the sheriff shook his head, "First out. First to die."

Creed nodded.

"Desert Storm," the man tapped his own chest. "I remember a K9 handler we had in our unit for a short time. He saved all our asses a couple of times."

Marine K9 units moved from one platoon to another for weeks at a time. For that reason Creed and Rufus were always the outsiders. And yes, everyone knew they were the first out, first to die. The platoon knew not to get attached to them, even though they depended on the pair to get them through fields of IEDs or booby-trapped buildings. What Creed and Rufus did—especially the dog's ability to warn them—it seemed a little bit like magic to the others. They were never sure whether the K9 team would end up saving them or getting them all killed. But one thing they knew for sure was that Creed and Rufus would be the first out, first to die.

"Hell," Krenshaw was shaking his head, "I owe you an apology."

"Don't worry about it."

"No, no, I am truly sorry." The man's entire demeanor changed. His arms went slack as his sides. "My wife keeps telling me I've gotten too damned cynical in my advanced age. Says I'm too quick to judge people on account of all the assholes I've dealt with over the years."

"Hey, I see you two met," a woman said as she came up from behind him.

"Norwich, I just made a damn ass of myself. You should have told me Mr. Creed was a Marine."

Sheriff Norwich shook Creed's hand then leaned down and gave her fingertips to Grace to sniff. She didn't attempt to pet Grace. The scent offering was her greeting, and Creed appreciated it.

"He has a young Army Ranger who works for him. Smart as a whip,"

Norwich said. "I worked with him last fall down in my neck of the woods."

Norwich was the sheriff of Santa Rosa County in Florida. Creed knew she was out of her territory. Probably on her day off.

"I've asked Jason to join me," Creed told both sheriffs. "Grace and I may need some help. This heat and humidity can wear a dog out pretty quickly."

"Does your Army Ranger have a little bitty thing like this, too?" Apparently Krenshaw still wasn't satisfied with Grace's stature.

Before Creed could answer, Norwich said, "Mr. Creed takes in shelter dogs and trains them for all kinds of scents. This little bit of a thing found that young woman in the river last year. Down in the forest. Come to think of it," and she glanced up at Creed, "She found Sheriff Wylie, too. Didn't she?"

Creed nodded. Both deaths had looked like suicides. It wasn't until later they were ruled homicides. When Grace found nineteen-year-old Izzy Donner, she was floating in the Blackwater River. He could still see the image of her dead body. Her jacket billowed around her. Her pockets had been filled with rocks and anchored her body to the bottom of the shallow river. Her eyes stared up at the sky.

He could still see Sheriff Wylie, too. He and Grace found him days later, along the river behind Wylie's cabin. Only he wasn't in the river. He was hanging from the branch of a huge oak tree.

Now, Creed scanned the horizon as more first responders and volunteers arrived. He had a feeling his catalog of images was about to get updated with a whole new category of gruesome.

"From what we know so far, it missed Smith Crossings," the sheriff was telling Creed. "Hit a couple of farms and homes on the outskirts. This here," Krenshaw pointed with his chin, his hands deep in his pockets, "took the brunt of the storm. On one hand, it's fortunate it missed those more populated areas. On the other hand, we have no idea how many people were here when it hit. Or how far it may have taken them.

"We just pulled out a bunch of travelers that were trapped in the restrooms at that convenience store."

Where the sheriff pointed, about thirty feet away, looked more like discarded rubble from a construction site—a pile ten feet high of cinder blocks, broken glass, dismantled shelves, shingles and two-by-fours. Three of the walls were sheered away. A section to the back remained standing. Creed guessed that was where the restrooms were. In front of the wall, an end cap display stood. It looked untouched.

Sheriff Norwich noticed where Creed's eyes had stayed and said, "Bags of potato chips. Still on the shelves. And that's not even the craziest thing you'll see today."

"This interstate exit has the convenience store, a gas station and a fast food place. You can see they all took a massive hit. Four fatalities. Nine sent off to area hospitals." He shook his head. "A couple of them...they didn't look too good. That's just what we've found so far. We have no idea what's waiting for us in the fields."

"I saw a stock trailer on my way here," Creed mentioned.

"Unfortunately, the driver will most likely be added to the fatality list. That is, if and when we find him. The response team's already pulled out a few people from their vehicles. They're trying their level best to get to as many as they can." He glanced at his wristwatch. "We're five hours into this. You know as well as I do, time is not on our side. I'm hoping that's where your dog comes in. Maybe speed this up a bit. Hopefully...Grace, is it?"

Creed nodded.

"Hopefully, Grace can tell us whether or not there are any survivors in some of these vehicles." Then he turned, put his hand up to block out the sun and added, "Or anywhere in those fields."

20

Quantico, Virginia

After Hannah's call Maggie left her friend, Gwen and headed back to her office at Quantico. Not much larger than a utility closet with bookcases and a desk, the space had always brought her a sense of comfort. It was her sanctuary despite all the horrific crime scene photos and files she had viewed over the years.

She had decorated with a smattering of personal items—here and there. Several file cabinets were stuffed full from an era before digital storage was possible. Maggie had occupied this same office ever since she came to Quantico as a forensic fellow. Had she pushed, she probably could have moved to a bigger one after she became an agent. But this place suited her. For some reason it didn't feed or prick at her claustrophobia. Most days, anyway. Besides, she knew exactly where everything was. Even now, she went immediately to a file drawer and pulled out the folder she needed.

Hannah Washington had asked Maggie for a favor. She knew Hannah well enough to know the woman didn't ask for favors. She was the type of person others went to for help and advice. So Maggie knew it wasn't easy for Hannah to call her.

"I've never heard Frankie so scared," Hannah had told her about her friend.

Maggie listened, taking mental notes and even writing down names on the back of a notepad that Gwen had quickly found in her handbag and handed to Maggie back at the restaurant.

In her file cabinet, Maggie found the Chicago detective's business card in the folder. A personal cell phone number was scrawled on the flipside. Maggie had met Detective Lexington "Lexi" Jacks last year. If she remembered correctly it was also in March. An unexpected snowstorm had greeted her at O'Hare International. Jacks picked her up. It was the first time the two women had met, and yet, Jacks had been concerned that Maggie didn't have a coat. Actually, Maggie didn't believe it was concern as much as impatience. But the two had bonded over the fact that both of them had even less patience for bureaucracy. She was hoping Jacks still harbored that particular impatience.

Chicago was an hour behind Virginia, but Maggie was still surprised when the woman answered on the third ring.

"This is Jacks."

"Detective, it's Agent Maggie O'Dell."

There was only a slight pause.

"Don't take this the wrong way, O'Dell, but it's a gorgeous spring day here. I hope you're not about to screw that up and tell me the FBI is interested in another of my cases."

"It's good to talk to you again, too." Maggie smiled.

"Sorry, I guess I should ask how you are. The last I heard you were in an isolation ward."

"It was just a precaution."

Ryder, Grace and Maggie had been exposed to the bird flu in the same case that Jacks referred to. It had gotten the FBI's attention and also prompted the CDC into cordoning off an entire floor of a luxury hotel on Michigan Avenue. Jacks had not been happy that her team of detectives and officers had been reduced to security guards while the federal agency figured out if Chicago had been exposed to a deadly virus. Truthfully, Ryder, Grace and Maggie had been lucky. Very lucky.

"Actually," she told Jacks, "I am calling about a couple of homicides that may have happened in Chicago this morning."

"Really? A couple? You're gonna need to narrow it down for me, because as I understand it we've had four and the sun hasn't gone down yet."

"These would have been early this morning," Maggie said, not wasting the detective's time. "Two young men. One looked like a home invasion."

"Wicker Park."

"Your department called it a home invasion, but I'm betting there's something about it that isn't that simple."

"What's the FBI's interest?" Jacks wanted to know. She was making this more difficult than Maggie liked. Maybe they hadn't bonded quite as much as she thought they had.

"The computer was stolen," she told Jacks. "I'm guessing his cell phone and any other electronic devices are gone, too."

"Okay, how do you know that? Or is it a lucky guess?"

"Lucky guess. What do you know about the victim?"

"Computer analyst for Park House Labs. Mid-level entry position, from what I can tell. Lived alone. His sister lives a few blocks away. She IDed him. Said he was mostly a computer geek. Not into drugs. Doesn't even drink."

"I need to know if you had a second homicide. On the street. Not far from the home invasion. Might have looked like an armed robbery gone bad."

"Another lucky guess?"

Maggie could hear in Jacks' voice that she was growing impatient, but the detective's lack of denial meant Maggie was right, and Hannah's friend wasn't just paranoid.

"If you were able to ID him, his name is Tyler Gates."

She heard a hiss of air. Jacks was clearly not happy.

"How the hell do you know this? We haven't released anything about the second hit."

"You already suspect the two are connected?"

"That neighborhood is not exactly known for random execution-style murders. But we haven't been able to connect the dots yet. You care to fill me in?"

Execution-style.

Hannah had told Maggie that Frankie Russo was still hoping her friend and co-worker had been injured. That maybe he was unconscious and in an emergency room somewhere. Or in surgery.

"How did you ID Gates?"

"Wallet was still in his jacket pocket. Cell phone is missing. We're still trying to see if any cameras in the area might have captured it or caught an image of the perpetrators."

Maggie sat forward, elbows on her desk. Frankie Russo had told Hannah that she and Tyler were video-chatting when two men approached him. She got a look at one, but feared that he also got a good look at her. Maggie now realized it didn't matter whether or not the man saw her. He had something even better to identify her than a quick peek over the device's small screen. As long as he had Gate's phone, he had access to much more, including her home address and possibly her texts and emails.

"So what gives, O'Dell?"

She'd almost forgotten about Jacks.

"The two men were friends," Maggie told her. "They might have hacked into a computer system and found something they weren't supposed to find."

There was a long pause.

"Okay," the detective said. "I think you better start telling me everything you know before I share anything more."

21

Frankie felt the adrenaline drain. Coffee no longer helped. It just made her have to pee, and she didn't want to stop unless she needed to fill the tank. Which meant gas station toilets and gas station coffee.

Earlier, she'd called Hannah using one of the burner phones to tell her she was driving down instead. Frankie told her about the men at the airport, how she recognized the one by the scar on his neck.

"Hannah, they knew exactly what gate. How is that possible?"

Hannah was one of the calmest, steadiest people Frankie knew, but she could hear the worry wrapped tight in Hannah's words.

"Just come on home, girl," she told Frankie. "Be careful. Be smart. We'll figure this out. And please, just let me know where you are. Even if it's a quick text."

For the first four hours Frankie constantly checked her rearview mirrors. She took unnecessary exits only to loop back onto the interstate. The whole time she watched to see if any vehicles stayed with her. She kept telling herself it was crazy to think they could have followed her from the airport. But then they had shown up inside the exact terminal at her flight's gate. Was it possible they had access to her credit card information? That still didn't explain how they knew what flight she'd booked.

Who the hell were these guys?

She shook her head and said out loud, "Tyler, what kind of mess did you get yourself into?"

Maybe they'd laugh about it someday.

She met her eyes in the rearview mirror and shook her head, again.

You know he's not okay. Why lie to yourself?

Maybe because she still had too many hours to go, alone and on the road. How did she forget it was a fourteen-hour drive from Chicago to the panhandle of Florida? In her defense, it had been over a decade since she'd driven the route. The rare times she went down to visit her father she had taken a flight that amounted to a couple of hours.

Her rental car didn't have a GPS. Her mistake. In her hurry, she'd forgotten to request one. She was just grateful to have a black Ford Escape waiting for her, right in stall I-24 with the key FOB and papers on the driver's seat. When she got to the exit booth and handed the printout, along with her driver's license, the attendant barely glanced at it.

For the first time since Tyler's phone call, she could breathe.

But it was short-lived. She had barely left the maze of rental car companies and felt like she was driving in circles, not sure what exit was needed to escape the swirl of interstate junctions that all seemed to lead to O'Hare. Quickly, she realized she needed directions.

She had pulled off into a fast food parking lot and tucked her smaller vehicle between two large SUVs. She'd never used a burner phone before and panicked when she realized it didn't have Internet access and couldn't even connect to Wi-Fi. She caved in and turned on her cell phone after promising herself that she wouldn't. But she desperately needed GPS just to get out of Chicago.

Later, at one of her first gas station stops, she asked the clerk if they had any road maps. He stared at her as though she were a Martian. Finally he told her "no." Then he added that the McDonald's up the road had free Wi-Fi access. She simply said, "thanks," not wanting to see the look on his face if she told him she couldn't use her cell phone. Despite her screw-ups, she knew the last thing she needed was to be memorable in case someone did come along behind her, asking about her.

Now here Frankie was, seven hours outside of Chicago. She passed an exit for Nashville. Signs announced there would be more exits for the city in the next several miles. Ordinarily, there'd be a few more hours of sunlight, but dark clouds were rolling in from the west. Frankie had noticed the temperature and humidity raised a notch with each stop for gas, fogging up her sunglasses as soon as she got out of the car. Only halfway to her destination, and exhaustion had begun to seep into her veins.

"Face it, Frankie," she told herself in the rearview mirror. With the darkening sky, she'd removed the sunglasses and could see her puffy eyes. "You don't have the energy to drive through thunderstorms."

Back at the gas station where she'd asked about maps—just outside of Indianapolis—she'd taken the clerk's advice and stopped at the McDonald's. She hadn't eaten anything except an apple back at the airport. At the McDonald's, she had backed into a spot under a tree where she ate and watched every vehicle that came into the parking lot. If the man with the scar was following her, she'd see him before he saw her. Or so she told herself.

The comfort food had not only settled the acid in her stomach, but it had also calmed down her anxiety a notch. Enough so, that she had dug out her cell phone charger and plugged it in. She turned on the phone no longer admonishing herself. But this time, she had looked up the rest of her route and jotted down notes including cities, exits and how many miles in between. It was a straight shot down I-65. That shouldn't have been difficult to remember, and yet, she felt more vulnerable without the GPS to direct her. Before she left the parking lot, she had sent Hannah a quick text:

JUST OUTSIDE INDIANAPOLIS. SO FAR, SO GOOD. XXOO

Now Frankie glanced at her watch, ignored that the stupid thing was telling her how many steps she was behind. Indianapolis was five hours ago. No wonder she was tired and hungry.

She started looking for exits with hotels. Not a motel, she decided. It had to be someplace with more than one door between her and anyone following. The hotel could be off the interstate but with an easy escape route. And someplace with more security than a guy at a front desk. Room service would be nice. She didn't want to leave once she settled in. And just in case they were tracking her credit card, she still had remembered Gordon's Visa number.

"Be smart," Hannah had told her.

Frankie followed the road signs and took an exit. She slowed down and watched to see who exited with her. Only one white car and when Frankie turned left, it turned right. Still, she drove a short ways and got back on the interstate. She took the next exit and relief washed over her when no one followed. And there in the near distance, she saw a sign for a luxury hotel brand she recognized. Six stories, a swanky lobby, room service, security cameras and keycard entrances. Everything a girl could want to feel safe and comforted. Yet, her eyes darted from one mirror to another.

"Are you back there somewhere, and I just can't see you?"

22

The first site the response team wanted Creed and Grace to search no longer looked like a vehicle. It had been thrown about 500 feet off the interstate. A state trooper and Sheriff Norwich led the way. They could reach the wreckage only by foot. Much of the way was flooded by ankle-deep water, and Creed hiked Grace up under his arm. Debris floated along the oily surface that glistened with shattered glass. He took careful steps over splintered wood and shredded metal. The scent of diesel permeated the air even this far away from the ruptured fuel lines at the gas station.

As they got closer, Creed could see that all but one of the car's tires had been sheared off. The hood and trunk were smashed in like a car crusher had prepared it for a garbage heap. The windows were gone, and in places even the paint had been peeled away. As Creed stood over the wreck he could see the roof looked like a huge claw had dragged over the top, cutting into the metal.

Though they had walked through running water to get to the vehicle, this section was dry. The tall grass around the smashed heap looked undisturbed. Creed examined the ground before he put Grace down and was surprised to find no pink insulation or shredded steel—not even a single piece of broken glass—tangled or deposited in the grass. It was as though the storm had sucked up the vehicle, chewed and battered and swallowed the pieces then spit out the empty hull. Creed realized that probably included the car's passengers.

"There's a body inside," the state trooper told Creed as if reading his mind.

The man had introduced himself as Jim Sykes. He was as tall as Creed with a sun-weathered face, unflinching gray eyes and a confident gait that gave Creed the impression he had seen things as gruesome as today's findings.

"It's still strapped in."

Creed lowered Grace to the ground, holding tight to her leash. She had on a vest that signaled to her that they would be searching for people—no drugs, no bird flu, no C. diff. Although, if Grace detected any of those, she would still alert. Multi-task dogs couldn't help themselves. It wasn't a credit to the trainer as much as the skill of the dog. In Grace's case, Creed knew he was simply her anchor, protecting her and keeping her safe while she did her job. He'd never had a dog quite like Grace.

"What makes you think there was anyone else in the car?" Creed asked, keeping his eyes on Grace.

Her nose was up, sniffing and twitching. She had been testing the air the whole time he carried her, but now she was already working a scent. It was probably the body inside. Even Creed could smell the ripe decomp beginning in the sun-baked heat.

The trooper hadn't answered yet, and Creed glanced up at him.

"The body's still strapped in. On the passenger side."

Norwich bent down to look inside the vehicle then jerked back and shook her head.

"I've seen plenty of car accidents in my day," she said, "but I'm always shocked by what a tornado can do to a person."

Creed took a good look and didn't flinch. He expected the mangled corpse to resemble the victims he'd seen after IEDs. But this surprised him. The passenger's seatbelt was buckled keeping him in place. The airbags hadn't had a chance to inflate. The man's shirt had been sucked off. Only the band of fabric around his neck was left, identifying that he had been wearing a blue crewneck T-shirt. His chest and face had been pelted with debris. Leaves and pine needles stuck to his skin. Pieces of glass and gravel were embedded like shrapnel. Something white like cotton had tangled into his hair. Streams of blood, now dried, had run from his ears and his nose.

The eyes were always what haunted Creed. Wide open, they conveyed the shock and horror of those last seconds.

"His wallet was still in his pocket," Trooper Sykes told them. "We usually take digital photos, just of the face to make it easier on the families. But it's always easier if we have a driver's license."

"Have you done that yet?"

"No, not until we're finished. Or you tell us we're finished."

Creed glanced back into the vehicle. As if reading his mind, Trooper Sykes added, "Don't worry. I'll close his eyes."

Grace tugged at the end of her leash. She was getting impatient at being ignored. Creed glanced down at her as he unzipped his daypack for her toy. He needed to praise his dog. If they found any blood or decomp material—even it wasn't exactly what they'd been looking for—he rewarded his dogs. It reinforced their effort to continue searching. For the dog it was a game. If a handler wanted the dog to continue playing the game then it was important to not change the rules.

His fingers found Grace's reward—her pink, squeaky elephant—inside the pack. But before he could pull it out, he realized Grace wasn't alerting to the remains in the vehicle. She didn't have time for the easy gimme. Grace had already moved on to another scent, and she wanted to go follow it…now.

"We've walked this entire area," the trooper told Creed when he noticed Grace with her nose poking up. "You think she already smells something?"

"In a situation like this there's a lot of scatter."

"Scatter?"

Creed focused on Grace. Her whiskers were twitching. Her head bobbed as she breathed in, sampling the air. The sun was beating down, warming the air and making it rise, but the humidity would make it heavy, trapping it.

He glanced up to find both Trooper Sykes and Sheriff Norwich waiting for an explanation. Normally, he'd be more delicate in his response, but these two were seasoned law enforcement.

"Any time you have a case where a body is dragged, flung or possibly ripped apart, there's what we call a scatter of scent. The dog's smelling blood and decomposition but that doesn't mean it's a body. It could just be blood. It might be pieces of a body."

"Would it help if I pointed out what areas we've already walked?"

"No. Grace directs me," Creed told him. "You're both welcome to come with us, but I need you to stay back ten to twenty feet."

"Grace, find," he said, though she didn't need a search word. She was already keyed in on a scent.

She peddled hard, trying to pull Creed along. Out here, the trees were stripped of their leaves along with the kudzu, but at least, some of the trees were standing.

"Slow down, girl," he told her.

There was hardly any shade, and the sun was relentless. Creed didn't want Grace to get overheated. The temperature edged into the upper eighties and the humidity made it feel even warmer. Scenting dogs breathed in 140-200 times a minute compared to a dog taking a walk and breathing in thirty times a minute. But it wasn't just breathing. Grace was taking in air, sending it in different directions, separating and identifying the scents. She could get dehydrated quickly. She wouldn't stop until she found her target. It was Creed's number one job to make sure his dog wouldn't hurt herself.

He also needed to make sure the tall grass wasn't hiding sharp objects.

Grace had always fought him on wearing protective boots, but no footgear could prevent razor cuts from shards of glass or punctures from boards with nails. The storm had reduced everyday objects and thrown them around to make a dangerous obstacle course. From what he could tell, most of the debris out in this field was contained to the solid heaps the storm had spit out. Or at least, that was what Creed hoped.

Along the way he saw dozens of soda cans, unopened but crushed. There were stray pieces of fabric and paper. Twice he bent to pick up a scattering of photographs. Smiling faces, family reunions, graduation, a wedding. He tucked them into his daypack.

At the far end of the field, a long line of pine trees had fallen on their sides, like dominos, one then another on top of each other. From what Creed could see they still had their pine needles. All the branches were intact. It looked like the wind had gently pushed them over. And that's exactly where Grace was leading him.

He glanced back. Norwich and Sykes followed behind, keeping a good distance. What Creed wanted to see was how far back the vehicle with the missing driver was. It had to be 100 feet away.

Grace kept a steady pace, her breathing more rapid. She zig-zagged and weaved, running perpendicular to the line of downed pines. She had zeroed in on something, crossing in and out of the scent cone. Grace slowed to skim her nose over some scrubgrass and stopped to sniff a bush. Creed was about to offer her water, but then she started pulling him, again, angling toward the fallen pine trees.

He glanced back a second time. She was drawing him farther and farther away from the vehicle and any other debris. A breeze had picked up, and he realized they were downwind from the area Grace led him. That was a good thing and yet, Creed couldn't see any signs of a target source. Was it possible she was smelling drugs or chemicals that were included in explosives? With all the stuff that had gotten ripped up and blown away, many of those toxic chemicals were undoubtedly in the air. He trusted

Grace, but her ability to track multiple scents meant she could be leading him to a scent he hadn't asked her to find.

He couldn't imagine that the driver of that vehicle had been flung this far, but he and Grace had discovered stranger things. It was hard to explain, but finding a body—no matter how damaged—was actually easier than not finding the missing person. Coming up empty, left questions. Did he miss something? Had Grace tried to tell him or lead him and he hadn't read his dog correctly?

Percentage-wise a good deal of searches ended with no victim. Sure, some finds were gruesome. Creed thought about the guy still strapped into the vehicle. The driver would most likely be in far worse condition. But no matter how gruesome, the find meant success and would bring an end to the search.

There was an old saying among K9 groups. *Grief belongs to the families. Dread belongs to the handlers.*

He wiped sweat off his forehead with the back of his hand.

Trust your dog, he reminded himself. Grace was rarely wrong.

Now, up close and along side the pine trees, Creed marveled at the sight. Not a branch was broken, not even the trunks. It truly looked as if the wind had gently pushed them down, one after another. The ground pushed up revealing roots still attached and holding on.

Grace pranced to a spot in the middle and poked her nose into the thick swath of pine needles. The branches on top of branches made it impossible to see underneath. Grace pulled her nose out and shook her head, sending stray needles flying. Then she turned to look up at Creed, finding his eyes with an intent stare that was her alert.

She had found her target and was ready for her reward.

23

FBI Crime Lab
Quantico, Virginia

Maggie sat down next to Special Agent Antonio Alonzo. What he called his office looked more like a film editing booth. A half dozen computer monitors lined the wall he faced, but his swivel chair allowed him to swing around to a more conventional desk that always seemed to be immaculately unadorned. Maggie couldn't help wondering if the desk was mostly for show, so that he didn't entirely throw off visitors who came into his office unprepared.

He eyed her as she placed the Starbuck's container next to his empty coffee mug. He recognized the bribe, and still rewarded her with one of his wide grins.

"You know I changed up a bit," he told her as he pulled the cup closer and inhaled deeply.

"A venti caramel latte," she said, "with three shots of espresso."

"Extra pumps of caramel?"

"Five pumps of caramel and one pump of mocha."

"You must want something big," he said as he snapped off the lid and took a sip. "Oh, that is some kind of wonderful. Go ahead, ask and you share receive."

Although Alonzo was considered a data wizard he defied the computer nerd stereotype. A fashion trendsetter in a building of drab navy, black or brown suits, Alonzo wore a bright orange button-down shirt that complimented his brown skin. His tie and the frames of his eyeglasses always seemed to match. Today, they were an indigo blue. He wore khakis and high-polished, brown leather shoes. He also, smelled good. Not ordinary aftershave. Something citrus with a hint of coconut.

"There were two homicides in Chicago this morning," she told him as she popped open a can of Diet Pepsi. "Two young men, middle twenties. Deacon Kaye was shot—execution style—in what looked like a home invasion. The other man, Tyler Gates, was shot on the street. Actually, just a few streets away. A possible botched robbery except they left the wallet. Took the cell phone. Both shootings took place in about the timeframe of an hour."

Alonzo sat back in his chair and sipped his coffee, listening, taking it all in. She knew he wouldn't interrupt her until she was finished.

"The men were friends. Kaye was a mid-level computer analyst for a chemical laboratory. Gates was a junior account rep for an advertising agency. They hacked into a company's computer email last week."

She paused and waited, letting him mull it over. He sat forward with his first question. "A military contractor?"

Maggie shook her head. "A cereal company."

"Cereal? As in Fruit Loops and Cheerios?"

"Not those two in particular, but yes, cereal and breakfast bars. It's a food company called Carson Foods."

"How do you know they hacked into the company's computer?"

"A woman named Francine Russo worked at the advertising agency with Tyler Gates. They're the account reps putting together an advertising campaign for the company's latest organic breakfast bars. Gates didn't like that the products were suspected of having glyphosate in them."

"Glyphosate? That's some sort of herbicide to kill weeds?"

"Or regulate plant growth. Sometimes it's used as a drying agent."

"But it's toxic?" Alonzo asked.

"It's been registered as a pesticide since 1974. The EPA says there are no risks to public health when glyphosate is used in accordance with its current label and that glyphosate is not a carcinogen. I'm quoting."

"I see." He put down his coffee and steepled his fingers.

"But the World Health Organization and some recent studies have labeled it a carcinogen that increases the risk of cancer."

"Ah, I get it," Alonzo said. "And Mr. Tyler's computer buddy at the chemical lab tested the breakfast bars, and indeed, found disturbing levels of this pesky pesticide."

"Yes. Russo was on the phone video-chatting with him about it when he was shot."

Alonzo whistled and tapped his fingers together. "I don't like where this is going. What do you need from me?"

In the past, Antonio Alonzo had been able to provide the unthinkable from satellite photos of a killer's gravesites to security camera feeds of a WalMart parking lot in the Midwest. He could track down the smallest piece of evidence, run it through databases and somehow find its relevance. He had been Maggie's right-hand man on several cases, accessing vital information in a remarkably short amount of time. On one occasion he provided life or death information. And he didn't just depend on computers and databases. The man was an encyclopedia of facts and trivia.

Maggie gave him the names of the three people involved: Francine Russo, Tyler Gates and Deacon Kaye along with any details Hannah had been able to share as well as the information from Detective Jacks.

"Anything you can find about Carson Foods and their CEO might also be helpful," Maggie added.

"I seem to remember a lawsuit regarding glyphosate. I'm pretty sure it wasn't a food company though."

"Maybe there's a connection. You think this could be about warding off possible lawsuits?"

He shrugged. "We both know people have killed for less." He was already making notes on a yellow legal pad. "Makes more sense than it being about cereal."

"Breakfast bars," she corrected him.

He looked up and smiled at her. "Right. That makes a big difference." He tapped his pen against the notepad. "You said the killer took Tyler Gates' cell phone?"

"It wasn't at the scene or on him," Maggie said. "Is that significant?"

"There's a whole bunch of information stored on a person's phone."

"But he'd have to know Gates' passcode."

"You said Gates was video-chatting when he met up with the guys. They wouldn't need the passcode. And a lot of people don't like to bother with passcodes. We live in an instant access society. Everybody wants to stay connected. They activate the REMEMBER THIS DEVICE. Social media accounts—Facebook, Twitter, Instagram—who signs out? Even their Amazon accounts and their email. A lot of people leave them open so they can quickly access them. Who has time to key in your password every time? The apps and accounts don't remind you to logout. They want you to stay connected. Did you ever notice they've even made it harder to find the logout?"

"So anyone who steals the phone also has instant access."

"Yup. And think about all the things we use our phones to do. Refill prescriptions. All you gotta do is scan the barcode. Same with checks. The bank lets you scan it and you see the amount in your account. If a person leaves that app open and doesn't logout, anyone who picks up the phone has instant access to all those accounts. Not only to their email and their texts, but their friends and family. In fact, the killers might be emailing or texting acquaintances before they discover Gates is dead. Especially if they're still looking for something—like who Gates might have shared information with from those hacked emails."

"That seems rude."

Alonzo gave her a look. "Yeah, we've never seen that before—a rude killer. Hey, I don't suppose you could get me a copy of the emails they hacked?"

"Not yet," she told him. "Russo said Tyler was sending her copies. I'm hoping to talk with her tomorrow. If she has anything, I'll see if I can get them forwarded to you."

"It'd be better if you can get me her email address and password."

Maggie was still waiting to hear from Hannah to see if Francine Russo had agreed to meet her. Or if the woman would even be able to. Two young men were dead in a matter of an hour. It had to be an orchestrated hit. Whatever Tyler Gates and Deacon Kaye stumbled upon was enough to get them killed. And if Alonzo was right, the killers already had plenty of information about Russo. Most likely, the woman wasn't just being paranoid that they would come for her next.

24

Creed's fingers fumbled around inside his daypack. He couldn't see through the pine boughs. When he finally pulled out Grace's pink elephant she didn't seem interested. Instead, the little dog kept prancing back and forth in front of the spot where she'd given her alert. She was more anxious for Creed to see what she'd found.

He looked over his shoulder. Norwich and Sykes had stopped about ten paces back. Creed guessed the wrecked vehicle was at least 300 feet away. Dread made him hesitate. He'd seen bodies in different stages of decomposition. Death was not kind. The smells that accompanied the dead rarely bothered him. In Afghanistan he'd witnessed corpses burned beyond recognition and ripped apart by IEDs. But he'd never seen anything like the body in the smashed wreckage. And that one had tons of steel surrounding and protecting it. He couldn't imagine what happened to a person flung 300 feet into the air and slammed back down.

"Did she find the driver?" Trooper Sykes called out.

"I'm not sure," Creed answered.

Grace kept her eyes on him even as she continued to pace. Every once in a while she would swing her head toward the downed pine trees as if she couldn't believe how slow he was.

"Good girl, Grace," he praised her, slipping the toy into the daypack.

She poked her nose through an opening between branches, clearly growing impatient with him. Creed dropped to his knees, craning his neck to see beyond the pine needles. It was too dark. He peeled a flashlight out of his pack and pointed the beam between the branches where Grace had stuck her nose. When he still couldn't see anything, he crawled closer. He parted the branches with his hands and then his elbows, thrusting his torso in between despite twigs whipping into his face and needles sticking his arms.

Finally, he saw what looked like the back of a car seat. It was muddy, lying on its side and plastered with pine needles. Then Creed realized it was too small to be a regular car seat ripped from a vehicle. He jerked away, throwing off his balance and falling backward out from the branches and onto his butt.

"What is it?" Sheriff Norwich was right behind him now.

Trooper Sykes offered Creed his hand. Grace batted him with her paw and started licking his face. He waved off Sykes and gave Grace a pat before he got back to his feet.

"I think it's a car seat," he told them.

Sykes took off his hat and scratched his head as he looked out toward the vehicle.

"Not the vehicle's seat," Creed said. "A baby's car seat."

"Oh my God," Norwich said under her breath.

Creed had done searches for lost children before, and always when one was found dead there was an eerie silence that overcomes even the most seasoned law enforcement officers. The three of them stood motionless. But then Creed noticed Grace. She was still prancing back and forth, impatient and bobbing her head toward her find.

To scent dogs, death was a game. There was no emotion attached to finding a corpse. Dogs could be influenced by their handler's moods and attitudes. It was why Creed emphasized to his new handlers to never show discouragement. But grief was more difficult to hide.

As if she was fed up waiting for her human counterparts, Grace poked her entire head between the branches. Creed wiped dirt from his hands and picked up the flashlight where he'd dropped it. When he looked again, he saw Grace disappear under the fallen tree.

"Grace, come back here." To Norwich and Sykes, he said, "She usually takes her toy. I'm not sure—"

A muffled sound interrupted him, followed by a whimper.

Creed dived back to his knees, pulling and snapping branches. He crawled and shoved his body forward, ignoring the sharp pokes and scrapes. He didn't stop until he could touch the car seat. The muddy, leather back faced him, but he knew Grace had made her way around to the front. All he could see was the tip of her tail, and it was wagging.

From behind and above him, Creed heard Norwich and Sykes trying to lift and break the branches. He elbowed up through the pine needles until finally he could reach over the car seat. A thin stream of sunshine allowed him to see the baby still strapped in. The child was caked in mud. Grace had licked clean the eyes and nose and mouth, and now she'd moved her tongue-bath to the left ear. The baby didn't cry. Outside of the whimpers and sniffles, it kicked its feet out. Tiny little hands fluttered. Grace tolerated the grabs and tugs and just kept licking.

Creed pulled the entire car seat, baby included, out from under the fallen pine trees. He draped his body to shield the child from being poked or whipped by twigs and needles. He felt the stabs in his back, scrapes across his arms and pinecones digging into his knees. By the time he made it out from underneath, the child was crying, more like screaming. Grace skipped alongside, desperate to settle the little tyke.

Sheriff Norwich and Trooper Sykes stood by to help, but now the desperate little hands clung to the front of Creed's shirt. Instead of trying to pry the child's hands free, he asked the others to disengage the car seat's straps. The baby grabbed fistfuls of Creed's T-shirt and held on tighter, burying its mud-caked head against his chest.

Sweat dripped down Creed's face, but instead of wiping at it he kept both hands on the baby. He rested his chin on top of the matted hair. Twigs and needles poked at him. As soon as the straps fell away he wrapped his arms around the child. Then he kneeled down, so Grace would stop trying to climb his leg. Her nuzzles and licks almost instantly stopped the baby's crying.

"My God," he heard Sheriff Norwich behind him. "How is it possible?"

"Can you guys check for injuries?" Creed asked.

He glanced up at the law enforcement officers who appeared paralyzed by the discovery. He didn't want to pull the child away and start the crying again. So instead, he sat back on his haunches and tried to run his fingers over one limb at a time.

Trooper Sykes knelt beside them. He started at the top, running careful fingers through the plastered waves of feathery hair, checking the baby's head.

Grace weighted her front paws up on Creed's thigh, supervising both him and Sykes. She was panting, her tongue hanging out and too far to the side.

Creed looked up at Norwich and asked, "Could you get us some water?" He gestured to his daypack.

She jerked into action. "Of course."

She fumbled with the zipper. He could feel her hands rummaging through the pack. Only then did Creed realize how discombobulated the sheriff was.

"There's a collapsible dish in there, too. For Grace."

While Sykes continued his slow and careful examination, Norwich opened and spilled water for Grace. At first the dog didn't want to be distracted from her guard post, but thirst changed her mind. Norwich held the bowl while Grace lapped up the water. The baby pulled away from Creed to watch.

"You want some, too?" Creed asked. "Are you thirsty?"

The baby's eyes met Creed's for the first time, and he was pleased to see they were focused, tracking and interested. He also noticed the baby's ears were packed with mud. Grace hadn't had a chance to clean them out entirely. Gently, he tugged a plug of dirt out of one.

"Are you thirsty?" he asked, again, and this time the child wiggled at the sound of his voice.

Norwich squatted beside them with the water bottle, still tentative as if trying to figure it out.

"You're really good with babies," she said.

He caught himself before telling her there wasn't much difference between babies and puppies. Not everyone appreciated that comparison.

Norwich awkwardly adjusted the bottle bringing it to the baby's lips, again, revealing how uncomfortable she was. She tipped it just enough for a small sip. Then another and another. Between Grace and the baby, they emptied the bottle. The little dog nosed Sheriff Norwich, wanting to take back her spot.

"Okay, okay, I'm moving," Norwich told Grace. She joked about getting out of the dog's way, but Creed knew the woman was glad to resume her distance.

"How old do you think?" he asked Sykes who had moved in front of Creed. Compared to Norwich, there was no hesitation.

"Not quite a year." Trooper Sykes ran his hands softly over the baby's legs, taking his time to feel for broken bones or wounds hidden by the mud. "My guess is ten or eleven months. I radioed for help earlier," he said in a low, calm voice. "Paramedics are headed back. They'll have IVs if necessary, but he doesn't look too dehydrated. I'm glad he drank some on his own."

"The pine trees provided shelter and shade," Creed said. He glanced around to check on Norwich and saw her examining the car seat. "It's almost as if they fell after he landed there." He knew when he told the story to Hannah later she would claim it was a miracle. It would be hard to disagree with her.

"Wait a minute. You said he? It's a boy?"

"Yeah, it's a boy." Sykes sat back on his heels and turned his head away. "And his diaper's full."

"Hey, your diaper would be full, too, if you flew three hundred feet in a car seat."

Sykes laughed, and the baby jerked his focus away from Creed and Grace to look for the sound.

"I found something," Norwich called out. Her hands were muddy as she rubbed at the top of the carrier. "There's a label with a name and address. They probably take this with them when they fly."

"That solves the problem of who he belongs to," Sykes said.

"Except he might be the only one who survived," she countered.

And once again, Creed was reminded that he and Grace still hadn't found the driver.

25

"Girl, it's about time you called!"

Frankie smiled at the sound of her friend's good-natured scolding. Of course, it helped that she was feeling snug and safe in her fourth floor hotel room. Right now, Frankie didn't even care if it might be a false sense of security. It just felt good to be inside and off the interstate where every second she'd felt exposed. She had kicked off her shoes and already ordered room service. Comfort food. All of her favorites.

Now she sat on the edge of the bed where she had a view of the only entrance to the hotel's parking lot. The rain pounded against the window. Lightning streaked across the sky. She was thankful she made the decision to get off the road.

"I'm in Nashville," she told Hannah. "I forgot how long of a drive it was from Chicago to the panhandle."

"Even longer when you're alone."

"You got that right."

"You feel safe where you are?" Hannah wanted to know.

Frankie hesitated then said, "Yes." She gave her friend the details of her choice and the precautions she'd taken. "It's the safest I've felt all day. Especially with the storms."

"I'm afraid you're going to be dodging storms all weekend. Now listen, before you drive all the way down here, my FBI friend wants to meet with you. Do you think you can get to Montgomery tomorrow about one o'clock?"

"Sure," Frankie said as she grabbed her notes and looked over her route. "That's four hours from Nashville. It shouldn't be a problem."

"I'm trying to cut a couple hours off for both of you. Maggie will be flying into Atlanta, so it's a two-hour drive for her. It'd be twice that long for her to come all the way down here to the panhandle. You can meet with her for lunch, and then you'll still have plenty of time to head on down. I'll have a room waiting for you."

"Hannah, are you sure? I've been thinking about this, and I don't want to put you and your boys at risk."

"After everything you and me have been through together? Girl, we'll do just fine."

But there was something in Hannah's voice that Frankie recognized. Her friend wasn't as confident as she sounded.

"Do you remember that meat-and-three this side of Montgomery? Southern Blessings?" Hannah asked.

"Of course. Your grandparents used to take us there. Miss Opal used to bring us extra biscuits. I can't believe it's still there."

"Miss Opal passed away a few years back. The new owners haven't changed a thing. And you need to bring some of those biscuits with you."

Frankie knew what Hannah was doing, trying to pretend that all was good and normal. She didn't stop her.

"I told Maggie that's where you'd meet her," Hannah told her. "At one o'clock. The place should be clearing out a bit, but on a Saturday, who knows. Her name's Maggie O'Dell. I'm sure you'll recognize her. She'll be the only Yankee in the place."

Hannah laughed, and this time it was genuine with the lovely melody Frankie was used to hearing. She smiled. She'd been gone almost as many years as she'd lived in the south, but being born there seemed to give a person lifelong credentials. And Hannah was right. Frankie would probably be able to pick the FBI agent out of the diner's usual lunch crowd.

"I know you haven't been able to check your email," Hannah said, her voice already serious, again. "You said Tyler mentioned he was sending you something. Is that right?"

"Yes, he did. I yelled at him about it. I can't believe I yelled at him." She couldn't think about that right now. "I haven't seen anything from him. My watch sends me notifications of my emails. Maybe it got dropped in my spam file."

"Do you mind giving me your email address and password? Maggie said it might be helpful if her computer analyst could take a look."

"Okay." Frankie gave Hannah the information. "So I guess if she agreed to meet with me, she doesn't think I'm just being paranoid."

"No. No, she doesn't. Maggie talked to a Chicago detective. Frankie, this is serious," Hannah said and her voice was filled with concern. "There's no easy way to say this. Tyler was shot. It happened not far from his friend's apartment."

"Oh my God! Is he okay?" Even as the words came out of her mouth, Frankie knew.

"I'm so sorry, sweetie. He's dead."

26

Florida Panhandle

Brodie didn't mean to interrupt Hannah's phone conversation. Hannah gestured for her to come into the kitchen then pointed to the freshly baked cookies. That was the aroma that had brought her back downstairs. Brodie still couldn't get used to things like this. Not just baked goods, fresh out of the oven and set there on the counter, but the idea that she could take one whenever she wanted.

"You get some sleep, sweetie," Hannah told the caller.

Brodie noticed that Hannah called several people "sweetie," but she called Brodie, "Sweet Pea."

"I'll see you tomorrow." Finished, Hannah looked at Brodie and said, "I don't know about you, but I could sure use a glass of milk and a cookie. How about joining me?"

Brodie nodded.

"Grab a couple of small plates. I'll get the milk."

Brodie washed her hands at the sink. Some days she wondered if she would ever feel clean enough. Thankfully, no one gave her a hard time about it, except for Thomas, Hannah's younger son, and usually it was only because he didn't want anyone expecting him to wash *his* hands.

The cookies were still warm, the chocolate gooey and the edges crispy.

"Was that your friend, Frankie?" Brodie asked.

Hannah nodded.

Over dinner, she had told Brodie about her childhood friend, that she was in some trouble and might be staying with them for a few days. Isaac and Thomas were excited. They called her Aunt Frankie. But Hannah seemed concerned that it was okay with Brodie.

Which was yet another thing Brodie wasn't used to—people asking and caring about her opinion. First, it was Ryder asking if it was okay for him to leave and now this. Brodie wished they didn't worry so much. She wished they didn't try so hard. She didn't want to be a burden.

It reminded her of the day she arrived. At lunch everyone had been talking, asking polite questions, but mostly just making conversation. Suddenly, she realized they had all stopped and were staring at her plate. She had dismantled her sandwich, separating the bread, tomato, lettuce, cheese and turkey. Then she carefully put it back together again and started breaking it into bite-size pieces. At first, she thought maybe she shouldn't be using her fingers. Was that why they were staring at her? But everyone else had their sandwiches in their hands.

It was Hannah who finally asked if everything was okay.

"Would you like something different?" she offered.

Brodie couldn't imagine what would be more delicious. It even had mayo on it and the bread was fresh, no green mold or flecks of insects. Iris Malone often hid drugs in Brodie's food, sometimes sneaking it in her favorites. Brodie hated the way the pills made her feel—not just groggy, but her body felt like it was disconnected from her brain.

"I'm sorry," Brodie had finally told them when she knew she'd never be able to explain. She remembered how her fingers stilled, and her eyes stayed on her plate all the while feeling the flush of embarrassment. Soon she heard laughter and she wanted to crawl under the table.

"Well, it looks like you started a new trend," Ryder said.

When Brodie looked up she saw that Isaac and Thomas had started breaking their sandwiches into small pieces and popping them into their mouths. It took her a minute to recognize the young boys weren't mocking her. They were enjoying a fun new way to eat their lunch.

In the weeks since then, Brodie realized she was becoming a bit of a hero—a strange unconventional hero—to Hannah's two boys. It wasn't just granting them permission to break up their food and eat with their fingers. There were other things. Two days ago she'd killed a spider on their bedroom wall using the palm of her hand.

Their mouths dropped open, and their eyes were so wide that Brodie immediately asked, "What? Was it poisonous?"

Though she was pretty sure it wasn't. As a girl growing up in the South, she had memorized what every poisonous spider and snake looked like. It had actually come in handy when she was confined to outdoor sheds and later, the basement prison.

It was ironic that Isaac and Thomas thought of her as a hero. They had no idea how much she had relied on them. One of her first lessons on manners came from Isaac. He kicked her under the table when she didn't immediately follow his example of saying, "thank you." Brodie hated to admit it, but she felt most comfortable with the two little boys. They didn't treat her like she might shatter into tiny pieces. And despite being twenty-seven years old, she knew her mind and social manners were probably more on their level than her adult counterparts.

Now, as Hannah sat across the table from her, Brodie could see she was still concerned about her friend. She had heard more of the conversation than she wanted to confess. But she wanted to make Hannah feel better. She'd done so much to make her feel welcome in her home.

"You make the best cookies," Brodie told her.

"Thank you, Sweet Pea. These are your brother's favorites, too."

"Have you heard from him?"

"Not since earlier. But they've been showing pictures on the news of the damage. Lord, have mercy! It's a miracle there weren't more deaths."

"Ryder and Grace, they're like heroes, aren't they?"

"Grace is, indeed, a special little dog. And your brother…well, he certainly has a gift with dogs. He knows dogs better than he knows people. And he's definitely more comfortable with them than he is with people."

"Jason says you can trust dogs more than you can trust people."

Hannah looked at her as if giving it some consideration then said, "Yes, I imagine that's true."

"Did Jason and Scout leave, too?"

"Yes, Sweet Pea. It's just you, me and the boys." Hannah paused before she added, "Until your mom gets here tomorrow."

She could feel Hannah's eyes stay on her, but Brodie's strayed out the window. She didn't want to think about her mother. The thought made her sick to her stomach. It reminded her of all the lies Iris Malone had told her. For years, Brodie had no idea they were lies. Even now, for some reason she couldn't stop her body from reacting.

Outside, dark clouds were ruining the sunset. She noticed they were gathering in the same spot as this morning. The same spot where Creed and Jason had gone.

"Will they be safe?"

She expected Hannah to reassure her, but the woman was already tense, worrying about her friend, so Brodie shouldn't have been surprised when Hannah said, "I pray to God they are."

Something in Hannah's tone made Brodie feel a sense of urgency. Her pulse started racing. Her eyes darted around the kitchen. She realized she didn't know where Kitten had gone. How could she have lost track?

"She's right here," Hannah told Brodie, knowing exactly what Brodie was looking for without a single word exchanged.

Hannah scooped up the kitten from under the table and deposited the ball of fur on Brodie's lap.

"Have you thought any more about names?"

"Names?" Brodie's fingers stroked the cat's soft fur, willing her mind to reset to calm.

In the beginning when she first found the kitten, Brodie would panic any time it was out of her sight. She'd never had someone she loved so much that it hurt like a kick to the stomach just to imagine losing her.

"Seems like she deserves a better name than Kitten," Hannah said.

Brodie tried to release the tension buckled between her shoulders. Kitten was fine. She was fine. She was in a warm, safe house eating cookies with a woman she could trust not to hurt her.

"How did you come up with the name Grace?" Brodie asked.

"That was easy," Hannah waved a hand at her like she was swatting a fly. "When Ryder found her, she was all skin and bones. Poor thing looked beat down. First time I saw her I told him it was by amazing grace that dog was alive. Almost immediately, we began calling her Grace. What was the first thing that came to mind when you saw Kitten?"

"I was glad she wasn't a rat."

Hannah stared at her for a second then she burst out laughing. Brodie caught herself smiling. She loved the sound of Hannah's laughter. It was like listening to music.

27

Southern Alabama

Creed was relieved when he saw Jason's SUV making its way through the barricades.

Two volunteers and another state trooper had taken Baby Garner. Michael and Elizabeth Garner were the names on the car seat with an address in Richmond, Virginia. Trooper Sykes confirmed that the driver's license they'd found on the passenger was that of Michael Garner. At this point, they could only presume that Elizabeth had been driving.

Grace had put the volunteers through a thorough inspection before she was satisfied enough to release the baby to the pair. Since then, Creed and Grace had walked a grid in the field, spanning out from the crumpled vehicle and tackling about a hundred-foot radius. This was after they'd walked the entire line of fallen pine trees twice.

Grace went through the motions, but she hadn't latched onto another scent cone. Creed worried that she'd gotten too overheated and too worked up over the crying baby. In this kind of heat and humidity Creed always kept an eye on his dogs. He restricted Grace to twenty-minute searches followed by thirty-minute breaks. She usually fussed about the breaks, but now she appeared bored.

He led her to a grassy patch, free of debris and pulled out her water dish. She did a lazy-sit and stared over his shoulder. She was distracted. She sniffed the air then stood back up. Creed recognized her agitation.

He glanced over his shoulder, and now, he recognized what was making her anxious.

Grace could smell the approaching storm.

Weather patterns produced their own distinctive odors, and Grace was like a canine barometer. She wasn't afraid like some of Creed's other dogs, but she did become restless by a drop in pressure, and she could sense any shift in the static electric field. From the curl of her tail and the pitch of her ears, Creed knew she was already on edge. The incoming storm was close.

He still hoped Jason and Scout could do a fresh search of the field. He didn't like the idea of leaving Elizabeth Garner out here to be battered by a second round of wind and rain. It no longer mattered whether she was alive or dead, he just wanted to find her. But the clouds were snuffing out the few hours of daylight that remained.

Sheriff Krenshaw waved at him and walked over. There was no hesitation as he sloshed through the receding water.

"We have to pull the response teams," he yelled to Creed. His hands were shoved deep in the pockets of his jeans. The man didn't look happy about it but also looked exhausted. "I have a couple of rooms reserved for you guys." He gestured back to the interstate. "You can get on and head up north toward Montgomery. About five miles."

"That's nice of you, Sheriff. You didn't need to do that."

"It's the least I could do. If it wasn't for you, we'd never have found that little one."

"Grace found him."

"That, she did." He gave her a genuine smile, but Grace had started pacing at the end of her leash. "She's picking up another scent?"

"No, it's the storm."

"Look, Trooper Sykes told me you've been beating down this field looking for that missing driver."

Creed rubbed at his bristled jaw. In the back of his mind he could hear the mantra: *Grief belongs to the families. Dread belongs to the handlers.* Did he do enough? Was it possible he missed something?

"Right now," the sheriff continued, "You need to go take care of yourself and your dog, but I hope you'll stick around the area tomorrow. Meteorologists are saying we're in for a helluva weekend. I'd sure appreciate having your crew nearby and available if that's possible."

"Of course." Creed's eyes were on Jason and Scout. Despite the darkening sky Jason had the tailgate up and was getting his gear.

"We might do one last search," he told the sheriff. "A fresh dog could make a difference." He saw Jason glance back at him, and Creed gestured to him.

"Just make it quick. You know the way it is down here. Sunshine one minute and the next, all hell breaks loose."

Scout was already bounding toward them. A couple of hours in the SUV would have the dog eager to get to work. He looked like an undisciplined jackass, practically dragging Jason, but the young black Lab had come a long way. And so had his handler. The two misfits made a perfect team.

Creed glanced over at the sheriff and saw the man's gaze lock on Jason's prosthetic. It was six months new to Jason and sometimes Creed saw the kid as uncomfortable with it as he had been with the empty hanging sleeve.

The technology was state-of-the-art, DARPA's newest and best, but it came in stages. Jason's version didn't hide the black metal. A skin-like material was still to come, along with more sensors. For now, he looked like a bionic man with a sleek black robotic arm, hand and fingers. Hannah's boys called him the Transformer, and Creed could tell Jason liked that. But then the kid would get out in public and practically hunch his body in a defensive mode. It had taken Creed a while to realize Jason's chip-on-the-shoulder attitude wasn't exactly all about the missing arm.

He introduced the sheriff to both Jason and Scout. Grace had come over to greet the Lab then she wagged in front of Jason until he reached down and petted her. They were close to the smashed vehicle, and Jason's eyes were already scanning over it.

To Jason, Creed said, "The passenger was found belted in, but the driver's missing. You might be able to get some scent from the inside. The seat, the floorboard. Maybe even the steering wheel." By now, Michael Garner's body had already been removed, but Creed knew Scout might still be distracted with the smells left behind from it.

Just then, Creed noticed the small door to the gas tank was open. The tornado had done strange things to the vehicle and prying open that compartment was the least of the strange things. But the gas cap hung loose by its cord. Would the storm's pressure be able to unscrew the cap?

He turned to look back up the incline to the interstate junction. First responders, law enforcement officers and volunteers were packing up. Where there were once buildings—a gas station, convenience store and fast food restaurant—now stood piles of bricks, shredded drywall, cinder blocks and two-by-fours. A couple of tow trucks and a trailer were loaded with the crumpled remains of vehicles.

"Sheriff, is there anyone up there who went through the storm?"

"Owner of the gas station is trying to salvage some of his inventory before the next downpour."

"Do you mind if I ask him a few questions?"

"What's this about?"

"Just a hunch."

Creed expected the sheriff to push for more of an explanation. Instead, he said, "Come on."

The name Roscoe was embroidered on the man's sweat-stained blue shirt. Gray dust clung to his trousers and ball cap. The scratches on his arms looked like he'd wrestled his way out of a tiger's cage. When he greeted Creed and the sheriff, Roscoe still had that glazed look in his eyes that

Creed had seen in others who had escaped death and knew it.

He was packing plastic containers with packaged food items from the shelves that appeared untouched by the storm. Bags of chips and candy bars had stayed on an end-cap, not a single wrapper torn. The shelf stood surrounded by bricks, ceiling tiles and pieces of drywall. Everywhere Creed stepped he heard glass crunch beneath his feet, and he was glad he'd put Grace inside his Jeep.

It didn't take much to get Roscoe talking.

"Out here there's no sirens," he told them. "My building faces the east. We never saw the damned thing coming. The wind picks up. Thunder. Lightning. Downpour. A little bit of hail. It's crazy. People pulling in off the interstate. They're putting gas in. Still running inside to buy crap."

He tugged his ball cap off and swiped his arm across his sweaty forehead. Plopped the cap back on and started again. "Then it calms. Y'all know how it is. That freaky, eerie quiet. And then it's right there. Wind blasting. Debris flying. It's throwing around stuff it picked up a mile away. The doors blew open. Glass shattered."

He shook his head and gestured to what must have been the front of the building. "I yelled for people to move inside. Told them to get to the back. Pile into the restrooms. Those are made of cinder block."

He looked back at the area, a portion of it still standing. A door hung from its hinges in a doorframe that was no longer connected to anything.

Suddenly, Creed's Jeep started up, the engine roaring to life just ten feet away from them. The sheriff looked at the vehicle then back at Creed.

"Your dog knows how to drive?"

"Heat alarm system. It's backed up with it's own auxiliary battery," Creed explained. "Turns the ignition and the A/C on when it reaches a certain temperature inside the vehicle." He wanted to get back on track. To Roscoe, he said, "I know it was crazy during that time, but do you remember a woman…"

Then he stopped himself. He realized he didn't know what she looked like. A name wouldn't matter. They didn't even know if the vehicle had been a car or an SUV. Some of the paint had been peeled away. He did remember seeing the Ford emblem. And the only remaining tire was small.

"She may have been in a white Ford sedan," he finally told the man. "Virginia license plates. She was with a man and a baby."

"You the one that found that baby?" he asked Creed.

"Yes sir. My dog did."

"Now you're looking for its momma, huh?"

"We're hoping."

"Let me think." Roscoe squinted, adding creases to a brow already filled with lines. "The place was going nuts. Pumps were full up. Cars pulling in just to get under the awnings." Then he blinked a few times and pointed like he was trying to get his finger on an image. "Wait a minute. There was a woman in line to pay. She was anxious to get back out. I think she may have said something about a baby."

"Did she go back out?" the sheriff asked.

Roscoe was quiet. Still thinking. He pulled his cap off, again, and did the swipe through his sweat-plastered hair. Tugged the cap back on and seesawed the brim like it helped him concentrate.

"Y'all know, I can't say for sure." Then he looked at the sheriff. "First paramedics took about five people just from around here. Maybe she was one of them?"

The sheriff looked from Roscoe to Creed. He turned around and Creed knew he was assessing how far away the vehicle was.

He looked back at Creed. "What makes you think they were here?"

"Gut instinct. And the gas cap was off. I know tornadoes do weird stuff but can they screw a gas cap off?"

The sheriff didn't reply. Instead, he fished his cell phone out of his breast pocket. By the time he walked the short distance to his patrol car he was barking out instructions.

28

Florida Panhandle

The lightning spiderwebbed across Brodie's bedroom wall. A rumble of thunder followed. Rain started tapping against the roof, a soft pitter-patter. It was a comforting sound, almost a lullaby helping her fall asleep.

Brodie pulled the blanket up around her neck even though the breeze coming in through the curtains was warm and damp. The blanket was so soft. So were the socks. Pink and fluffy, they made her feet forget about the cold and damp concrete and all the cuts and scrapes she had learned to endure. Ryder had bought her a whole drawer full of socks, waiting for her when she arrived.

The drawer of socks was just one of the luxuries of living in this house surrounded by a beautiful forest. She wasn't cold or dirty or hungry. No rats. No foul smells. Instead, fresh air brought the scent of blooming flowers and wet pine. She could feel and hear the comforting purr of Kitten curled up in the nook of Brodie's knees.

She already missed Ryder. She had felt safe just knowing he was close by. It didn't feel right with him being gone. She liked Hannah. She trusted her. She liked Jason, too, and Dr. Avelyn. They'd all made her feel welcome. But Ryder made her feel safe. He had been there when she woke up in the Omaha hospital room back in October. He had promised that he wouldn't let anything happen to her.

In the shadows she could see the basket Hannah had left on the table in front of the window. Her eyelids were heavy, but it helped her sleep to think about the good things that surrounded her. Today the basket was filled with two bananas, an apple and an orange.

Shortly after Brodie arrived, she started finding a basket of food inside her room whenever Hannah left fresh towels or linens for her. The basket usually contained fruit. Sometimes there was also a freshly baked muffin or a few cookies, each individually wrapped and tied with a ribbon. They reminded Brodie of little gift packages given for a special occasion. But there were no special occasions, and yet, the gifts continued.

Brodie mentioned the baskets to Ryder once when she still worried that perhaps all that food wasn't meant for only her.

He told her, "Hannah believes food can feed the soul as much as the body. It's probably her way of telling you that you'll never go hungry in this house."

Brodie didn't really understand the part about the soul, but she certainly knew what it was like to go hungry. Iris Malone had withheld food as punishment dozens of times. And when she did feed Brodie, too often there were drugs hidden inside.

The drugs played games with Brodie's mind. They blurred her vision and sometimes incapacitated her so much she felt paralyzed. Almost always they made her sick to her stomach. Sicker than going without food. And now, she still broke apart her food, unconsciously looking for the capsules, the pills, or the powder that didn't belong. It wasn't that she didn't trust Hannah. It was like her fingers did it on their own.

She thought she'd gotten better, but over the last several days she found her mind playing tricks on her. The memories, the nightmares seemed to trigger something inside her. And then, it took concentrated effort to tamp down the unwanted thoughts that came without warning. There were voices, too.

For a long time after she'd been rescued she still heard Iris' voice, so close, so real. And it sounded exactly as it had so many times before: Iris lecturing her from the top of the basement stairs or outside the locked door. Lately, it wasn't Iris that Brodie heard. Instead, it was some version of Brodie's own voice, whispering to her, reminding her of things, raising suspicions, questioning her judgment.

But tonight Brodie listened to the storm outside. Her eyelids closed against the flicker of lightning that danced across the ceiling. The thunder remained in the distance, a low, gentle hum that couldn't possibly hurt anyone. The rain increased its tempo, the tapping now accompanied by running water flowing through the gutters and downspouts.

She had no idea how long she'd been asleep when something startled her. Brodie jerked awake. She glanced around sensing someone's presence. A flash of lightning illuminated the bedroom, and she bolted upright when she saw the child standing in the open doorway.

"Issac? Thomas?"

A second flicker of light revealed that it was neither boy. The little girl had long, stringy hair. The front of her dress was stained. Her shoes muddy. She gestured for Brodie to come follow her.

"Charlotte?" The question came in a whisper that Brodie barely recognized as her own. "What do you want?"

A crack of thunder woke her up for real this time. Brodie sat up. She was drenched in sweat. Her jolt startled Kitten. Her eyes darted to the doorway and strained to see. The door was closed. She scrambled out of bed and hurried to check the doorknob. It turned easily in her hand, and relief washed over her so overwhelmingly, so completely that she felt a deep chill.

She pulled the door open and peeked around the frame. There was no one in the hallway. Her pulse raced. She found herself tiptoeing to the top of the stairs, clinging to the railing as she walked. She was breathing hard. No, not breathing...panting, almost ready to hyperventilate. And yet, she wished she could hold her breath as she passed each door, straining to listen. In the back of her mind she could remember walking down another hallway, dark and quiet. Each door she passed eased open just enough for eyes to peer out at her. A door had opened a sliver more, and she saw the little girl watching her.

"Who are you?" Brodie remembered asking the girl.

"My name is Charlotte. Who are you?"

Then another door opened. Another little girl. Down the hall, a third door and another pair of eyes.

Brodie shook her head, wanting the images gone. Her knees wobbled as she crept passed the closed doors. Her pajamas were soaked with sweat and she was shaking from the wet dampness. She made it to the top of the stairs and her legs collapsed under her. At the bottom of the stairs a shadow emerged, and her heart skipped a beat. Her hand flew to the railing, gripping it and hoping she had the strength to pull her body away. She needed to move. She needed to hide. But already she heard a door opening behind her, down the hall.

"Brodie?" The voice called from down below. "Are you okay, Sweet Pea?"

It was Hannah! Not Iris. Iris Malone was in a prison a thousand miles away.

Relief unclenched her fingers from the railing. She let her body slide back to a sitting position on the top step. Something brushed against her side and startled her until she felt the soft fur against her arm. Kitten climbed up into her lap.

There were footsteps behind her and before she turned, Isaac sat down on the step beside her.

"Sweet Pea, there are no locked doors that you can't unlock," Hannah called up to her.

It wasn't about the doors. It was what was on the other side. The eyes peering out at her. Little girls that looked exactly like her. All of them named Charlotte. Just like her.

But then she remembered what Hannah was talking about. Something similar had happened one of her first nights here in this house. She woke up and didn't recognize where she was. She'd raced out of her room and down the stairs, straight for the front door, frantically searching and pulling and twisting at locks.

The next day, Ryder had taken her around the entire house. He showed her every single door and explained how she could undo every single deadbolt and every simple push-button doorknob lock.

"Are you okay?" Hannah asked, again, but she didn't attempt to climb the stairs. She'd give her space. In the beginning, Brodie had flinched from their touch, not used to being hugged. Actually, she wasn't used to being touched without it coming with pain.

She nodded that she was okay. She tried to relax and breathe. Tried to calm the pounding of her heart. Then she realized Hannah might not be able to see her nod in the shadow of the stairwell. She felt Isaac lean against her, and something brushed her on the other side. It was Thomas squeezing in between her and the railing. He was rubbing the sleep from his eyes.

Now, Brodie hoped Hannah wouldn't be upset that she had wakened the boys.

"I'm okay," she said.

Before she tried to explain, Isaac asked, "Can't sleep?"

He said it like one kid to another.

Brodie looked down at him and nodded.

"Monsters?" Thomas asked from the other side.

She startled at his question. What did he know about monsters?

"When we're afraid of monsters hiding in the closet or under the bed, mom says we should sing."

"Sing?" Brodie was sure she hadn't heard him correctly. His voice was as groggy as his eyes.

"Something cheerful," Isaac told her as he reached over and began petting Kitten.

"Yeah," Thomas said. "Monsters hate when boys and girls are happy.

They want us to be afraid."

"You know what else helps?" Isaac looked up at her, genuinely serious about helping her.

"What?" Brodie asked.

"Milk and cookies."

"That's right," Thomas agreed. "Mom, Brodie needs some milk and cookies.

She realized she wasn't shaking anymore. Kitten purred beneath her fingers. As silly as it seemed, she suddenly felt safe flanked by these two boys and a cat. Her eyes adjusted to the dim light and the continuous flicker from the outside. Down below she could finally see Hannah's face. Despite the furrowed brow, Brodie could see she was smiling.

DAY 2

Saturday, March 9

29

South of Montgomery, Alabama

Creed was surprised to find less than a dozen guests in the hotel's breakfast area. He told the sheriff last night that he didn't want to take two rooms away from people who may have been affected by the tornado. The sheriff assured him that most of the other first responders and volunteers were close to home or staying with family. From the half empty parking lot, he realized there were very few travelers. Yet, as soon as he and Grace walked into the dining area a manager rushed up to him.

"Sir, we don't allow dogs in the public areas."

"She's a working dog."

The man looked down at Grace, and she wagged at him as if showing off her vest.

"Sorry, rules are rules."

He was about a decade older than Creed and a head shorter, but he stared up at him with unflinching authority. He didn't seem to mind that he had the attention of all his guests. The place had gone so quiet that a clink of a fork against a plate sounded like thunder. Before Creed could answer, Jason came around the corner with Scout at his side. The man's head spun so quickly Creed almost laughed.

"Mornin'," Jason said to both of them. Then he noticed the whole room watching and stopped.

"No dogs are allowed . . ." the man paused when his eyes caught a glimpse of the black mechanical hand at the end of Jason's shirtsleeve.

Creed was curious to see if it would change the man's mind.

"These dogs aren't allowed in the public areas."

Nope, it hadn't changed anything.

"Hey, wait a minute," one of the women called from a nearby table. "Are you the men who found that baby yesterday?"

"Yes, ma'am," Creed said. He gestured to Grace. "She found him."

"You're all over the news," she said, pointing up to one of the three televisions. "Someone caught a part of it on their phone."

That surprised Creed.

"What seems to be the problem?" asked another guest, an older gentleman sitting with three others. He was addressing the manager.

"We don't allow dogs in the public areas," the man told him, but his voice had lowered.

"I don't think any of us mind," the woman said, looking around. "Any of you mind if these men and their dogs have breakfast with us?"

Creed watched the manager from the corner of his eye as the room erupted in agreement with the woman. The man's neck started to redden against his white collar.

"Well . . . just this once," he ended up saying before marching out the door.

"Thanks everyone," Creed said, waving a hand to the group.

"Someone has to stand up for heroes," the woman said.

He was grateful when they all went back to their breakfasts and conversations. He didn't want to talk about Baby Garner. He was anxious to get something to eat and head back out.

Jason found a table by the window far enough away from the others. Creed sat down and told Jason to go ahead. He'd settle the dogs. He could see the kid eyeing the buffet line even when the manager was still trying to throw them out. To his surprise, Jason brought him a mug of coffee and set it on the table in front of him then bee-lined for the food. Sometimes Creed was still amazed at how much the young vet had changed.

The first time they met, Jason had a chip on his shoulder the size of Montana. An IED had blown off half his arm and sent him home. It had also left him belligerent and morose. He'd even admitted to Creed that he had fantasies of suicide and was proud of the fact that he had hoarded enough pharmaceuticals to do the job right.

As different as the two men were, Creed could relate. He'd been sent home from Afghanistan by an IED, too. Alone and missing his K9 partner—the only good thing in his life at the time—he had been angry and depressed. The first time he met Hannah he was drunk and had started a brawl with three men in the bar she was tending. She saved him. Lectured him then listened to him. Helped him figure out a way to give his life purpose.

When Creed recognized a glimpse of himself in Jason, he took a chance that Jason needed the same thing. He gave him a puppy. Told him if he wasn't going to stick around, he'd need to give the dog back. It wasn't fair to the puppy to get attached then have his master off himself. Creed had been blunt, made it sound like he didn't care what Jason did to himself. That was his decision. But he wouldn't let Jason desert a puppy he'd committed to taking care of and training.

Creed bent down and petted the black Lab that sat next to his boots watching and waiting for his handler. Scout and Jason made a good team. Both hardheaded and full of energy. Creed often described Scout as a jackass, but he meant it in a good way. Scent dogs needed that over-the-top curiosity and addiction to adventure. The stuff that drove ordinary dog owners crazy, or sadly prompted them to give up the dog, was exactly what Creed looked for in a search dog.

He saw Jason's tray piled high and wiped at the smile on his face. That was the other thing the handler and his dog had in common, both of them were eternally hungry. Both loved food, but were lean and muscular—not an ounce of fat on either from working hard.

"Is there anything left?" He asked Jason as the kid unloaded from his tray to the table. There were several plates and saucers overlapping and filled with scrambled eggs, bacon, biscuits and gravy along with a tall glass of orange juice and another of milk.

"Very funny."

The dogs had already been fed before they'd left their rooms, but Scout was licking his chops, eyes fastened on Jason's hands, ever hopeful for a dropped morsel.

"Aren't you getting yours?" Jason asked, sitting down and ready to dig in, but again, waiting and trying to be polite. It was obvious this was a new habit for the kid.

Creed lifted his mug. "I will. Just having some coffee first."

When Jason still hesitated, Creed added, "Go ahead. I don't mind."

In between bites, Jason said, "You're worried about Brodie."

A statement, not a question.

"Hannah said she had a nightmare last night. And another panic attack. Found her at the top of the stairs like she was getting ready to race down and out of the house."

Jason washed down a mouthful before he said, "She hasn't done that in a long time."

"Not since the first week. She did it in Omaha pretty often."

Creed let his eyes wander out the window. Blue skies, not a hint of the storms predicted for later in the day. He realized that was sort of how Brodie was. She nodded and said all the right things. She wasn't afraid of any of the stuff he expected her to be afraid of: bugs, spiders, rats . . . even thunderstorms. Instead, she broke her food into tiny pieces, sometimes in an unconscious frenzy. She chopped at her hair until it was uneven, short and spikey. She washed her hands over and over again as if there were invisible stains that only she could see. There seemed to be an internal storm still brewing beneath her surface, though she pretended everything was blue skies.

He knew that PTSD worked differently in everyone. He had dealt with his own on his own terms. But he also knew that it could sneak up on you when you least expected it. When you thought you'd put it behind you. Just when you felt safe and secure.

"Back in Omaha, I was always afraid she'd run out of the facility and get hurt." He glanced over and was surprised to see Jason had stopped eating to listen to him. "They couldn't lock the doors. That only made things worse. Sort of like Molly. Remember when we tried to put her in a dog crate?"

Jason nodded. "She rammed her head against the grate so many times she made herself bleed."

Molly was the mixed breed they'd found after a mudslide in North Carolina. The vehicle she was trapped in had been buried by the avalanche of mud and debris. Molly was the only one of her entire family inside the car to still be alive. Her story was one that Jason had shared with Brodie. Now, Creed realized the two had something in common. Both had panic attacks when locked inside small spaces.

"You know," Jason said while he picked up a piece of bacon and started working on the rest of his breakfast, "I think she's so much stronger than we all think. She survived for sixteen years. You and me didn't even finish our tours of duty." He paused to take a few bites, but was also measuring Creed's reaction. Satisfied, he continued, "The first time I met her, do you remember what she said to me?"

Creed had been so worried about how Brodie would respond to all the new surroundings that he hadn't paid any attention to introductions. He shook his head.

Jason held up his prosthetic hand and flexed the fingers.

"Most people are fascinated or appalled. Or a combination. Like 'oh my God' and 'what the hell.'"

Creed smiled. The kid had come a long way to how he felt about it, too, but Creed wouldn't remind him right now. Instead, he just listened.

"But Brodie," Jason said while his eyes flitted to somewhere over Creed's shoulders. Creed had gotten a glimpse of his eyes and was surprised at the emotion he saw there before Jason tucked it back away and continued. "She asked me if it hurt really bad. She senses stuff, you know. She sees things that we don't even notice anymore, because we're so used to seeing them." He rubbed his good hand over his jaw.

Creed knew what he meant. A couple of weeks ago, one of the first warm evenings they'd had since she arrived in Florida, Brodie convinced him to pull out sleeping bags so they could look up at the stars all night. It was something they'd done as kids in their backyard. She made him point out different constellations, stuff he hadn't thought about in years.

Creed's phone started ringing, and he grabbed it out of his pocket. It was a number he didn't recognize.

"This is Creed."

"Mr. Creed, it's Sheriff Krenshaw. Sorry for the early call, but I wanted to catch you before you headed back out. We found Mrs. Garner."

Creed felt his jaw clench. He hoped his silence would coax the answer. Creed could feel Grace staring up at him, already sensing his tension.

"Turns out you were right about them being up there putting gas in. She'd gone in to pay and was trying to get back out to the car when it hit. Knocked her clean off her feet."

At least her body wasn't still out in that field tangled in some mess of debris. That's what Creed was thinking about when the sheriff continued. Creed almost missed the part Krenshaw said about her being unconscious.

"Wait a minute," Creed said. "She's alive?"

"She was asking about her baby even as she was in and out of it. They had to take her in for surgery. Internal injuries. She's still in critical condition, but they're telling me she's expected to recover. Prospects of that look much better now that she knows her little boy is still alive."

"That's great."

"It's supposed to get wicked again this afternoon. I wouldn't blame you if you took off for home, but I'd sure appreciate it if you two stuck around. I have your rooms booked through the weekend."

Jason was finishing the biscuits and gravy, and Creed realized that maybe he had an appetite now.

"We'll stick around and head on home tomorrow."

He didn't want to stay away any longer than that. He knew Jason was right about Brodie. She was strong, but he also knew she was still terribly vulnerable. And it probably wasn't a coincidence that her nightmare happened the first night he was gone.

30

Birmingham, Alabama

Willis Dean had slept on the sofa in his office. It wasn't the first time he'd spent the night at the television studio, but it was the first time he felt like he had to. It wasn't a problem. He kept a change of clothes and a toiletry kit. Shaving was tricky, and he had nicked himself good. He'd need to get makeup to cover it for him. And of course, his back was yelling at him that he wasn't a young man anymore.

As soon as he woke up he checked his email and text messages. It wasn't the ones from the National Weather Service that he was anxious to see. There were half a dozen of those already. Instead, it was the text message that wasn't there.

What did he expect? Did he really believe his son could be right? That Beth would change her mind.

For the first time in his marriage he hadn't called or alerted his wife that he wouldn't be home for the night. He always called. It was instinctive after all these years. So much so, that twice he'd caught himself tapping out a message, only to stop himself and delete it.

He didn't know how this worked now? He had no idea.

When there was no text message or voice mail from Beth, Willis regretted his decision to not send something, anything. He couldn't blame her for not extending those common courtesies if he didn't do the same.

But then a little voice in the back of his mind told him, *But you weren't the one who asked for a divorce.*

Clearly, he had a lot to learn about this new world he was entering.

By the time he made it down to the weather desk in the studio, his mind was back to where it needed to be.

On the television monitor in the corner he could see Mia was on the air. They'd be taking turns all afternoon and probably into the evening. What they called their weather desk was really a small room. The separation gave them enough privacy and quiet to talk with each other, communicate on-line with storm chasers and make phone calls.

A large glass window allowed them to look in at the studio. He could watch Mia in front of the green screen if he wanted, but the television monitor allowed him a view of what she was actually pointing to on the weather map.

Willis immediately started reviewing the latest information. On a day like today, it would be changing and streaming in constantly. He couldn't remember the atmosphere being like this in early March. All that moist air drifting up from the Gulf of Mexico was unseasonably warm, downright hot, and the trough coming from the Rockies was unusually cold. Yesterday those two systems started to clash. All the ingredients had been brewing and simmering, drifting into place. Now they were starting to come to a boil.

The entire Tennessee Valley was under weather alerts for a weekend filled with dangerous thunderstorms capable of producing tornadoes. But the added threat was that this system would stall right over Mississippi, Alabama and Georgia. And Willis knew that meant that they were in for several consecutive days of violent storms.

All maps and computer models confirmed the potential for significant and widespread tornado outbreaks. He glanced at the monitors. Just to the west, across the border in Mississippi the radar was already blooming. Green patches with bits of red and yellow splashes were popping as a squall line started forming.

A news anchor replaced Mia. Willis glanced up and saw her grab two bottles of water then she came in and took the seat next to him.

"Are these numbers correct?" he asked her.

"Yeah, there're crazy, aren't they? Wind shear is off the charts." She handed him a bottle of water. "I'm glad it's the weekend. I hate when we have to worry about school kids."

"Except people don't pay attention to us on the weekends. As long as the sky's blue, no worries."

"Willis, you're starting to sound jaded." She smiled but didn't look over at him as she added, "Besides, they hardly ever pay attention to us."

He shot her a look and saw her smile widen. Her eyes were tracking across the monitors. It was difficult to explain to others the camaraderie true weather nerds shared. Only they understood that surge of adrenaline and the electric-charged energy that supercells triggered inside them. Willis had felt it since he was a young boy, and most true weather nerds—Mia admittedly so—had also felt it. But it was difficult and almost embarrassing to try to explain it to a layperson. How could someone be so excited about a phenomenon that caused so much death and destruction?

"NWS is saying yesterday morning's storm was an EF4," she told him.

"Thank God, it didn't stay on the ground for long. Smith Crossings would have been smack-dab in its path."

"Did you hear about the baby they found alive?"

"What? No." Willis said. He hated to admit he hadn't been home. He hadn't even had his regular commute last night or this morning to listen to the radio.

"A ten-month-old boy was thrown from his parents' vehicle. A search and rescue dog found him clear out under some fallen pine trees."

"Really?"

"We've been running the video a motorist took from the highway. It's a bit grainy but makes me tear up every time I see it."

An alert dinged on the monitor dedicated to the National Weather Service. Both of them turned.

"A tornado warning," Willis said. "Here we go."

31

Atlanta, Georgia

Maggie had taken an early morning flight to give herself plenty of time for the two-and-a-half hour drive from Atlanta to Montgomery. She could have waited for and caught a connecting flight, but the March day was gorgeous. That was only part of the reason for her choosing to drive. The other reason—Maggie hated flying.

Originally, she had hoped to meet Frankie Russo at the Atlanta airport, but the woman got spooked when she thought she'd been followed to the Chicago airport. Hannah told her Frankie rented a car and had driven to Nashville last night without anyone trailing her.

Maggie didn't ask how she was sure she hadn't been followed. She knew Hannah was already worried sick about her friend. Yesterday, when she told Hannah what she'd learned about Tyler Gates and Deacon Kaye, Hannah had gone quiet on the other end of the line for so long Maggie finally had to prompt a reply, "Hannah, are you okay?"

"Those poor young men. They definitely stumbled onto something, didn't they?"

After a couple of back and forth phone calls, Maggie had Frankie's email address and password to give to Alonzo. And Hannah had arranged for her to meet Frankie just outside of Montgomery, Alabama. It'd cut two or three hours of drive time for Maggie. She knew Hannah was being practical, but she couldn't help being disappointed. If she'd driven all the way to the Florida Panhandle to K9 CrimeScents she would have been able to see Ryder.

Hannah obviously sensed this, because without any encouragement she told Maggie that Ryder and Jason were working a site devastated by a tornado.

"It's just south of Montgomery," Hannah told her. "I'm sure he'd love to see you."

She wondered if that were true or if it was Hannah simply wishing it to be true. Maggie knew she had pushed Creed away. The closer they got, the harder she pushed. And yet, just the idea of seeing him made her palms sweat and her pulse race. She was thinking about all that while Hannah was trying to give her directions to where she was to meet Frankie Russo.

"It's a meat-and-three called Southern Blessings. Big parking lot right across from a truck stop. On the south side of Montgomery. Just off the interstate. You are going to love the biscuits," Hannah told her as though this were a simple lunch date.

Maggie had jotted down all the directions and instructions before it occurred to her to ask, "I know it's a diner or restaurant, but what's a meat-and-three?"

"Oh sweetie, I'm sorry. You choose your meat and three sides. It's a little slice of heaven. And speaking of slices, make sure you try the butterscotch or pecan pie."

It made Maggie smile even this morning as she remembered the conversation from last night. Hannah, herself, was a fantastic cook who sincerely hoped and believed she could soothe the soul and solve most problems with her food.

Maggie's mouth watered thinking about Hannah's smothered fried chicken and black-eyed peas. She'd have to settle for airport food or road trip food. Before she headed out to pick up her rental car, she found a corner table in one of the terminal's small cafés. She ordered a bagel, cream cheese, fresh berries and a Diet Pepsi. She needed to check her messages. She had left Agent Alonzo with a long wish list, and she was anxious to see his progress.

One of the many televisions mounted all over the airport terminal hung ten feet in front of her. She thought about moving to another table but liked this corner. She could see the entrance and her back was to the wall. All were important ingredients for a seasoned FBI agent. After ten years she figured she was allowed to call it seasoned instead of jaded or paranoid.

Then her eyes caught the closed caption crawling across the bottom of the television screen. It read: MAJOR FOOD COMPANY CEO AND SENATORS SIGN GLOBAL INITIATIVE TO FEED THE WORLD'S HUNGRY.

She turned her phone from airplane mode to ON and immediately noticed she had a text message from Alonzo. It was short and simple:

CALL ME AS SOON AS YOU LAND.

Maggie dug out her wireless earbuds as the waitress brought her plate.

"Those berries look wonderful," she told the woman.

"We aim to please. But I'm afraid you'll need to settle for Diet Coca Cola instead of Pepsi. You're in Atlanta, you know."

"That's fine. Thanks."

And as she tapped Alonzo's phone number, she also dug a bottle of water out of her travel bag. Her eyes darted back to the television screen. The news conference with the food company CEO and the senators was still in progress. Now the closed caption identified that company as Carson Foods. Of course it was. Before she looked away she saw a face she recognized standing alongside the senators back behind the CEO. She shouldn't have been surprised to see her boss, Assistant Director Raymond Kunze.

"Hey, Maggie." Alonzo answered.

"I realized I'm asking you to do this on a Saturday."

"And this is probably why neither of us are in relationships."

She knew he meant it as a joke. So why did it sting a little?

"Have you seen the news? Carson Foods' CEO is on TV right now."

"Their wonderful global initiative," he said. "Sounds like they're so generous, right? They actually stand to make billions."

"A.D. Director Kunze is there."

"For sure. His homeboy, Senator John Quincy is sponsoring the initiative."

"I don't want to get you in trouble with Kunze. I'm doing this as a favor to a friend, but you—"

"Maggie, don't worry about it. I can already tell you something doesn't look right about this whole thing. Listen," he paused and she heard him moving around, "I worked some magic last night. Don't ask any questions as to how or what, okay?"

"Okay."

"I can track Tyler Gates' phone."

"We already know where he was before he got shot. Frankie said he was at Deacon Kaye's apartment."

"No, no. Not where he's been. I'm able to track the phone since it got taken."

It took her a few seconds to realize what he was saying.

"Okay," she said, waiting for more.

"Remember I told you the killers may have stolen the phone because it would be a treasure trove of information? They'd have access to Gates' emails, his texts, contacts, all of his accounts especially social media, subscription services, any apps he had downloaded."

"Okay, but would they keep the phone turned on? It's harder to track it if they've shut it off."

"True. But they didn't shut it down, and why would they? If they shut it down they'd need to figure out what his passcode was to turn it back on. Why go to that extra trouble when they could just keep it on? Charge the battery every now and then."

"Unless you can tell me exactly where these guys live in Chicago, I'm not sure how tracking them helps us," she told Alonzo as she slathered cream cheese on her bagel.

"Except they're not in Chicago."

"Again, if we don't have an address—"

"Maggie, listen to me for a minute. I can't give you an exact address, but I can narrow it down to one of two hotels that are across the street from each other. Listen carefully, across from each other in Brentwood, Tennessee."

"Brentwood?"

"It's a suburb of Nashville. Just off Interstate 65."

She placed her knife on the edge of the plate and sat back. Took a deep breath, because she felt like she'd just had the air knocked out of her.

"They're still following her," she said. "How is that possible? They have his phone, not hers."

"My best guess? They were able to use his email to gain access to hers."

"That's possible?"

Alonzo laughed, a genuine full-throated laugh that had Maggie tapping her earbud to reduce the volume. The café was getting crowded with a wave of passengers. Her eyes scanned the new faces coming into the café while her mind raced.

This was much bigger than she expected. More serious than she realized. And with Assistant Director Kunze involved? No way could she tell him what she was doing. But what about Frankie Russo? She needed to alert the woman. Tell her she was right. She was being followed.

Maggie glanced at her watch. Russo had to already be on the road.

Then her stomach took a nosedive.

Maybe they'd already killed her.

"Sorry Maggie," Alonzo finally said, and she couldn't even remember what he was apologizing for.

"Too little sleep," he continued, "and too much caffeine. To answer your question, yes, it's possible. If they tapped into her email account they may have seen a hotel confirmation. Even if she paid in cash, the hotel probably asked for her email for that purpose or to send a receipt. Most people aren't going to have a problem with it. We give out our email addresses as easily as we do our phone numbers. Ms. Russo probably wouldn't think twice about it."

He paused. When he came back on his voice was lower, "I have to tell you, if that's what happened, this is a level of sophistication that goes beyond Tyler Gates and Deacon Kaye hacking into a corporation's internal email system. These killers are not a couple of thugs. They're definitely professionals."

"Do you think they already took care of her?" Maggie asked.

Now Alonzo went quiet. The silence lasted so long she knew he hadn't thought about that.

"Truthfully? I don't know. But then that's your area of expertise."

"I need to check on her. Call me if you find anything else."

"Let me know what you find out."

Hannah had given her the number for Frankie's burner phone, and Maggie had programmed it into her contacts. It had been a long time since she'd used one, and now she wondered if burner phones had caller I.D. The woman might not answer. She found the number and hit the call button, silently praying for the woman to pick up. Maggie did not want to have to call Hannah. How could she explain to her that she may have already failed her?

On the other end she could hear the phone ringing.

Pick up, Russo. Please pick up.

32

Alabama

Sometime during the early morning hours, Frankie Russo had been at the window watching when she saw them make the turn into the entrance to the luxury hotel. At first, she thought she must be mistaken. She was dead tired. Her eyes could barely stay open. Exhaustion had overwhelmed her after her room service meal, and yet, she still couldn't sleep.

So at four o'clock in the morning, she had perched in front of the window, staring out from her fourth floor window, almost as if she had expected them. She had chosen this hotel because it had just one entrance into the parking lot. And now in the dark, with only the pole lights to illuminate the inside of the vehicle, Frankie could see the huge square head of the driver, like a block on top of shoulders that looked like a tank.

At that time of morning, the parking lot was empty of people but packed with vehicles. Instead of driving around, the black sedan pulled up under the carport. He got out of the car and there was no doubt in her mind that this was the man with the scar on his neck even though she couldn't see the scar. She knew it was the same man she saw kill Tyler; the same man she saw at the airport searching for her. The other passenger stayed in the vehicle and out of sight.

Frankie had scouted out and planned her escape route before she had even gone into her room. She'd even timed it. Her bag stayed packed, and after her shower she'd put on fresh clothes instead of pajamas. When she saw the car, she slid into her shoes and gathered the few items she'd scattered on the desk and in the bathroom. One glance out the window had told her it was still parked at the front door.

Within minutes, Frankie had taken the back stairs to an exit at the rear of the building. She had parked her Ford Escape just a few steps from that door where it was out of sight of the front entrance. The one entrance to the parking lot had been an advantage for her to see them, but she knew she'd need to leave another way. In the back of the hotel she'd found a landscaped berm that connected the hotel's lot to another parking lot next door. Just as Frankie had hoped, her small SUV glided over the area without trampling any of the plants. She was on the interstate in less than ten minutes.

Now here she was, just an hour outside of Montgomery. She was still gripping the steering wheel. Her eyes continuously watched her rearview and side mirrors. She knew the only thing she had going for her was that she was ahead of them. But she'd have no idea when, not if, they discovered she had left the hotel.

Were they an hour behind her? Two hours? Twenty minutes?

How the hell had they found her?

Ever since she left—as soon as she could breathe again—her mind kept trying to go over what she'd done that might have tipped them off. How was it possible? If they were able to track her phone, they might know she was in the Nashville area, but how did they know exactly what hotel she had chosen?

She had told no one, except Hannah. And Hannah wouldn't have told anyone. Except… Did Hannah tell the FBI agent?

Frankie's mind went back to what her assistant had said about the men waiting for her at the agency. They told her it was something "official." Was it possible they were law enforcement?

"No," she told herself. She shook her head and met her eyes in the rearview mirror. The FBI agent was a friend of Hannah's. Someone she trusted.

"You're just getting punchy from too little sleep. Come on, Frankie," she told herself out loud. "Law enforcement officers don't gun down computer hackers in the street."

At her last stop for gas—and gas only—she texted Hannah to let her know she was on her way. She didn't share with her friend anything else. Hannah was already worried sick. Frankie wouldn't add to that. Besides, there wasn't anything else her friend could do for her.

She was so paranoid she kept the burner phone off. It didn't help matters that dark storm clouds were gathering on the western horizon. It was warm and muggy, but the rain had washed everything clean. After a long Chicago winter, Frankie should have been enjoying all the green with pops of color along the roadsides. Instead, she couldn't take her eyes off the vehicle's mirrors.

Somewhere behind her, she knew they were following.

33

Florida Panhandle

Brodie dreaded the visit from her mother, but she had promised Ryder that she would allow it. Now that it was here, she didn't want to think about it.

"You need to cut her some slack," Ryder had told her.

"But why aren't you close to her?" Brodie wanted to know.

The silence that followed told her more than his answer.

Those first days in the Omaha hospital were such a blur. Brodie had been dehydrated, malnourished and battling the residual effects of being drugged. She remembered waking and seeing Ryder sitting beside her bed, but in the beginning she wasn't even sure who he was half the time. He was a man instead of the fourteen-year-old boy she had left behind. Complicate all that with the nightmares, along with Iris Malone's voice still occupying a segment of her mind.

One of Brodie's first introductions to her mother was her television show. Ryder channel-surfed on the hospital TV until he found it. And that was another thing that bothered Brodie. Why was she Olivia *James*? Not Olivia *Creed*? She had asked Ryder, and he simply said she'd need to ask their mother.

As for why the two weren't close? Ryder had told her, "It's a long story. It has nothing to do with you."

"Are you sure?"

"Yes. And it doesn't matter anymore. She wants to be a part of our lives. You have to at least give her a chance."

After everything he'd done for her, Brodie agreed to at least try. Even her therapist applauded the idea and reminded her, "Your mother is not the villain that Iris Malone said she was."

Brodie knew that Iris had lied to her, but it didn't make it any easier to erase everything the woman had told her over and over again for the last sixteen years. It didn't help matters that Iris' lies fed off of Brodie's guilt. She did, after all, disobey her parents. Why wouldn't they be angry? Why wouldn't they want to punish her?

Last night's nightmare, along with the rain, brought the beginning back so clearly. Too clearly. Sometimes it felt like ages ago. Other times, it felt like yesterday.

It had been raining that day. She and Ryder were reading their new books that Gram had given them while their dad listened to the football game on the car radio. He was in a bad mood the entire drive. Their mom had stayed with Gram, and Brodie just figured he was upset that they had to go home without her.

They stopped at a rest area so Brodie could go to the bathroom. It seemed silly, but even now she could remember how happy and carefree she skipped through the puddles, her new book still under her arm. The rain made all the taillights and truck lights blink and glow—red and orange, yellow and green. She didn't feel scared at all.

The little girl was standing at the sink when Brodie finished using the toilet. She was thin and her long hair stringy. At first, Brodie thought the girl was using the bathroom because she was sick. Her face was so pale, and she looked sad. She said her name was Charlotte, and she asked if Brodie would like to see her new puppy.

Brodie realized too late that it should have been a warning signal. Why did the girl look so sad if she had just received a new puppy? Maybe she didn't want the puppy. Maybe she was going to offer it to Brodie. But then,

Brodie became mesmerized by the RV that Charlotte showed her. The girl scrambled up the steps, and Brodie followed. Inside it looked like a house on wheels. It was so pretty. The smiling woman invited her in. She showed her how they could sit on the sofa, watch TV—"go ahead, sit down"—and cook their meal while they rode along the countryside.

Brodie had never been inside such a vehicle before. Iris had offered her a ride, just a short one for her to get the feel. Brodie paid little attention to the man behind the steering wheel or the boy in the passenger seat. She'd barely noticed that there wasn't a puppy anywhere to be seen.

When Iris pulled out her phone and said she'd call Brodie's parents to see if it was okay, Brodie only nodded while she sipped the milkshake that the woman had already prepared for her and Charlotte.

She remembered being fascinated by how high up they rode. By the time she wondered how this woman knew her parents, she was feeling sleepy, so sleepy she could barely move her arms.

It was her fault. Her bad decision. That was what Iris Malone told Brodie so many times that Brodie knew it had to be true.

When Iris told her that her mom and dad didn't want her back, she believed her. She wanted to talk to them. She pleaded with Iris to let her explain to them that she was sorry, but Iris said it was too late. Iris said they didn't want her back.

"They told me to keep you," Iris said. "But you're so naughty, I don't know if I want you."

When her parents didn't come to get her, Brodie knew it had to be true. Iris told her that she had given them directions, told them exactly where to come to get her. When you're eleven years old you believe the adults around you. After all, why would they lie?

Dozens of times Iris Malone got on the phone and talked to Brodie's mother. Now she knew Iris only pretended to talk to her parents. But back then, Brodie heard the one-ended conversations and believed them to be real. Iris made them convincing enough that knots tied up Brodie's stomach and tears smeared her face. By the time she realized Iris Malone was an evil woman, she had forgotten what was true and what were lies. She was too scared, too hungry, too tired or too cold. She couldn't remember whether she was Brodie or whether she was Charlotte. And after a while, she no longer cared.

At some point, even she was relieved to be free of Brodie. Brodie was a frightened crybaby, a naughty, selfish girl who disobeyed her parents. But Charlotte…Charlotte was brave and strong.

When Ryder first told her—back in the hospital—that he and their mother had traveled all over the country for years trying to find her, Brodie wasn't sure she believed him.

He saw her cynicism immediately and said to her, "I tell you what. I promise never to lie to you."

"No matter what?" she had asked.

"No matter what."

"Even if the truth is painful?"

She could still remember the look on his face: a combination of sadness, concern and a whole lot of hesitation.

"The truth can't possibly hurt as much as the lies already have," she told him that day, not having a clue about the heartache and sorrow that would result from what he had to tell her.

The death of her grandmother happened only months after Brodie had been taken.

"It wasn't your fault," Ryder had insisted. "Gram was sick the last time you saw her, remember?"

"And dad?" she asked. "What happened to him?"

It took Ryder longer to tell that story. How he had found their father with a bullet in his temple.

"Mom blamed him, didn't she?" Brodie asked.

"She didn't have to. He blamed himself."

"Is that why they got a divorce?"

"You'll need to ask her."

At first, it was too much to comprehend. The idea that her disappearance had caused such devastating consequences to her family, to everyone she loved. Her knee-jerk reaction was to take on the blame. It was her fault. *All her fault.* Iris Malone had drilled that into her head. She was so stupid for following the little girl named Charlotte.

Something occurred to Brodie at that moment that she hadn't considered before. Maybe she was lucky that Ryder didn't blame her. That, despite all of Iris Malone's lies, her mother didn't blame her for walking away and getting into that RV. But how could Brodie not blame herself?

34

South of Montgomery, Alabama

Maggie felt the tension forming a knot in her back. She adjusted the rental car's seat even as she changed lanes. Frankie Russo wasn't answering her burner phone. Maggie had left several voicemails, but obviously Russo wasn't checking them.

The woman wasn't checking them or she wasn't able to check them.

If Agent Alonzo was right, sometime in the wee small hours of the morning, the man who had murdered Tyler Gates and stole his phone had made it to the same hotel where Russo was staying. If the woman had been able to escape, she still had to drive from Nashville to Montgomery without the killer interrupting her trip with a car accident. Maggie knew that was a four-hour drive.

She glanced at the car's navigation panel. She'd be at the restaurant in ten minutes. Soon enough she'd find out. The problem was, she didn't know what she was going to do if the woman didn't show up.

Maggie had spent most of the trip from Atlanta bargaining with herself. If Russo didn't answer her phone by the time she crossed the Georgia/Alabama border, she'd call Hannah.

The border came and went.

Then she decided if Russo didn't call her back by the time she stopped to fill the gas tank, she'd call Hannah. Each time, Maggie talked herself out of her own deal, telling herself there was no reason to worry Hannah until she knew something. But the truth was, she worried she had already let Hannah down.

At the last stop Maggie did call Ryder. She had tried to sound as casual as possible. Her pulse was racing from all her second-guessing about Russo. Or at least, that's what she told herself.

"Hannah said you're working a site close to Montgomery. Are you still there?"

"Yep, Jason and I are sticking around. Weather's supposed to be crazy all day."

When she heard that Jason was with him she went from disappointed to relieved in a matter of seconds. And then she wanted to kick herself. That feeling of relief simply confirmed how much of a coward she was. Gwen was right.

"I'm meeting Hannah's friend for lunch at a diner just south of Montgomery before she heads down to your place. If you and Jason have time, you want to meet for coffee later? Before I head back to Atlanta?"

"Yeah, that sounds good."

There had been no hesitation in his voice. He sounded genuinely pleased. She gave him the address of Southern Blessings, and that was that. She still had no idea what she'd do if Frankie Russo didn't show up. Then she realized that Ryder would help if she needed to search for the woman. There was something very comforting in knowing that. The two of them had dealt with more difficult situations than this one.

Now, as she maneuvered the exits and streets she allowed herself the flutter of excitement. She wanted to see Ryder. Months ago she'd convinced herself that she needed to give him space to deal with his sister, but to be honest, she was having some difficulty dealing with her own feelings…denying her feelings. She had gotten good, almost too good, at compartmentalizing her emotions in order to manage and cope with all the things she experienced at crime scenes. All the psychological fallout from profiling madmen and serial killers. She told herself things she wanted to hear. But Gwen was right. Maggie knew she wasn't being fair to Ryder.

She almost missed the entrance for the restaurant. She'd expected a small diner tucked away in the middle of a busy crossroad intersection. Instead, she saw that Southern Blessings was a large freestanding building with its own parking lot. Across the street, 18-wheelers filled every slot, filling up their tanks at the gas station/mini mart. Some of them were parked off to the side while truckers walked over to the restaurant.

She was early and parked in a far corner, pulling under the shade of the beautiful magnolia trees that were blooming. She opened the car window and was hit by a blast of hot, humid air that immediately fogged up her sunglasses. She closed the window and started the car again, so she could wait with the A/C.

The entire trip she had watched the blue skies disappear as clouds gathered. Now they were starting to look more threatening. There wasn't much blue left, but Maggie had been in the South before. Thunderstorms rolled in, dumped rain and rolled out. Certain times of year, it was a daily occurrence. She hadn't turned on the radio because she didn't want to miss a call from Russo.

She checked her phone. No messages from Russo or Agent Alonzo. She pulled up the photo she had downloaded and compared it to a couple of women going into the restaurant. More diners were leaving than entering. Hannah had been smart in choosing one o'clock.

A few cars pulled out of the parking lot. A trucker left his rig at the gas station and walked across the street to the restaurant. A black sedan came into the lot and drove slowly up and down the aisles like the driver was looking for a place to park. Except there were plenty of spots. Maggie raised her phone, so anyone who noticed her might think she was reading her text messages. But as the car crossed her aisle, she snapped several photos getting a profile of the driver in one and the license plate in another.

She watched the car drive the final loop, and then just like that, it exited the lot. Her eyes followed it all the way to the interstate entrance. From what she could tell it had turned onto the northbound entrance.

Maybe it was nothing. A lost traveler or someone having second thoughts about the restaurant. She pulled up the photo with the license plate and messaged it to Agent Alonzo. It had taken her a minute at the most to send it, and yet, the next time she looked up she saw a small SUV pull in and do almost the exact same thing.

Up one aisle and down another. The woman's head pivoted from side to side as though she were looking for the best spot. She finally settled on a space in the far corner. She backed into the slot, and only then did Maggie see that in doing so, the woman had a direct shot out of the parking lot.

Maggie sat back, holding up her phone again and blocking her face. It didn't matter. The woman hadn't looked her way as she left the vehicle. She had a tangle of dark hair. She wore blue jeans, a T-shirt, running shoes and oversized sunglasses. Her head swiveled back to the street then the gas station across from the restaurant. She definitely had someone else on her mind, but she walked with purpose. So maybe she knew that she was being tracked.

Maggie watched her all the way to the restaurant door then whispered to herself, "I am so glad to see you're still alive, Frankie Russo."

35

Southern Blessings
South of Montgomery, Alabama

Frankie Russo felt like every nerve ending in her body was on high alert. She had been functioning on adrenaline since she'd left Nashville. Her mind wouldn't shut off. Her eyelids felt like lead shutters. The humidity had turned her thick hair into unruly waves. At one point she had looked in the rearview mirror and didn't recognize the image staring back at her. But as soon as Frankie walked through the restaurant's door the scent of fresh baked bread and batter-fried food brought back a wave of good feelings and good memories.

The entire drive she kept telling herself she just needed to get to Southern Blessings. Just get there! But she quickly reminded herself that this place definitely brought a false sense of security. She couldn't let her guard down. Not here. Not yet!

The hostess led Frankie to a table in the center of the restaurant.

"Would it be possible to have that booth by the window instead?"

The hostess didn't look pleased. Frankie could tell they were finishing a busy lunch hour, and the booth she was asking for still had dirty dishes.

"I've been cooped up in the car since sunrise," Frankie told the woman, slipping into an old familiar southern accent. "It would do my soul some good to be close to the window."

"As long as you don't mind waiting while we clear."

"Not at all."

It took two minutes at the most before Frankie was able to sit down. A waitress handed her a menu while she set a glass of water in front of Frankie and placed a bowl of fried dill pickles in the center of the table.

"What can I get for you, Hon?"

Odd as it seemed, the waitress looked familiar, and Frankie wondered if she had worked here when Hannah and Frankie had come as children. The woman looked to be in her fifties, tall and skinny with deep creases around her mouth and at the corners of her eyes. Painted on eyebrows gave her a look of being eternally anxious for your order. Frankie glanced at her nametag.

"I'm waiting for a friend, Rita, but I would love a cup of coffee."

"You got it, Hon."

Frankie picked out one of the fried dill pickles as she surveyed the rest of the guests. She had made a good decision choosing this booth. With her back to the wall she could get a good look at everyone inside and anyone who came in the door. Several people waited to pay their bills. There were probably about a dozen guests still eating or waiting to be served. A large man in a ball cap occupied a booth close to the door. Sitting at the counter, a well-dressed older gentleman was eating a slice of pie. Two women were being served their lunches at a table next to where the hostess had originally wanted to seat Frankie. In the other corner, a middle-aged couple had only coffee cups left. His arm stretched across the table to touch her hand. She was blushing and smiling too much. It had to be a new relationship.

Frankie felt a wave of relief when she realized the man with the scar wasn't here...yet. But her anxiety kicked up a notch when she also realized that the FBI agent wasn't here either.

Rita brought her coffee and a small covered basket.

"Something for you to snack on," she said, "until your friend gets here."

Frankie lifted the cloth napkin and could smell the buttery, warm biscuits. Her mouth watered. She finished the fried dill pickle and plucked one of the biscuits out from under the cover. In the window she caught a look at her reflection even while she scouted the parking lot.

She ran her fingers through her hair, trying to smooth down the wild curls. This restaurant and her reflection reminded her of the first summer she'd spent with Hannah and her grandparents. Hannah's grandmother had tried to tame Frankie's hair with bows and barrettes. After Frankie pleaded with her, the woman finally did up Frankie's hair in cornrows to match Hannah's.

When her father saw her, he'd laughed, so hard. Frankie hadn't seen him laugh like that before, or since. It made her smile just thinking about it.

Her father loved and respected Hannah's grandfather so much he would have been pleased to have him and his wife raise Frankie full time. And it would have been better if they had. Instead, Frankie had to live with her father's regret and despair, all the while looking forward to the next time she could escape to Hannah's.

For the first time, she noticed the sun had disappeared completely. She'd watched storm clouds gather in the west the last hour of her trip. But still, the sun had been relentless. The temperatures spiked in the upper eighties but the humidity made it feel like a slow boil. Inside the rental SUV she had hardly noticed until she was forced to stop and refill the gas tank. She'd left Chicago needing a jacket, not realizing she'd be wishing for a pair of shorts twenty-four hours later.

A man and a woman came in the door. Frankie thought they were together until the man seated himself at the counter and the woman waited. A teenaged boy joined the woman before the hostess came to seat them.

The man wore khakis and a green polo shirt, a designer one with a little logo on the breast pocket. He was older. Maybe in his fifties, possibly early sixties. She used to be better at reading people when she first started at the advertising agency and was obsessed with demographics. One thing for certain, there was something about this guy that bothered Frankie, but she couldn't quite put her finger on it. For some reason, he didn't look like he belonged. He didn't look like the type of guy who dropped in at a meat-and-three for lunch on a Saturday. Maybe it was the exhaustion, but her gut instinct had saved her ass already several times. Before she could study him further another woman walked in.

And just with a glimpse Frankie knew. This was the FBI agent.

Shoulder length auburn hair, taller than average, blue jeans and leather flats. A V-neck T-shirt but with a lightweight collared shirt over it, unbuttoned, sleeves rolled up, tails untucked and billowing so it could hide the shoulder holster. No one would notice the strap or the weapon unless they were looking for it.

The woman glanced around the restaurant, taking off her sunglasses and allowing a second for her eyes to adjust. But that's all it took was a second or two before she found Frankie and headed directly for her. She slid into the booth across from Frankie, put her hands on the table and laced her fingers together.

Then she smiled and said, "Hi Frankie. I'm Maggie O'Dell."

36

Florida Panhandle

Ryder had told Brodie that their mother had wanted to be at her side in the Omaha hospital. Brodie didn't remember. While her body was hooked up to IV fluids and connected to a variety of machines, her mind went into a delirious fever. Ryder said she slept in fits and starts, waking up wild-eyed, fists flying, legs kicking and not recognizing him or where she was. In the midst of all the chaos, one thing seemed certain. Her mother's presence panicked her, so much so, that after several days the doctors asked she leave.

Although Brodie didn't remember any of that, she'd never be able to forget her last days before she was rescued. Like a nightmare looped in her memory, it played over and over again. Instead of her sweat drenched hospital bed she was still imprisoned in the Christmas house where Iris Malone had left her.

The old rundown farmhouse, less than a mile from Iris' house, had been abandoned when Iris and her brother Eli Dunn had committed their mother to a nursing home. The old woman had loved Christmas, and the entire place remained as she had left it, untouched for years, forever decorated and ready for the holiday.

For Iris Malone, the Christmas house was the last stop for the Charlottes she wished to be rid of. She left them there for her brother, Eli to pick up and do whatever he wanted. Some he sold. Others he murdered and deposed of after he was finished with them.

Iris Malone claimed she didn't know what her brother did with the women. Now that the man was dead—along with Iris' son, Aaron—the woman could say whatever she wanted and no one could contradict her.

The last years of Brodie's captivity, and especially the last days, she had been starved. The Omaha doctors said it would take a long time for her to recover from the damage her malnourished body had endured. When they found her, she was severely dehydrated, too. Dr. Rockwood had tried to explain to Brodie how the mind tried to compensate, sometimes shutting down for long periods.

"Survival mode," she called it.

All Brodie knew was that almost five months later she still felt the panic kick in every time she thought about her mother. Intellectually, she understood it wasn't really her mother who caused the feeling. It was Iris Malone's lies that had entrenched themselves firmly and completely inside Brodie's mind. Without effort and without warning, Brodie could hear them:

"You're such a naughty girl, your mother and father said they don't want you anymore. Your mother told me to keep you. She never wants to see you, again."

The woman had been so convincing Brodie never doubted her. Many times she'd tell Brodie these things even as she held a telephone receiver in her hand, as if Brodie's mother was actually on the other end of the line at that very moment.

Brodie knew it wasn't right to keep punishing her mother by keeping her away. She'd been so patient, following the rules of the doctors and then the rules Brodie had put in place. She knew it wasn't fair, and yet, she still couldn't keep from feeling nauseated. Her mother was the last link, the last reminder of Iris Malone's evil manipulation.

Brodie had watched her mother on television hoping it would trigger good memories. Her show, *Life in Style with Olivia James*, was on every day, and Hannah rarely missed an episode. But the woman on the TV screen acted and talked so properly that Brodie hardly recognized her. She suggested linens and decorations and delicious recipes while she created a masterpiece right there in an hour.

Olivia James was a celebrity and looked much taller and younger than the woman now standing in Hannah's kitchen. She was still dressed very nicely in colorful soft fabrics that made Brodie almost want to reach out and touch a sleeve. Almost.

"Hello, Brodie," Olivia said, a smile caught at the corners of her mouth. The expression reminded Brodie of her grandmother, and she realized this older version of her mother looked very much like Gram.

Brodie couldn't find her voice and simply nodded.

Hannah promised that she would stay with them. Both mother and daughter agreed they needed a mediator. Now Hannah turned around from the counter and gestured for them to sit down at the table. Instinctively, they chose seats across from each other.

A box on the edge of the table distracted Brodie. Its flaps were pulled back. She gave the contents a half-hearted glance then her eyes darted back. She stood up to get a better look.

At first she thought it was an interesting assortment: books, movies, toys. A white dragon captured her attention. Then she realized it wasn't just any white dragon. It was hers—Puff the Magic Dragon, one of her favorite Beanie Babies.

She started looking at the rest...really looking, coming in closer. Standing above the box, Brodie could see Pokemon trading cards, more Beanie babies, Harry Potter and Lemony Snicket books and a purple plush dog with pink ears. Her fingers touched the dog.

Without thinking she said, "Puppy Surprise Eliza."

The fur was still as soft as cotton candy. She glanced up at Hannah and told her, "Each dog came with puppies inside. You didn't know how many you'd get until you opened the box and opened her tummy. You might get two, three or four. My Eliza had five."

Her hands hesitated.

"Go ahead," Olivia told her.

Brodie picked up the stuffed dog and turned her over. Carefully, she pulled open the Velcro sealed tummy. Gently she plucked out all five little puppies. Kitten rubbed against her legs, anxious to see, and she bent down to show the cat. When she stood up again, her eyes found Olivia's.

"You kept all these things?"

"Of course. There's lots more, but I brought some of your favorites."

Brodie touched the spines of the Harry Potter books, remembering how she and Ryder had read these out loud to each other. But she didn't remember there being so many volumes.

As if reading her mind, her mother said, "I kept buying the new ones every time they came out. Ryder didn't want to read them without you, but I guess I thought...*or hoped...*"

"I can't believe you kept all these things."

"They were pieces of your life. I simply couldn't bear to part with anything that reminded me of you."

This time when Brodie looked at her mother she saw the tears in her eyes. All those years that Iris Malone had lied to her, Brodie had never once considered the pain and loss her mother had suffered. Instead, she had spent sleepless nights, painful weeks wondering why her parents didn't come for her. They'd speak to Iris on the phone, but they never asked to speak to Brodie. She was so devastated, so lost, so hurt, so convinced that they had abandoned her.

"I'm sorry," she whispered, eyes down and staring at Kitten, her fingers still clutching the toy dog. She didn't know what else to say.

"You have absolutely nothing to be sorry about."

Brodie glanced up to see her mother wipe her eyes with a careful, almost stiff composure that seemed contradictory to the emotion she had just displayed. And Brodie couldn't help thinking that she was glad her mother didn't attempt to hug her. Not just yet.

37

South of Montgomery, Alabama

Creed and Jason loaded all their gear into Creed's Jeep and set up Scout's crate alongside Grace's. Despite Scout being three times bigger than Grace, he knew she was the boss of him. He wagged and humbled himself to her as he climbed up into the back. Scout hesitated a couple of times like he was waiting for her permission.

"Why are you taking me with you?" Jason asked.

"What? You don't want to go?"

"Won't you two… you know, want to be alone or something?"

"We're having coffee before she heads back to Atlanta. What were you thinking this was? A booty-call?"

Creed glanced at the kid. Jason's head turned to look out the window, but he could see his grin in the reflection of the glass.

"So this friend of Hannah's, is she pretty hot?"

"She's too old for you."

"Isn't Maggie older than you?"

Creed shot him a look, and Jason put up his hands in surrender. "Hey, I'm just making conversation."

"Anybody ever tell you that you stink at it?"

"Actually, all the time."

It had rained overnight. Just enough to make the streets wet and the air heavy with moisture. It was sweltering. Loading up the gear had left Creed sweaty, his T-shirt sticking to his back before he could blast the A/C. Clouds were rolling in. Ominous and bulging gray, they hung so low they looked like they could snag on the treetops.

Jason fiddled with the radio while Creed took the ramp to the interstate.

"We're already in a tornado warning," Jason said. He found a station reporting the weather and left it there.

"Sheriff Krenshaw said it would be like this all weekend."

"We've both been to Afghanistan. How bad can it be?"

Creed didn't answer. He was remembering the Garner's vehicle. It certainly looked like an IED had blown it up. The gas station had been reduced to piles of bricks and boards. Pine trees snapped in half. He'd seen mortars demolish entire Afghan villages to empty hulls. But it was hard to wrap his mind around the fact that this destruction had been caused by forces of wind, and not explosives.

They hadn't driven for more than ten minutes when dark clouds started gathering in the west. This section of the interstate, the north and southbound lanes were separated by a wide median filled with hardwood trees, so thick and so tall it was impossible to see what was on the other side. Occasionally, through a sliver between trees Creed could see the oncoming lanes of traffic.

Behind them it continued to grow dark enough that the vehicles following now had their headlights on. Creed kept glancing at his mirrors and each time the gray mass seemed to creep closer, swallowing every last piece of sky.

He craned his neck until he could get a glimpse of Grace in her crate. She had her nose pressed against the metal grate of her door.

"You okay, Grace?" he asked, and Jason twisted in his seat to take a look back.

"They can feel the storm," Jason said.

"She can smell it."

Jason was still turned looking out the rear window. "Man, it's getting wicked back there."

Just then, the radio started blaring with the emergency broadcast system. The robotic voice told them a tornado had been spotted on the ground six miles west of Hayneville moving north, northeast. A tornado warning was in effect for Lowndes County.

"Where's Hayneville?" Jason asked as he pulled out his cell phone and started tapping up map coordinates.

"Looks like Lowndes County is up above Butler. Isn't that where we were yesterday? And we're now in…" He looked back at his phone. "Montgomery County. It must be behind us."

The emergency broadcast ended and a weather report came on with the meteorologist repeating the information. Creed clicked up the volume:

"Folks in Hayneville, you need to take cover now. Go to the lowest level of your house. If you're in a trailer, get to your neighbors. Get off the road and into a building. You need to move to the middle, away from windows. Cover your head. And folks in Montgomery County, you need to prepare for this tornado. The National Weather Service hasn't issued a warning for Montgomery County yet, but I'm telling you, if you're in the southern part of Montgomery, you need to be looking for this tornado to be headed your way."

Jason twisted in his seat again to look out the back window, "It's really dark back there."

Creed glanced into the side mirror in time to see the cloud-to-ground lightning. It illuminated the entire sky.

An 18-wheeler roared by in the lane next to them, and Creed started looking for an exit. There were no signs promising any escape in the next several miles.

"Maybe we should get off the interstate." Jason said, as if he were reading Creed's mind.

"Some of the back roads wind in all directions. That might not be a good idea. We could get trapped."

Another truck zoomed by, its wake shoved at the Jeep, almost knocking them aside. Were they oblivious to the warnings or trying to outrun the storm?

"So maybe you need to speed up," Jason said.

Creed still couldn't see anything to their left. The continuous mass of trees blocked the horizon. But he did notice the black clouds coming over the tops of the branches. They were churning and so was his stomach.

The rain came as a downpour. No droplets. No pitter-patter. A sudden sheet of water that the windshield wipers couldn't keep up with. All Creed could see ahead was the blur of taillights. Cars were still passing on his left. The trees blocking the horizon started to sway.

The first ping of hail rattled him into a white-knuckled grip on the steering wheel. The clatter on the roof that followed sounded like it could break a hole in the metal. He worried it would shatter the windshield.

"Son of a bitch," Jason said.

Creed could feel the kid's tension. He wanted to tell him to calm down, but he was pretty sure he had every right to feel tense. They were in trouble, and he didn't even need to look at Grace to see how true that was.

38

Creed wondered how it was possible. The faster he drove, the darker the sky got. It was pitch black behind them. He still couldn't see a thing to the west. The ridge of trees in the median continued to block his view. The hail had stopped, but the rain continued.

"It just looks like a massive thunderstorm," Jason said. He was turned and straining against his seatbelt, so he could watch out the rear window. "I don't see anything resembling a tornado. Maybe it's not even close."

Still, Creed turned up the radio, but the meteorologist had a whole new list of other tornado warnings in other counties. Willis Dean kept reminding them, "Even if I didn't mention your county, watch the sky. Conditions could change very quickly."

Creed glanced down at the compass in the Jeep's dashboard. The meteorologist had said the tornado was moving north, northeast. They were traveling northeast. Just when he told himself they were moving along right in its path, the rain let up. The sky in front of them seemed to lighten.

He felt like he could breathe again. Up ahead the ridge of trees in the median would be ending soon. Now, between the trees he could see a few on-coming headlights on the southbound lanes. His foot even eased up on the accelerator.

"We should be able to see better pretty soon," Creed told Jason and gestured to the empty median.

The tree line finally ended. Their view was, indeed, better.

"Oh my God! It's right there!" Jason whispered.

Creed glanced over then did a double take. The trees had been hiding it. There was no mistaken the black swirling wedge emerging from the gray mass. He swore he could feel its energy. A bolt of lightning illuminated its core.

"You can see debris in the air. That thing is massive," Jason said.

The radio started squawking the emergency broadcast system warning for a tornado on the ground.

Jason punched the volume down. "Yeah, no shit!"

Creed stepped on the accelerator.

"Ryder, what the hell are you doing?"

"Trying to outrun it."

"It's coming right at us. You need to speed up."

"That's what I'm doing."

"You're gonna have to go faster. Give it some gas."

Creed glanced down. He was already going ninety-five.

"Oh my God, we're not gonna make it." Jason braced his hand against the dash. "You need to stop."

"We can't stop. We'll be right in the middle of it."

But even as the Jeep's engine jolted to one hundred miles per hour Creed could already hear the roar of the storm. It was alive and churning and spewing and heading right for them. It was almost on top of them.

Another truck barreled around them. But Creed couldn't see any other vehicles following.

"You're not gonna make it," Jason was yelling over the wind gusts that started to shake the Jeep.

The rain came again, but this time there were pieces of twigs and pine needles along with other debris hitting the windshield.

"We need to turn around," Jason told him. "Turn the hell around."

"I can't turn around." There were guardrails and the median still had trees and brush. No way he could drive over all that.

"It's gonna hit us!"

Jason was yelling, again, and Creed could barely hear him over the rumble that now reverberated through the entire Jeep. Just then, his ears started popping and he knew they were already inside the storm.

Creed slammed on the brakes. The Jeep skidded on the wet asphalt. He tightened his grip on the steering wheel. This was not the time to roll it out of control.

"What the hell?" Jason said while he reached for the grab handle.

Creed didn't allow the Jeep to come to a stop. It was still skidding on the slick asphalt when he jammed it into reverse. The vehicle bucked. Then he floored it.

His heart hammered against his chest. He kept his eyes forward as the Jeep flew in reverse. He couldn't look away from the black mass that continued to spin toward them. Debris flew everywhere now. He watched the backup camera and didn't ease up on the accelerator. There was one set of headlights in his lane, and he still didn't slow down. The car pulled onto the shoulder and out of his way. There were no others.

The black wedge only seemed to grow. Pieces of debris pummeled the Jeep, thumping and smacking the roof and the hood.

"It's crossing!" Jason said. "Look it's crossing the interstate." Jason pointed with his prosthetic hand even as he braced his other against the dash. "Oh my God, it's crossing right where we were."

Creed eased up a bit, but kept backing the Jeep away.

"That car's too close," he said. The vehicle that had pulled onto the shoulder to get out of his way had stayed put. "What the hell's wrong with them? Did you see who was behind the wheel?"

"Hell no! I haven't taken my eyes off that monster."

Everything was a blur through the rain. But Creed could see electrical poles snapping in half, one after another. Power lines swung free and whipped around. A billboard went airborne. Its steel pole bended over.

"Look at that." Jason pointed to an object flapping out of the column of black. "Wow! That's a roof. A whole roof! It must have picked it up from somewhere else and it's tossing it out."

They were far enough away now that the debris wasn't hitting them. Creed finally brought the Jeep to a stop. He kept his foot on the brake. He didn't shift into park. He wanted to be able to go again if he had to.

"It might be headed for Montgomery," Jason said "And it doesn't look like it's lifting up. God, that thing is massive."

Creed put the Jeep in park, but left the engine idling. He clicked out of his seatbelt and twisted around to the dogs. Both of them were wide-eyed and panting. Grace clawed at the grate when she saw she had his attention. He reached his hand over the console and offered her two fingers.

"You okay, girl? How bout you, Scout? It's okay. We're all okay."

"Oh man, look at that! It just hit that building."

Creed glanced over his shoulder just in time to see a two-story cinder block explode, flinging bricks and glass. Shipping crates and trailers crumpled like tin cans. Some of them got sucked into the black whirling mass. The lights along and inside the small industrial complex flashed and blinked out. The roof of another structure peeled away.

In the distance a blue-green flash lit up the black sky.

"A transformer must have blew up," Jason said.

They watched in silence. The storm seemed to devour the horizon to the north of them as it moved west to east. The lightning flickered inside just enough to show the steady rotation. It looked like a living, breathing creature, and only as it crept away from them did Creed realize how deafening its sound had been. They didn't need to shout any more.

That's when Creed said, "Do me a favor. When you tell Hannah this story, don't tell her how close we came to being sucked up into the storm."

"Right, sure," Jason said. "Hey, where did that vehicle go?"

Creed turned back around to face the windshield. The car that had pulled over to the shoulder to get out of his way was gone.

39

Birmingham, Alabama

"This one is massive, folks," Willis Dean talked to the camera. "If you're in Hope Hull, you want to take cover right now. Montgomery County, you should be hearing sirens go off. Everyone to the south of the city, go to your safe place."

He kept one eye on the monitor to know where to point. The radar was exploding with angry red and yellow bursts.

"This is the tornado right here. One of our storm chasers watched it earlier as it approached Interstate 65. We'll show you some of the video when it comes in. Again, this is a very dangerous wedge tornado. It's rain-wrapped, so please don't let it deceive you. At times it may look simply like a big, wide thunderstorm. Make no mistake, there's a tornado inside there.

"So if you're out shopping or having lunch, you need to go to an interior hallway. Get away from windows. Cover your head. Do not try to drive around this. This is a very dangerous wedge tornado."

Mia brought a new list of warnings, and he handed the reins to her. By now they were transitioning smoothly. She walked on, he walked off. In his younger years they would have had to drag him off the set, but these days he understood the necessity for refueling, keeping fresh and having time to review all the information coming in at a rapid pace. People's lives were at stake. Nothing could be missed or left out.

They were already receiving photos of damage even as new tornadoes were being sighted in other counties. The sky was falling around them.

Paul handed Willis a stack of messages as he entered the weather desk. Then he gestured to one of the city's video cams. A hulking mass was creeping into the viewfinder.

"Wow! Which camera is that?" Willis asked.

"The airport. It's pointing south toward I-65."

"Any word from Gary and his crew?"

"Gary checked in but the new guy's gone silent."

Willis glanced up at Paul. "He's the one that was driving alongside it, right?"

"Yeah." Paul shrugged. "Maybe his equipment got knocked out."

"His cell phone would still work."

"Mia just got some info. A cell tower went down."

Willis was protective about their chasers. Most of them were volunteers. He still trained a good deal of them. "Keep trying to get him, okay?"

"Absolutely," Paul told him and left.

Willis hated that the kid's name wasn't at the tip of his tongue. He remembered he was set to graduate in May from Auburn, but he hadn't grown up in the south. He'd come down to college from Kansas.

"Kansas...Simon."

Now Willis remembered because he tried to explain to Simon how Tornado Alley was different than Dixie Alley. The young man had spent his teenaged years racing across Kansas and Nebraska chasing funnels.

"On the plains," Willis told him, "you can see them in the distance. You can watch them form and drop out of the clouds. Here, the trees hide them. And half the time so does the rain."

Simon had nodded and said, "I guess I'm not in Kansas anymore, Dorothy." Dorothy from the Wizard of Oz. It became a running joke.

The NWS monitor started pinging out another warning. It didn't stop at one.

40

Southern Blessings

"Both men were in the vehicle?" Maggie asked.

"I believe so. The big guy with the scar on his neck was driving."

"You could see the scar?"

"No, but I recognized his profile." Frankie lowered her voice and leaned closer over the table. "He has a block-shaped head and big, square shoulders."

"Is he here?"

Maggie saw a spark of fear in Frankie's eyes before her chin jutted up and her eyes darted around the restaurant. It only took a few seconds, because Maggie had already noticed that the woman had been watching the door.

"No, he's not here."

Maggie was trying not to be distracted by her food, but somehow she had managed to fork her way through half of her Conecuh blackened chicken. The waitress had talked her into adding a side of cheese grits and those were almost gone, too.

"This food is delicious," she told Frankie who munched on her sweet potato fries but had barely touched her pecan-crusted catfish.

"Hannah and I used to come here when we were kids." She smiled. It was the first time since Maggie sat down that she saw the woman relax.

"How about the other man?" she asked, quiet and calm, trying not to jumpstart Frankie back into panic mode.

"I've never seen him."

"Not even a glimpse on the phone screen when you were talking to Tyler?"

"I don't think so."

"Think about it. Just for a minute. Go back to your conversation. Close your eyes if you need to. Relax and try to replay it in your mind."

Frankie closed her eyes, but there was no relaxing. Her brow creased, and it looked like she had clamped her jaw tight. The waitress appeared to fill Frankie's coffee cup, and Frankie's eyes flew open. It was obvious she looked a bit fluttered.

The waitress glanced at Frankie and said, "You okay, Hon?"

"We're just talking about, you know, yoga and meditation," Frankie explained returning to the southern accent she had used to order her lunch. "I'm not very good at it." And she gave a forced laugh.

"You're tired, Hon. All those hours in the car." She topped off the mug and asked Maggie if she wanted a refill on her Coke. "Y'all, let me know if there's anything else I can get you." Then she moved on to the next table.

In that brief exchange with the waitress Maggie could see how exhausted Frankie was. She noticed Maggie studying her, and she pushed a lock of hair back away from her face, notching it behind her ear.

"When they were at my office," Frankie said, "my assistant thought they looked or sounded official. I can't remember exactly what she said. Is it possible they're law enforcement? Tyler and Deacon did hack into a corporation's computer system."

"Only one problem with that," Maggie paused and glanced to the nearest occupied table. The older women were laughing in between bites. "Law enforcement officers don't normally execute a suspect on the streets."

Maggie immediately regretted being so blunt. Frankie's olive complexion paled and her eyes darted out the window. Maggie's eyes followed. Both she and Frankie had been checking the parking lot. But in the last few minutes Maggie couldn't help notice how dark the sky had become.

The corner light poles had turned on. Across the street, the lights above the gas pumps were on and most of the vehicles headlights, too. All of them triggered by the sudden change. But otherwise, it looked quiet. Even the trees were stock-still. There wasn't a hint of a breeze.

Maggie's cell phone buzzed on the table beside her. A new text message from Agent Alonzo. Frankie finally started eating her fish, pretending not to be interested. Maggie held the phone up, so no one could read it but her. She was hoping Alonzo had an owner for the black sedan, though she hadn't seen the vehicle return. She'd been watching for it over at the gas station.

His message was only two words:

HE'S THERE.

She tried to keep her reaction from registering on her face. She could feel Frankie's eyes on her. But Maggie didn't look up. She continued to stare at the phone. Then she tapped back a message:

INSIDE?

Alonzo knew where she was. He said he was mapping out everywhere the tracking device had led him, getting as close as possible. But this morning when he told her about the killer being at Frankie's hotel, Alonzo hadn't been able to distinguish if he was exactly at Frankie's hotel or the one next door.

His answer came back quickly:

DON'T KNOW. 100FT RADIUS.

Her eyes darted back out the window before she could stop herself.

"What is it?" Frankie wanted to know.

"Did you tell anyone you were coming here?"

"Just Hannah. What's going on?"

"By text?"

"Yes and we talked."

"Did you use your phone or the burner?" Maggie kept her voice calm, but she could see Frankie becoming visibly shaken. And every time Maggie scanned the parking lot, Frankie's eyes shot out the window, too.

"I think I've been using the burner. I can check my emails with my watch."

"Your watch?"

Frankie flexed her wrist. "It's a smartwatch."

"It keeps you connected to your email account?"

"Email and text messages."

Maggie didn't say anything. She kept quiet and watched as the realization swept across Frankie's face.

"Oh no," she whispered and her eyes met Maggie's. "Can they track this?" Her fingers were sliding the band up and down her wrist. Maggie could see the skin turning red. She put out a hand and stopped her.

"It's Bluetooth," Maggie said. "It's possible."

"And you think they're here, don't you?"

"Just relax, okay?" Maggie noticed the wind had picked up, and now, fat drops of rain started hitting the window.

"Folks," a short, stout man came into the middle of the restaurant. His bald head glistened with sweat. He was waving his hands for their attention. Maggie hadn't see where he'd come from, but he was wearing a stained apron.

"Folks," he tried again, and everyone quieted. "My name's Hank. I'm the head cook. I need to tell y'all, we're in a tornado warning. Nobody needs to panic," he said.

Even as he said this, Maggie saw the two waitresses hustling through the restaurant, picking up and delivering and finishing, reminding her of flight attendants when a pilot comes on to warn about turbulence.

"We have a small basement. It's nothing fancy, but y'all might want to consider coming on down. At least until we know it's safe. It's over this way." He gestured to the back of the restaurant and started walking in that direction, but no one followed.

Maggie looked to Frankie, but she was so busy studying the parking lot that Maggie wondered if she had even heard the man. And now, Maggie could see the wind had gotten stronger. Trees swayed. The rain was coming down in sheets.

There was a crash of thunder. No warning. No slow, distant rumble.

Lightning flickered in the dark sky and so did the restaurant's lights. A second crash sent almost all the guests to their feet.

"Everyone, please, let's head this way," Hank said and now the two waitresses were encouraging people.

"Oh no!" It was the trucker sitting in the booth close to the front door. He bolted up out of his seat. Just as he turned, the glass in the front doors exploded.

"Let's move it!" Maggie shouted as she raced across the room and started herding people to the back.

She looked over her shoulder to check on Frankie and saw her helping the two older women who had been seated close to them. A teenaged boy pulled and pushed at the woman with him, despite her being paralyzed by the loud roar that blared through the shattered glass door. Hank was already out of sight, yelling for guests to hurry. Maggie could barely hear him over the wind.

The couple that had looked like new lovers started running for the back, but the man was three steps ahead, glancing back but not waiting for the woman. The man in a polo shirt followed. He stopped to loop his arm through the woman's and pulled her along.

The trucker stopped to help one of the waitresses. He was motioning for Frankie to hurry with the other two women.

"Go," Maggie shouted to Frankie when she saw her stop and look as though she might wait for her.

Maggie turned back around to gather the last waitress. She was nowhere in sight. Maybe she had gone ahead and Maggie missed her. Was that possible? The only other place was the kitchen or the restrooms. Over the counter she could see into the kitchen area. The grill was abandoned. There was no one. Maybe the woman had already gone down.

"Rita?" she called but the howl drowned out her voice.

She saw the older man, the one with salt and pepper hair who had been at the far end of the counter. For some reason he was clear across the restaurant close to where Maggie and Frankie had been seated. He looked like he was searching for something.

"We've got to go," she yelled at him.

He didn't seem to hear her.

More windows shattered. Another crash followed by a boom. It sounded like explosions. The lights flickered. Maggie felt her ears pop just as lunch plates took flight. One of them sailed into her forehead before she could duck. It knocked her off her feet. Blood dripped down her face as she crawled. One blurry-eyed glance out the door and she saw trees swaying erratically. Behind the trees a cloud of black smoke was spitting out ash.

Then it occurred to Maggie what it was, and her heart started banging against her ribcage. It wasn't smoke behind the trees. And it wasn't ash. It was the tornado spewing debris, and it was heading directly for the restaurant.

She pushed to her feet fighting against the wind and being pelted by what it brought with it. She felt her way along the wall, hoping she was heading in the right direction. Chairs and tables were skidding across the floor. More glassware crashed against the walls.

"Come on," a deep voice called. "Hurry!"

Objects were pummeling the roof. There was a scream of metal ripping away and a new draft overhead. She didn't dare look up. Suddenly, in front of her was a hulk of a man reaching his hand out to her. It was the truck driver.

"Hurry!" Frankie yelled from behind him.

Maggie stretched her arm toward them. He grabbed her wrist and pulled her the rest of the way. She stumbled down the concrete steps, descending into dark shadows. She saw that the older gentleman had made it down before her. There was a landing. Her hand pressed against the cool concrete. Before she turned to descend down the next set of stairs, the door above her slammed shut.

Maggie couldn't help feeling that they were going down underground only to be buried.

41

Above them, the storm raged. To Maggie it sounded like the building was being ripped apart. Loud crashes were followed by the entire structure vibrating. Wood cracked. Glass shattered. Floorboards moaned too close overhead. A thunderous roar only seemed to grow louder. A single light bulb cast a dim glow over the area.

Around her several people had pulled out their cell phones. Their faces were an eerie blue-white. Hank commandeered the stairwell with the lone flashlight, shooting its beam up around the corner and towards the door at the top. It was almost as if he expected the storm to break through.

When her eyes adjusted, Maggie scanned the area. Cinder block walls and a concrete floor. Two steel support beams took up the center. Both were bolted into the ceiling joists and into the floor. Shelves with boxes lined one wall. An old chest freezer was squeezed into the far corner. The restaurant above was probably 2,000 square feet, but this room was, at best, a quarter of that.

Just then, a loud boom sent debris raining down. Maggie looked up and saw how low the ceiling was. Exposed wood beams were so close she could reach up and touch them with her fingertips.

So close. Too close.

Nausea immediately kicked in without warning. She needed to breathe or the claustrophobia would take over. Once upon a time a killer had locked her in an old chest freezer, not unlike the one in the corner. Ever since then, she found it difficult to tolerate small, enclosed spaces, let alone small spaces crowded with a dozen other people. Her pulsed raced. Her chest ached from the throbbing of her heart. But right now, she was grateful to be down here instead of upstairs.

Above them, the storm thrashed and pounded. Furniture screeched as it was shoved across the floor. Large objects were being hurled and dropped on top of them. More debris rained down. The roar made it difficult to hear anything else. It sounded like being underneath the tarmac as jet engines revved over their heads. She couldn't hear anything else, but Maggie could see one of the older women's lips moving, her hands together, fingers laced. She was praying.

For a brief moment, Maggie envied that kind of faith. Her father had had it when he ran into a burning building as a firefighter. When she was a child he'd given her a religious medallion, a duplicate of the one he wore. He promised that if she wore it she would be protected from evil. For a short time, she'd kept it on a chain around her neck, out of respect for and remembrance of him, not because she believed. After all, his medallion hadn't protected him. She'd taken it off and never put it on again the day she'd seen real evil and knew the only metal that could stop it was a bullet.

But times like this she wished she believed, because what was happening above truly sounded like a demon from hell. A demon that pummeled them and at the same time clawed and ripped, trying to tear them out from their hiding place.

She tried to concentrate on the others in the cramped quarters. Frankie was crouched down beside her. On a bench next to them the woman praying huddled with her friend. The teenaged boy allowed the woman, who was most likely his mother, to wrap her arms around him.

The older gentleman who had been sitting at the counter held onto the wooden shelving unit, one of the few solid pieces of furniture. Up in the restaurant Maggie thought the man looked familiar. There was something about his composure that she recognized. Maybe he was retired law enforcement. Shadows prevented her from getting a look at his face, but he held a wad of bloody napkins to his jaw. One of the waitresses stood close to him, holding onto another part of the shelving unit.

The middle-aged couple braced against the wall in the far corner. Maggie had thought they looked like lovers earlier. Now, neither comforted the other. In fact, they stood at arm's length.

The man dressed in a polo shirt and khakis had been at the counter, too. He stayed close to the stairwell.

The truck driver had lost his ball cap. Long, thin strands of hair whipped around his head and looked as wild as his eyes. He stood close to Hank, staring up the stairwell like he was ready to push the door open as soon as the storm stopped. But he was holding his arm. In the dim light Maggie could see the stain of blood growing on his shirt. When he turned, she could see something protruding from the back of his shoulder.

It reminded her of her forehead and her fingers found the open wound. Then Maggie realized something else. Her eyes darted around, checking faces, searching the far corners. The other waitress—the one who had served Frankie and her—wasn't here. She had looked for her and had hoped the woman had already escaped down the stairs. But she wasn't here.

Maggie listened to walls collapsing overhead as the storm punched and scratched and beat down on them. She felt the crushing weight of the woman's absence. There was no way she could survive whatever was happening up there.

Just when Maggie didn't think things could get any worse, something exploded above them. The beams creaked and groaned. The concrete wall vibrated. A second boom shattered the light bulb sending them into darkness. A slow moan grew into a high-pitched screech.

Then suddenly, the ceiling started collapsing down on top of them.

42

Creed carefully maneuvered the Jeep through the mess. Power lines dangled from broken poles. They tried to drive to the industrial area they had watched take a direct hit. A gigantic cell tower had toppled over on top of the interstate, so they had to backtrack to another exit.

Creed weaved along a side road, stunned by what he saw. Branches cluttered their path. Cinder blocks and bricks were scattered everywhere. Electrical transformers six-stories high were bent over and twisted into the ground. In an area where trees had blocked their view of the tornado, now Creed could see all the way to the horizon.

He slowed and they rolled down their windows to listen for calls of help, but an eerie silence had replaced the roar of the storm. And in the quiet they could hear the tinkling of shredded metal that hung from the few trees that remained standing.

"Oh man, over there," Jason said as he pointed to the right. A few blocks away was the entrance to a residential area.

Creed saw flashing lights of rescue units arriving at the other end of what used to be a housing complex. Three blocks wide, for as far as he could see, foundations looked swept clean, but beside each one stood a pile of rubble. If not for the concrete slabs it would have been difficult to tell where one house ended and the other began.

People wandered around. Some looked totally lost. Some were bleeding. A few first responders were already in the streets. Sirens filled the air. Confetti littered the lawns with shattered glass, toys, shoes, books, dinner plates and twisted pieces of chain link fence. Yet, at the end of one driveway stood a stainless steel refrigerator, upright and unmarked as though someone had just delivered it.

Across the street, not a house looked touched, except for the corner lot. The wall facing the street was sheered off, making it look like a dollhouse. Furniture, rugs, wall hangings remained in place. Creed was stunned to see that even the pillows on the sofa hadn't been disturbed.

The path of the storm was very distinct. To the right, every single tree had been uprooted, stripped of leaves and bark or dumped on top of what used to be a house. But on the other side of the street, huge oaks weren't missing a single branch. Magnolia trees still kept their blooms. The only indications of a storm were the pieces of pink insulation clinging in between the leaves like cherry blossoms.

Creed felt a bit numb. He backed the Jeep and pulled up off the street into an empty lot, getting out of the way of a fire truck.

"We should take the dogs," he told Jason, "and do a sweep. See if there's anyone trapped."

When Jason didn't respond, Creed glanced over at his profile. Behind his sunglasses Creed could see the kid staring out the windshield. His hand was rubbing the elbow of his other arm. It was a familiar gesture, a habit Jason had gotten into after his arm had been amputated, but Creed hadn't seen him do it since he'd been fitted with his new prosthetic.

"You okay?"

Jason blinked a couple of times before he turned to look at Creed.

"It looks like a war zone," he said.

"Yeah, it does. One big difference," Creed said. "Rufus and I usually came in before everything exploded."

43

Florida Panhandle

Hannah had saved Brodie from the anxiety of having lunch with her mother.

What a spectacle that would have been!

Brodie could only imagine the look on Olivia James' face as soon as she started breaking apart her entrée into tiny, little pieces. Here was a woman who instructed and lectured on the appropriate utensils used to serve particular foods. She remembered an entire episode dedicated to silverware placement that included a total of four separate forks.

But now, as they sat across the kitchen table, Brodie didn't know what to do with her hands. She had picked up Kitten at one point, trying to settle the cat on her lap. Even Kitten must have felt the woman's disapproval. The cat insisted on jumping back to the floor and disappeared as she often did when she didn't want to put up with whoever or whatever upset her.

Brodie was quickly learning that Kitten didn't possess the same loyalty Hannah and Ryder's dogs had. Still, the cat had become a sense of security to Brodie. She couldn't explain it. The animal calmed her like nothing else.

The kitten had appeared inside the Christmas house along with two paper bags full of grocery. She wasn't sure if the person who left the food had also left the kitten. It didn't matter. Whether a mistake or an intention, Brodie immediately thought of the cat as much of a gift as the food.

Now, Brodie wished her fingers were stroking Kitten's soft fur. Instead, she was hiding them and wringing her hands under the table.

Thankfully, Hannah filled the silence. Her voice was smooth and steady and peaceful. She talked about recipes, the storms and about Ryder and Jason. She told Olivia about Isaac and Thomas, and Brodie wished the two boys were here. They would understand her discomfort, but they would also be impatient and wanting to play with the toys inside the box.

At first, Brodie tried to keep up, listening and nodding, but now her heart was pounding too loudly. Her ears were filled with a rushing sound. She glanced at her mother to see if she could hear the thumping. Olivia James' lipstick was too perfect. Her fingernails were trimmed and painted. Not a single chipped one. No jagged skin.

Under the table Brodie looked at her fingernails. Several were bitten to the quick. She fought the urge to take care of a cuticle on her thumb. Unable to bring it to her teeth, she started to pick at it with her fingers.

Olivia James' hair was pretty, too. There were highlights of gold and the ends swished softly under her chin. Both sides were even. Brodie resisted forking her fingers through her short-cropped hair. Only recently had she tried to stop cutting swatches of it out. In her mind, long hair was what had attracted attention. It was one of the reasons she was taken. Iris wanted to replace her daughter Charlotte, and Charlotte had always worn her hair long.

Brodie had hated the dirty, unwashed strands clinging around her neck like a noose. As soon as she had access to a pair of scissors, she started to cut it and didn't stop until it was shorn so close she could see her scalp in places.

*Those scissors…*she remembered now. The image flashed before her. She had driven the metal blades deep into Aaron's neck. Above the rushing sound in her ears Brodie could still hear his howls of pain. She could still feel his warm blood splatter her face. She didn't attempt to pull the blades back out. No, if anything, she pushed them deeper.

She gave her head a small shake, wanting to get rid of the image. She looked up to find Hannah and her mother staring at her.

When had Hannah stopped talking?

Brodie could see the concern lined on her forehead. Her mother was watching her like a person watching a scary movie and not knowing what came next. Brodie wanted to tell her that this was exactly what she was getting herself into. She wasn't her innocent, little girl anymore. She didn't care about pretty things or old toys. Instead, she was thrilled to have a drawer full of socks and warm blankets and chocolate chip cookies. She wanted to tell her mother that she was as strange as she looked with sunken cheeks and skinny legs. She was inappropriate. She ate with her hands…hands that were still chapped and scarred; fingernails manicured by teeth.

But instead of saying any of those things, what she said next surprised her as much as it surprised Hannah and her mother.

She blurted out, "I killed a man."

44

Just South of Montgomery, Alabama

Creed and Jason geared up. They grabbed helmets and added extra batteries for the flashlights already inside their pre-loaded daypacks. Creed squeezed in a couple more water bottles in case someone needed water. Both of them had wrap-around sunglasses to protect their eyes from falling debris, but they also had goggles for themselves and for the dogs.

Grace didn't mind goggles, but it was impossible to get her to accept boots. Most of their dogs came to them after being abandoned. As a result, some had particular issues, and Creed took all of those issues into consideration when he began training. Lately, he regretted that he hadn't tried harder to get Grace to wear protective footwear.

As Jason put Scout's all terrain boots on, Creed applied a breathable wax balm to Grace's pads. *This,* she allowed. It protected her from the hot asphalt and toxins, keeping her pads strong. But it wouldn't protect her against sharp objects like Scout's boots would. Creed had tried to put Grace in every kind of footwear available, even the less obtrusive ones that Dr. Avelyn, his veterinarian, had recommended. Grace didn't resist having them put on. She didn't chew or tug them off. No, she simply sat. She wouldn't move. She refused to move.

They put the dogs' vests on and attached short leashes. Creed checked the GPS devices to make sure the batteries were full before zipping one into the pocket of each dog's vest.

Jason and Scout headed down one street. Creed and Grace took another. They agreed to meet back at the Jeep in an hour. The dogs would need a break. The sun was blazing hot and the air thick. The extra moisture from the storm made it difficult to breathe.

It amazed Creed how people reacted to dogs in a disaster zone. Dogs brought normalcy back to their lives. Some even stopped and asked to pet Grace, despite the shock in their eyes or the blood on their clothes. Grace's presence, her prancing and genuine joy to get to work, also gave Creed a sense of calm. Still, he could feel the tension as the two of them walked through these very personal and private ruins of strangers. He couldn't help but feel like a trespasser.

After a natural disaster, the primary search for first responders had to be for surface victims. It would keep them busy doing triage and getting survivors to hospitals. But Creed and Grace had to concentrate on those victims trapped, buried, or pinned beneath the crushing weight of their demolished homes.

Time was never on their side. Buildings compromised by the storm could collapse completely. It wasn't just the structures they had to worry about. There were downed power lines, gas leaks and flooding. Life threatening injuries could quickly turn a rescue into a recovery.

"She must be in here," a woman was screaming.

Two men teetered on top of a rubble pile that just hours before had been a house. They were ripping up layers of shingles, beams and drywall. They tossed down bent window frames with pieces of glass flying as the frames hit the pavement. The younger man stopped and waved at Creed.

"Mr. Creed. Deputy Mitch Huston. I was out at the interstate site yesterday."

Without his uniform, Creed didn't recognize the man. Truthfully, there had been dozens of responders, and he'd only met a handful, but he pretended to remember.

"This your neighborhood, deputy?"

"Yeah," he said. "I'm across the street. We were lucky. Unbelievably lucky." He sheepishly pointed to one of the houses that escaped damaged, survivor's guilt already taking hold. "These are my neighbors, Bud and Alice."

"My mom is somewhere in this mess," the woman said to Creed, gesturing to him with a cell phone in her hand.

"She was home. I was talking to her on the phone when it hit. She's in there somewhere."

She tapped her phone's screen and a few seconds later everyone stopped at the muffled sound of a phone ringing. It came from deep inside the debris pile. Creed could tell they'd already done this—call the number and listened to the ringing. They knew where they needed to dig, but now, they all stared at him, watching and waiting.

He ventured closer. Toward the back, another section of the house had collapsed into a mess of splintered boards and drywall. Creed found a tangle of clothes and shoes. Carefully, he tugged free a canvas tennis shoe. He held it up, showing it to Alice.

She was speechless, suddenly overcome with emotion. She simply nodded before he asked if it belonged to her mother.

"Hey, Mister." It was Bud calling down to him. "No disrespect, but we could sure use a hand up here. It sounds like her phone is straight down underneath us."

"Sir, hold on a minute," Creed told him.

He squatted down in front of Grace. He presented the shoe to her, allowing her to sweep her nose over it. She sniffed the surface then dipped her nose inside. He could have chosen any of the woman's clothing. If she had worn the item recently there would be skin rafts with her individual scent. But Creed trained his handlers to choose shoes if they had a choice. Few people laundered their footwear, so the scent stayed longer.

He could feel all three of them watching. Most of the time, he'd insist family members move away while his dog did her job. A family's emotions could distract a scent dog. Sometimes people physically got in the way or simply asked too many questions. But last fall Creed had found himself in the position of being one of those family members and defending his right to be included. At the time, they were searching the graves of a madman and believed they might find the remains of his sister. So he knew how it felt to be pushed out of the way. For all he knew, Grace would alert to the exact spot where they were already digging and confirm the woman's location.

But that wasn't at all what Grace did.

She poked her nose in the air. Circled once. Then she turned her back on the mountain of debris and headed in the opposite direction.

45

Frankie felt the crushing weight but couldn't see what was on top of her. There was a lot of scrambling in the dark. Flashes of blue light as people found their cell phones. Someone was crying. It was better than the screams from a moment ago. And the fact that she could hear again, should have brought relief that the storm above them had stopped. Actually, it had stopped so suddenly Frankie didn't trust that it was finished.

"Are you okay?" Someone asked. Before Frankie could respond, someone else answered and she realized they weren't talking to her.

Could anyone even see her? It was so dark she could hardly see. Her back was against the cold concrete floor. When had she fallen down? She tried to move and pain shot up her leg.

"Oh my God, you're bleeding!"

This time the voice was too far away, and Frankie knew it wasn't directed to her.

The chaos around her didn't seem to include her at all. More flashes of blue and white light as more cell phones came on.

"I can't get a signal," a woman said.

Then suddenly a stream of light hit Frankie in the face.

"Frankie? You okay?" It was Maggie O'Dell, though she couldn't see the woman on the other side of the blinding light, she recognized her voice.

Finally, the stream moved down. "Can you move?"

"I'm stuck," Frankie said as she lifted her head to see what the light revealed.

It made her stomach lurch, and she tasted bile in the back of her throat. Her legs were pinned underneath one of the steel beams that had been holding up the basement ceiling. It looked like part of the building had also caved in on top of her. In a panic, she twisted and wiggled and tried to pull herself out.

"Hold on," Maggie told her with a hand on her shoulder. "Hey, I need some help over here!" She yelled.

Frankie pointed to Maggie's forehead, "You're bleeding."

The FBI agent swiped her fingers over the wound and wiped the blood on her jeans.

"I think it's okay," she told Frankie. "Probably just needs a couple stitches."

The older man who Frankie remembered had been at the counter before the storm, was the first to respond. Except his jaw was bloody now, and his salt and pepper hair glittered with glass and dust. His white shirt with his carefully rolled up sleeves was torn and stained.

"Do you think we can lift it?" Maggie asked him. She didn't wait for his answer. She was waving someone else over.

He crouched down and stared at Frankie as if it were important for him to know the identity of the person he was helping before he gave the beam a single glance. Frankie guessed he was in his sixties. Close up, his skin looked weathered from too much sun, and his hair was more salt than pepper. But his forearms looked lean and strong. And yet, Frankie almost sighed with relief when she saw the giant of a man over Maggie's shoulder.

It was the truck driver who had helped her earlier. He had kind eyes and muscles that looked like he could lift a car off a person. But there was blood running down his arm and his shoulder hung at an odd angle.

"Wait a minute," Maggie told him when she noticed his arm, too.

"What's your name?"

"Ronald."

"Ronald, turn around."

She pointed her cell phone's flashlight at his back. Frankie saw the shard of glass, and panic quickly replaced any relief. A four-inch chunk stuck out of the top of his arm. It didn't help matters when Frankie saw Maggie's response. The woman looked visibly shaken. Was it the blood? It did look gross. But she was an FBI agent. Didn't she see worse stuff?

"We need to take care of you, Ronald," Maggie told the man. "You can't help. You need to sit down." She grabbed the edge of a bench and dragged it over. Then she turned back around and called out, "Hey, anyone know first aid? I'm talking major wound. And I need some muscle over here."

"We're trying to pry open the door," a voice called back. Frankie thought she recognized it as Hank's.

Maggie looked down at the older man who was still kneeling next to Frankie.

"What do you think?" she asked him. "Can the two of us lift this?"

"If it was just the beam. But all this other stuff. Maybe we should wait for the paramedics."

"What's your name, sir?"

"Friends call me Gus."

"I'm Maggie. How about we give it a try, Gus," Maggie told him.

Despite Maggie's best attempt to hide it, Frankie heard the urgency in her voice, and it kicked up Frankie's anxiety. Did she think they couldn't wait until the paramedics arrived? The pain was almost unbearable now. She bit down on her lower lip. The beam had most likely broken at least one of her legs, if not both.

Gus shrugged then nodded. He examined the beam looking for someplace to put his hands. Maggie did the same.

"You ready, Gus?" Maggie asked. "On the count of three. One. Two.

Three."

The beam didn't budge. It didn't shift even a little bit. It simply didn't move.

Frankie tried to concentrate on breathing. They were going to try, again. She breathed in. Then out. Another breath, in and out.

It still did not move.

Frankie stopped. She held her breath this time. Then she sniffed the air and her eyes darted to Maggie's. She smelled it, too.

"Don't panic," Maggie told her.

How could she not panic? The storm had broken a gas line, and now the fumes were filling their small, incredibly cramped area.

46

Grace led Creed across the street. Her nose was working the scent. Her tail curled up over her back. Deputy Huston had skidded down the debris pile to follow. Alice was close behind. Her husband, Bud stayed and continued to dig.

"My mom was in the house," Alice shouted at their backs. "She didn't leave the house." But she still trailed behind them.

Grace strained at the end of the leash. Once she shot a look back at Creed to hurry up. He cringed as she trotted over broken glass. She threw her head back and sampled the air without stopping. Her breathing grew rapid and her eyes fixed ahead. He tried to steer her around oily puddles and two-by-fours with nails.

"This is the little dog that found that baby," Deputy Huston was telling Alice. "He was thrown out of the car. It had to be over 200 feet."

Creed tried to tune them out. He thought about stopping and asking them to stay back. But at this point, he didn't want to stop Grace. And the deputy brought up a good point. Tornadoes threw people around. But at the same time, he wanted to warn them that the storm had thrown the woman's belongings around, too. There was a chance that Grace could be tracking something that had belonged to Alice's mother. Something that simply had her scent on it along with some blood.

She led them between rescue vehicles and through groups of first responders. Most hardly noticed them. Creed glanced over his shoulder. They were cutting a diagonal line that already crossed two streets. They came around a debris pile almost two-stories high, and now, Creed could see where Grace was taking them. Jason and Scout were already there with a team of firefighters. Grace tugged even harder.

The small park and half a dozen huge live oaks had survived, although all the leaves and some of the bark were stripped away. Under the second tree, Scout jumped at the trunk and peddled the air with his front paws. Then he sat down. Creed could see Jason already pulling out Scout's rope toy to reward him.

The block of white glistened against the stark black and brown. Cradled in the branches above was a bathtub.

Creed stopped and turned around. He put a hand up to stop Deputy Huston and Alice.

"Hold on a minute," he told them. To Grace, he said, "Good girl." She was already staring up at him, waiting. His fingers fumbled with his daypack's zipper. He found the pink elephant and handed it to Grace. Pleased, she took it in her mouth and made it squeal, again and again.

"I don't understand," Alice said.

"Where did your mother usually take shelter?" Creed asked.

"Very few of us have basements. Bud and I have a closet under the steps. Mom usually goes to the bathroom and gets—" She stopped and her eyes flicked over his shoulder and up at the tree. "No. It can't be."

They let the firefighters do their job. They were supposed to wait for a fire truck to maneuver its way through the downed power lines. There was no secure way to climb up and look inside the bathtub without a ladder. And yet, the men were already tossing a rope over one of the few branches that wasn't bearing the weight of the bathtub.

The youngest of the firefighters was stripping out of his gear, tossing off anything and everything that might obstruct his climb.

To Creed, he asked, "Can your dog tell…"

He stopped himself and checked to see if the family members—by now Bud had joined Alice—were back far enough to not hear him. Deputy Huston had made sure of that.

The firefighter continued, "Can your dogs tell if she's dead or alive?"

It was complicated. Creed didn't want to get into a lengthy explanation of how fresh this scene was. Both dogs were trained for search and rescue, but both had also been trained for recovery. There was a distinct difference in the scent of a live person and a decomposing body. But a person who may have died only hours ago?

"No, sorry," Creed told him.

"But you're sure someone's still in there? Isn't it possible she was inside and is gone, but her scent is still there?"

"I guess anything's possible," Creed said. He'd seen stranger things. But he trusted his dogs. "Both dogs believe she's still there."

The man simply nodded. To the other firefighters, he said, "Okay, let's do this."

He was short and compact. When he grabbed hold of the rope, it quickly became clear why he was chosen. He shinnied up with little effort. In no time, he pulled himself up onto a thick branch adjacent to those cradling the bathtub.

Creed watched the man's face and within seconds he knew the bathtub was, in fact, a coffin.

He joined Jason under one of the other oaks, far enough away to give the family and the firefighters room to assess, to work, to grieve. The dogs were taking a break in the rare patches of shade. Jason had already given them water and retrieved their reward toys. Both of them lay with their hind legs kicked back. They watched the action and chaos around them, curious but at the same time, disinterested, almost as if they knew they had already done their jobs.

Jason pulled out his cell phone. With one hand he was holding and scrolling. His prosthetic fingers were capable of intricate touch, but the kid had gotten so used to doing many things with one hand. It was almost as if he forgot he could use the other.

"What was the name of that restaurant where we were meeting up with Maggie?"

"Southern Blessings." He glanced back at Jason. His thumb was still scrolling. "Why do you ask?"

"One of the firefighters said it took a direct hit."

"What?"

"I'm looking to see if there's any information on-line."

Creed patted down his pockets in search of his own cell phone.

"Are you sure that was the name?" he asked, hoping Jason may have heard it wrong.

"Yeah, I'm sure."

Creed found his phone and had to turn it on.

"How can you be sure?"

"Because I kept thinking it was ironic that a place with blessings in its name would get hit by a tornado."

Creed's phone was finally ready. He tapped a text message to Maggie:

ARE YOU OKAY?

Then he waited.

47

Maggie knew she wasn't good at this. Crime scenes. Dead bodies. No problem. But victims, injured and bleeding with glass sticking out of their flesh and steel beams on top of them? That was a problem. She wasn't a first responder. She remembered CPR, but that was all.

The gas fumes were making her lightheaded. She couldn't think straight.

Hank couldn't get the door open at the top of the stairs. There was something blocking it. While both of them called for help, she could see Hank was getting a better response. More of them were interested in getting the door opened than aiding those who had gotten injured.

Two of the men were trying to ram the door with one of the fallen beams. The guy in the designer polo shirt had stayed at the foot of the stairs, constantly checking his cell phone. He looked anxious to get back out the door ever since they'd come down. Maggie had heard Hank call him Max.

The other man, Maggie had nicknamed Loverboy. Perhaps it was a misnomer, because ever since the storm began, the man had nothing to do with the woman he'd been so enthralled with earlier over lunch.

The beam that had fallen on Frankie had taken part of the ceiling down with it. For a brief moment, Maggie thought it might be a possible escape route. But on closer inspection, she could see that a metal object had sealed the hole. Right now, all she cared about was getting this beam off of Frankie. The longer it crushed her legs, the more likely the woman might lose them both. But Gus didn't seem to share her urgency.

"I think I could help," Ronald, the truck driver, still offered. "I can use my one arm."

That was yet another dilemma. Does she leave the shard of glass in? She knew from personal experience that taking a knife out could cause a victim to bleed out quickly. Was it the same for a big-ass piece of glass?

And where the hell was everyone else? The older women stayed praying close to the stairs. The other lovebird? From what Maggie could tell she was texting on her cell phone. Maybe, hopefully, she was getting them some help.

Finally, the waitress came over to take a look at Ronald. She removed her apron and tried sopping up the blood dripping down his arm. To Maggie she said, "Do you think he needs a tourniquet?"

Maggie noticed her nametag and asked, "Do you know how to do one, Val?"

"Yes, ma'am," she said and she started ripping the ties off of her apron.

She was younger than Maggie had noticed before. Probably in her twenties. The other waitress was older. The waitress who called her and Frankie, "Hon." The one Maggie didn't save.

Maggie kneeled down next to Frankie. Sweat beaded on her forehead. Her eyes were closed but she was biting her lip. It was bleeding. Maggie looked across the beam at Gus. He seemed content to let her call the shots. He also seemed content to wait for the paramedics. He leaned against the wall, watching and waiting.

Suddenly, Maggie realized her feet were wet. Frankie's hair was wet, too. Somewhere water was seeping in. The rest of them could stand. Frankie couldn't.

Now Maggie's eyes darted around the crumbling basement. She stood and turned, shooting her cell phone's flashlight over the walls, the shelves, the collapsed ruins. She double-backed and started searching the area. A five-foot length of steel pipe had come down with the ceiling. She grabbed it, pleased with how heavy and sturdy it felt.

"Come on, Gus," she said, gesturing for him to come over to her side of Frankie. Val had finished her makeshift tourniquet and Maggie called to her. "Can you give us a hand?"

Maggie shoved the steel pipe under the beam, keeping it away from Frankie's legs.

"Val, when Gus and I lift this beam, I need you to pull Frankie out from under it."

Frankie's eyes were open now, wide and hopeful. She couldn't disappoint her.

Val came around behind Frankie and helped her bend forward enough for Val to get her hands under Frankie's shoulders. Then Maggie motioned for Gus to join her. They would push all their weight down on the pipe and hope it would lever the beam up enough for Val to pull Frankie's legs free.

"Okay, here we go," Maggie told them.

She and Gus pushed and strained and the beam lifted only inches. It wasn't going to work. How could this not work? Frankie's eyes watched, waiting and waiting. But it wasn't enough. Then suddenly, another hand reached over and gripped the pipe.

Ronald added his weight. The beam began to lift. The other debris slid off and the beam lifted more. Val pulled and dragged until she had Frankie completely free.

"We need to get her up out of the water," Maggie told them before they could celebrate.

They lifted her up onto one of the wooden benches. With her back against the wall, the bench was long enough for her legs.

"How you doing?" Maggie asked her.

"Better." She offered a weak smile. Then she jerked and grabbed Maggie's hand, squeezing it tight. She grimaced and panic filled her eyes, again, as she said, "I still can't move my legs."

48

Florida Panhandle

Hannah had suggested Brodie go "take a lie down." She was too old for Hannah to tell her to go take a nap like she did with Isaac and Thomas. Brodie didn't argue. She welcomed the retreat. She needed the relief. Another minute longer and she was sure her heart would explode right out of her chest.

She found Kitten and curled up on her bed. But she didn't reach for the book on her nightstand. The stories, the wonderful adventures had been her escape. There was no escape from this. How could she get rid of the images and the memories when they had wrapped themselves so tightly and so firmly around her mind that they had managed to become a part of her?

Then she saw the notebook and pen also next to the bed. Brodie sat up and grabbed the journal. She found the first empty page and began filling it:

My name is Brodie Creed.

My name is Brodie Creed.

My name is Brodie Creed.

Brodie was the problem. She was weak, a scaredy-cat, a crybaby. Although Brodie hadn't shed a tear in many years.

No, not Brodie. Charlotte hadn't shed a tear.

She readjusted the pen in her hand and wrote:

My name is Charlotte.

My name is Charlotte.

A soft tap on her door stopped her. She jerked and threw her legs over the edge of the bed, prepared to run. The reaction was so instinctive she didn't realize how silly it was until Hannah peeked around the door.

"You okay, Sweet Pea?"

"Yes."

"May I come in?"

"I suppose." She pulled her legs back up and pushed herself into the pillows, using the headboard as a brace. She held the notebook, the page with the words clutched against her chest. "Am I in trouble?"

"Oh, Sweet Pea. No, not at all."

"When is Ryder coming home?"

Hannah smiled at her, and she wasn't sure why. "He should be home tomorrow."

"I don't want to talk to her anymore," Brodie said, but now she couldn't meet Hannah's eyes. She didn't want her to see how weak and cowardly she was.

"You don't have to. You take as much time as you need."

"Is she leaving?"

"The weather is nasty up through the route she needs to take. I asked her to stay the night. Is that okay with you?"

Brodie shrugged like it didn't matter to her. It wasn't her mother's fault.

"I can't make the memories go away," she whispered, so softly she really meant it just for herself.

Hannah sat on the edge of the bed and reached out a hand. The first time she'd done this Brodie didn't know what to expect. She placed her rough and scarred hand in Hannah's. Hannah's was soft and warm and smooth, but firm and strong.

"I'm no expert," Hannah said, "but maybe we could try putting some good memories back inside your mind."

"How do we do that?"

"Well, you're already doing it every time you enjoy being with Isaac and Thomas. When you feel the warm sunshine on your face. Remember when you and Ryder slept outside under the stars? And Jason sure does like telling you about the dogs and showing you what they can do."

Brodie tried to listen, really listen. She realized she was gripping Hannah's hand like she needed to hang on.

"Sweet Pea, you've had to be strong and brave for so long."

"Charlotte was." It came out before she could stop it.

"Charlotte?"

"She was the brave one. Brodie was always weak and frightened. She cried all the time." She looked up to see Hannah's reaction.

"*You* are the brave and strong one. And you have always been, Brodie," Hannah squeezed her hand and tilted her head to make sure Brodie didn't break eye contact. "Brodie may have been scared but she grew strong. Brodie became brave and fought back because she knew what it felt like to be frightened, and she didn't want to feel that way anymore. *Brodie* was the one who survived. Charlotte was just a name Iris Malone called you. She couldn't make you be Charlotte. She tried, right? She tried over and over again to make you Charlotte. Isn't that right?"

She waited for Brodie to nod.

"She tried and she couldn't do it. You know why? Because Brodie wouldn't let her."

Brodie stared at her and finally nodded.

"None of us, including your mother, expect you to be that little girl anymore. But you don't have to push her aside. She's still a part of you. She gave you your love of reading, your kindness to animals, your fascination with the stars. Sweet Pea, somehow you need to stop blaming her. It wasn't her fault. None of it was your fault."

"That's what Dr. Rockwood said."

"Maybe starting on Monday we can see if you can talk to Dr.

Rockwood every week."

"But she's in Omaha."

"She said she could talk to you over the computer or the phone. A video-chat. Or you could go back to Omaha for a little longer."

Brodie shook her head, almost too violently as she said, "No, I don't want to leave home."

Hannah smiled, again, and this time Brodie furrowed her brow, questioning what she had said that made Hannah smile.

"That's the second time you called this home." Hannah squeezed her hand, and Brodie noticed she had eased her grip. "Now, you get some rest. Maybe a little later—only if you're up for it—your mother brought some home movies. Some good memories. Would you like to watch?"

"With Isaac and Thomas?"

"Of course, but oh Lord, you'll have to be prepared for them poking fun."

Hannah stood, and Brodie let go of her hand.

"Get some rest. I'll fix some special movie treats for all of us to munch."

Brodie watched her leave. She stroked Kitten. Then suddenly, she remembered the notebook she still had clutched against her chest. She looked at the words. She tore the page out. But instead of crumpling it and throwing it away, Brodie folded it carefully, protecting the words inside the fold. She folded it a second time then hid it clear to the back of the drawer in her nightstand.

49

Just South of Montgomery, Alabama

Creed's phone dinged, again. He glanced at it and wanted to throw it against a wall. They were heading back to the Jeep. Between sending messages that "failed to be delivered" to Maggie, Creed argued with Jason. The kid wanted Creed to leave him and Scout to continue searching while Creed drove to the restaurant. Scout's tongue dangled sideways. Both dogs were panting. The humidity was stifling. He wanted to get both dogs inside the Jeep.

"I can't risk leaving you without some A/C relief for Scout," Creed said.

He knew he didn't need to remind Jason that sometimes dogs couldn't cool off fast enough on their on. Although dogs sweated through their paw pads, panting was their only way to circulate air and cool their bodies. Because scent dogs breathed more rapidly while working a scent, there was a risk of them becoming dehydrated quickly or worse. Within a very short period, an overheated dog could suffer heat stroke causing damage to the brain, heart, liver and nervous system. Creed wouldn't forgive himself if he lost a dog to heat exhaustion. That was why he'd installed the alarm systems in all their vehicles as an extra precaution. All his handlers carried the supplies necessary for subcutaneous injections in case they needed to rehydrate a dog more quickly.

He knew Jason only meant well. He wanted to make sure no one else was missing. Creed finally convinced him to give one of the firefighters a business card with his and Creed's phone number. After all, they were only a mile or two from the restaurant. They would come back. But even as Creed promised, he noticed the horizon growing thick and dark with another round of storms.

Now, ready to leave, he tapped one last message to Maggie as he started the Jeep.

"We did see that cell tower down over the interstate," Jason told him.

"But weren't you just on the internet?"

Jason pulled out his cell phone. "It was really slow. And I never really connected. Not getting anything now. I've got her number in my contacts, I'll keep trying while you drive."

Creed punched the address of the restaurant into the GPS. He had a feeling they'd need to try more than one way to get there, and they wouldn't be able to look up directions or maps. He was relieved when he saw that they really were only three miles away and according to the GPS, they'd be there in less than five minutes.

"I'm sure first responders are there," Jason said. "The firefighter told me about it—" He glanced at his watch, "Like half an hour ago. Maybe they already got everybody out."

"Let's hope so."

Jason turned the radio on, and the station was broadcasting more weather advisories. He turned up the volume.

"Folks, this is Willis Dean at WALC-TV in Birmingham, Alabama. Please pay attention this afternoon and evening. I know we have some folks who were already hit. Damage reports are coming in, and we'll get you information as we get it. But folks, as bad as it's been we can't let down our guards. There is another line of storms developing."

Creed's phone dinged, and Jason punched the radio volume down. Creed handed him his phone while he weaved his way around more downed power lines.

"It's Hannah," Jason said. "She wants to know if we're okay. They're probably just hearing about the damage."

Another ding and Creed shot a look of hope.

"Hannah, again. Said Dr. Avelyn and Penelope Clemence are coming up to help. She wants to know what the hotel is where we're staying. I'll text her back on mine."

He handed Creed his phone then started tapping on his own.

"So we must have service if her message got through."

"I'll text Maggie, again."

"Thanks."

"The damage must be more widespread than what we're seeing if Dr. Avelyn and Penelope are headed here," Jason said.

Creed knew that Dr. Avelyn belonged to a national group of veterinarians that responded after natural disasters. They worked with local authorities to treat injured pets. Penelope Clemence helped reunite displaced dogs with their owners. The woman had made it a mission to rescue abandoned dogs and find homes for them, even working with shelters to raise funds. To her credit, she'd turned almost a dozen facilities across the country into no-kill shelters. Some of Creed's best scent dogs had come by way of Penelope.

Only a few miles after exiting the housing development, and Creed could see it wouldn't be a simple trek. Up ahead, a jumble of debris blocked the road.

"I guess we're taking the long way around."

Twenty-four minutes later, they still hadn't heard back from Maggie. Although one of their texts finally claimed it was delivered. Flashing lights of rescue crews could be seen from half a mile away. Vehicles lined both sides of the highway. Only a couple of units had made it all the way into what used to be the parking lot. A HAZMAT unit in full gear had taken over what used to be a gas station on one side of the street. Eighteen-wheelers were flipped on their sides and upside down vehicles were scattered everywhere. Some of them were crumpled like tin cans.

"Where's the restaurant?" Jason asked just as Creed's phone dinged.

Finally, a text from Maggie:

HANGING IN THERE. HOPING A RESCUE CREW IS ABOUT
TO BUST US OUT OF HERE!

Creed scanned the area. Though the gas station pumps had been destroyed and the vehicles tossed, the cinder block station was still standing. He noticed a sheriff's patrol car and recognized Sheriff Krenshaw. He shifted into PARK, left the engine to idle and the A/C on.

"I'm gonna ask Sheriff Krenshaw. I'll be right back."

He grabbed his K9 CrimeScents cap and pulled it on. It usually gained him entry and allowed him to pass through most barricades. Turned out, he didn't need it. Krenshaw saw him and waved him over.

"Mr. Creed, good to see you, again. We've got quite a mess."

"We heard a restaurant got hit."

"Yup. A bunch of people are trapped in the basement."

"Have the rescue crews reached them yet?"

He shook his head and grimaced. "We're gonna need more than a rescue crew. They've got some earthmoving equipment coming, but I'm afraid that next round of storms will beat them here."

The sky had already started to darken.

"Sir, I have a couple of friends trapped inside."

"No fooling?" His wince was more pronounced this time. "I'm sorry about that. Have you been in contact with them, yet?"

"Finally got a text."

"You might give them a heads up about another round of storms. But Mr. Creed, I wouldn't tell them how bad this looks. Hate to take away a person's hope."

"How bad is it, Sheriff?"

He turned around and pointed to a parking lot littered with debris. At first, Creed couldn't tell that there had ever been a building. Then he saw the concrete foundation and one wall still standing in the rubble. But everyone's main focus was on what had landed on top of where the restaurant used to be—an 18-wheeler, its trailer on its side and split open. And it was right on top of where Maggie and Frankie were.

That wasn't all. The storm had tossed and rolled the huge blue containers that the truck had been hauling. And now Creed could see members of a HAZMAT team inspecting the barrels.

"What's in those?" Creed asked, but the knot forming in his stomach told him he might not want to know.

Krenshaw shrugged. "Don't know yet. Trying to call the company. Driver didn't make it. But I will tell you this, I know for a fact that chemicals are Alabama's second largest export. I'm just hoping none of those containers broke open."

50

Birmingham, Alabama

Willis didn't like the way the radar map kept lighting up. He couldn't believe what he was seeing. Inflamed commas—the signature of a hook echo—seemed to be forming in a blink of an eye. Storm chasers had already called in four different tornadoes on the ground, and that still didn't account for what he was seeing on the radar. Across the border in Mississippi another group of storms were getting organized, lining up and marching east/northeast. He hadn't seen anything like this since 2011.

The tornado that Simon had called in earlier had hit an industrial complex. Photos were coming in of a residential area where homes had been flattened. The same tornado plowed through a gas station and restaurant before lumbering on, skimming the southern edge of the Montgomery. From recent reports the monster was still on the ground, raking across the state.

As violent as that storm appeared, it wasn't the only one. It was a juggling act keeping up. As soon as one warning expired, another supercell would replace it. The news team faced the same challenge. Hundreds of photos, livestream video and damage assessments flooded their social media pages. Reporters were out on the roads and trying to get to some the areas hit. There were fatalities, though in the early hours it was best to wait for the authorities to confirm. It became a challenge to sift through what was real and what were rumors gone wild in the chaos of the moment.

Willis looked up from the monitors, and Paul handed him a new printout.

"They're saying people are trapped underneath that restaurant," Paul told him. He sat down and gestured to the television monitors. One of their anchors was talking about it right now.

Willis glanced up then did a double take.

"Is that a semi trailer?"

"The truck stop across the road got hit, too. I know this place. It's not far off the interstate. My wife and I have eaten there."

Willis shook his head. "Any word from Simon?"

Out of the corner of his eye he saw Paul wince and look away.

"Nothing yet."

"Don't wait too long, Paul. Send someone out to check."

"Roads are blocked. Where do I even send them?"

"The last place that Simon called from. Please, just do it. I don't have a good feeling. This was the kid's first Alabama tornado. We shouldn't have sent him out."

"We didn't send him, Willis. He went out on his own. We only send teams."

Willis turned and stared at the man. Paul was a twenty-year-plus weather veteran, most of those years here at this station.

"We have hundreds of spotters and chasers, Willis. We can't take responsibility for all of them."

Willis stopped himself from reminding Paul that the last he checked, he was still in charge. Instead, he simply said, "Send someone, Paul." Then he swiveled his chair back to the radar screens.

Paul barely left and another one of their interns leaned into the doorway.

"Mr. Dean, you have a call on line one."

"I can't take any calls right now. I don't take calls."

"I know, I'm sorry, sir," the young woman was visibly flustered. "It came in on the news desk. They told me it was really important. They said it was your wife."

"They'll need to take a message."

Why in the world would she call him in the middle of a storm outbreak? He was irritated. Beyond irritated. In all their years together she'd never interrupted. And suddenly, it hit him. She wouldn't dare interrupt unless…

He tapped one of the screens until it brought up his own neighborhood. No, it wasn't close to any of the tornadoes. Though some of the thunderstorms were severe.

He stood and hurried to the door. He couldn't remember the young woman's name. It didn't matter. She was already gone. His eyes darted to the phone on the wall and he saw that line one was still blinking.

"Suck it up, Willis," he told himself and pulled the receiver off.

"Beth? I'm a little busy here," he said.

"Willis, I'm so sorry. I'm so very sorry." Her voice sounded far away, a bit muffled and gargled like she was calling from under water. "I'm trapped."

"Beth, I can hardly hear you."

"I was at Southern Blessings."

"What's that?" He had no idea what she was talking about.

"The restaurant. A tornado hit."

His eyes flashed to the television screen. It was still showing the semi trailer. There was a HAZMAT team.

"We're trapped, Willis. And I'm scared."

51

Southern Blessings

Maggie was desperate to find some relief for Frankie. Ronald's arm had stopped bleeding and Val was keeping watch over him. Gus had joined Max and Loverboy convincing them to try another tactic other than brute-force, which wasn't working. She finally had Hank's attention.

"Is there any way to stop the gas leak?" she wanted to know. She could taste it as much as smell it. At this rate, they would all die from carbon monoxide poisoning before they could be rescued.

"It must be a break in the line," he told her. "The grill in the kitchen is gas."

"What about an emergency shut-off?"

"If the line's broken it won't matter. Our only chance is to break through that door."

She pointed to the maze of pipes that ran in between the ceiling beams.

"Could you check?"

He shot the flashlight up and around following the pipes that were still intact and inspecting the ones that were broken. His bald head shined with sweat. The air was hot and stifling down here. Maggie's T-shirt stuck to her like a second skin, but it didn't matter if she couldn't breathe.

"Here," he said. "This one is gas."

"Are you sure?"

He followed the pipe with his flashlight, stepping over debris and around the two older women. She noticed their feet sloshed through water. How much higher was it?

"Oh dear," one of the women said. "Did the gas line break?"

Hank ignored them and zigzagged all the way to the far corner and over the chest freezer.

"There." He pointed to a lever. "This is the gas shut-off."

"Hold this," he told her and shoved the flashlight at her. "Keep it right there."

He climbed on top of the freezer so he could reach it. He gestured for the flashlight and pointed it directly on the lever, stopping first to read what was written. Then he grabbed it and pulled it down.

"We still need to close off those broken pipes," he told her. There'll be residual gas in the lines."

He hopped off the freezer and took the flashlight back. He started searching the boxes on the shelves and sorting through items left on a workbench. He picked up a couple of things and moved back under the pipe.

"Hold this, again." He handed her the flashlight.

She pointed it up while he stuffed a rag into the pipe. Then he started winding duct tape around and around until she couldn't see the rag. Could it be that simple?

"There's another break over here," he said and waited for her to point the light.

They did this three times. Maggie couldn't tell if it worked. Her nostrils were already filled with the smell. Her chest ached from breathing in the fumes.

"They'll shut it off at the main," the woman said from her place, sitting next to her friend.

Again, Hank ignored her, but Maggie asked, "Is that standard procedure?"

"I believe so, but it depends how bad the tornado was. It may have compromised the main, too."

"Thanks. I'm Maggie, by the way. Are you two doing okay?"

The woman put her arm around her friend whose face looked pale. "We'll be fine. I'm Clara and this is Adele."

Maggie looked to Hank. He was still standing beside her. She had expected he would be anxious to join the men at the door, but he swept the stream of light around their surroundings. It flicked over the hole in the ceiling where the support beam had pulled down a chunk with it. Maggie saw Hank's eyes go wide.

"What is it?" she asked.

He shot the light back and forth as though trying to get his bearings.

"We're directly under the kitchen," he said. "That must be the grill or the dishwasher."

She waited for more of an explanation. She could see him working his jaw as his eyes examined the ceiling.

Finally he said, "I just realized, that's a lot of weight above us."

He skimmed the flashlight everywhere now, shooting it in people's eyes. He was looking for something or someone.

"Rita's not down here," he said with a hint of panic. "I don't see Ann Marie or Sofia either."

Maggie realized that it only now occurred to him to look and see if his co-workers had followed him.

The other waitress, Val overheard. She stayed by Ronald's side, but to Hank she said, "You know Ann Marie is scared to death of going down underground. They probably went back into the restrooms. Isn't that where they always tell us to go?"

Maggie watched the two of them exchange glances. Hank looked up, shooting the ceiling above the freezer with his flashlight beam as if he might be able to see if the women were safe in the space above.

Maggie already felt guilty about Rita. How did she miss seeing the other two women? She couldn't think about it. There was nothing she could do for them now. Hopefully they were safe.

"Any chance there's another flashlight down here?" she asked Hank.

"I have no idea. I'm guessing all this crap is the previous owner's. We never came down here."

"So it'd be okay if I looked around?"

"I'm sure it's fine." He pointed to her cell phone. "Have you been able to send anything? Mine doesn't have a signal, but it's about five years old."

"I received one. Not sure if mine got delivered."

"It's hit or miss." The woman who Maggie had pegged as one of the lovebirds had been tapping since the storm ended. "I was able to get a call through."

"You talked to someone?" Maggie asked.

"Yes. But only briefly before my call got dropped."

"I'll keep trying then. Let me know if either of you hear anything," Hank said and he left for the stairs, taking the brightest light with him.

"I'm Maggie," she told the woman.

For the first time, she looked up from her phone.

In the stark white light Maggie could see laugh lines around her mouth and at the corners of her eyes. She was probably in her late forties, maybe fifty. She was pretty with intense blue eyes and chin-length blond hair.

"I'm Beth," she finally said. Her eyes caught a glimpse of the shoulder holster inside Maggie's unbuttoned shirt. "You a cop?"

Maggie glanced around then bent down and lowered her voice. "FBI. I would appreciate it if you didn't mention it."

"No problem. We all have secrets."

It was a strange thing to say, but Maggie expected the woman might be in shock. After what they'd all been through it was no surprise that emotions would be skidding a bit over the edge by now. She was fighting her own battle with claustrophobia.

"Maybe we can keep each other updated," Maggie told her. "If we get a connection."

"Sure." And the woman went back to her phone.

There was something in her tone that told Maggie she probably wouldn't share. After all, she hadn't mentioned the call before now. Maggie knew how a chaotic situation could press one person to fend for herself, while another would risk his own pain from glass in his shoulder to help another. It wasn't up to her to pass judgment, but she learned quickly the people she could rely on and those she would not.

She went back to the shelves along the back wall. She turned her phone's flashlight on. She needed to conserve her battery. Maybe there was a flashlight on the workbench where Hank had found the duct tape. No such luck. She skimmed the light over the boxes. Some were labeled. Most of them were taped shut. She glanced back at Frankie to see how she was holding up. In the dim light, Maggie could see the pain etched on her face.

She shoved a couple of boxes around. Then in the back, she found one that interested her enough to pull forward. She peeled off the packing tape and shined the light down inside. Maggie pulled out one of the bottles in the case and ran the light over the label: Conecuh Ridge. Clyde Mays Alabama Style Whiskey. 85 proof.

Finally, she found something that might take Frankie's mind off the pain.

52

Creed offered for he and Jason to work a grid with Grace and Scout. The gas station and the restaurant were just off Interstate 65, which meant travelers coming and going. Just like yesterday it was difficult to know if anyone might still be missing and possibly in the rubble.

Sheriff Krenshaw told Creed that all the staff at the gas station was accounted for. Several motorists and truck drivers had already been taken by ambulance to an area hospital. Some were still being cared for at the scene.

"I'm afraid I can't let you do that," Krenshaw told him. "Too dangerous. Lots of spilled fuel. Couple of the 18-wheelers are all busted open."

"How about the restaurant?" Creed asked, wanting to get closer. He wanted to see what was left. "Are you sure everyone made it safely underground?"

"Actually, they already pulled three people from what they think was the restroom."

"Were they able to tell you how many others might be trapped?"

Krenshaw stared at him for a moment, clearly not understanding what Creed had asked. Then he saw the realization sweep across Krenshaw's face. "I'm sorry, son, I should have said three fatalities."

Creed's pulse started racing. He hadn't asked Maggie about Frankie. But she would have told him. Or had she told him, and the text hadn't come through yet?

"Are you able to talk to your friends?" Krenshaw asked.

"Not really. A text message finally came through."

"One of the carriers is bringing in a mobile station." The sheriff craned his neck and looked at the access road. "Should be here soon. Or they might be setting up a bit farther out. Getting some generators trucked in, too."

"Have you guys been in contact with anyone trapped down there?" Creed asked.

"I think they had a couple of 911 calls, but they keep getting dropped before they got much information. Without knowing names, we don't have a number to even try. Family'll be showing up soon. But you know how that works. Sometimes they can be more of a problem than a help. Rumors start flying, and it's hard to sort through."

His eyes kept scanning the roads. Suddenly, he looked back at Creed. "Actually, if you can get through to your friend, you might be able to get us some information. My biggest worry right now is that we won't have time to do a damned thing before those storms get here."

Creed glanced at the western sky. He could see the gray mass approaching, the lightning inside the clouds illuminated the motion and the layers.

"Hey, mister," Krenshaw called to someone behind Creed. "Only first responders are allowed on this side of the line."

Creed turned to see a giant of a man in Ray Ban sunglasses, dark trousers, a white collared shirt soaked with perspiration and the shiniest leather shoes he'd ever seen at a disaster site. Instead of answering Krenshaw, the man lifted the ball cap in his hand and pulled it on, struggling a bit. The cap was too small for his square head. The letters on the navy blue cap surprised Creed. They surprised Krenshaw, too.

"What the hell is FEMA already doing here?"

"This isn't the first storm in the area," the man told him as if that was explanation enough.

Creed thought the guy certainly had the attitude of a federal administrator. But having served in the Marines, Creed would have guessed the guy for ex-military. There was something about his stance. He was taller than Creed, broad chested, square shoulders and square head to match. An ugly scar poked out of his shirt collar adding to Creed's suspicions. He figured he'd leave it for Krenshaw to handle.

"I'll check in with you later, Sheriff," he told him, and Creed headed back to the Jeep.

As he turned away he tapped his cell phone, looking and hoping to see a new message from Maggie. What he did see was three bars. Instead of attempting another text, he hit the call button.

It was ringing on the other end. That was more than he'd gotten earlier. Still, he expected the call to get dropped when someone answered.

"Maggie?"

"Yes, yes! Ryder? I can't believe you got through."

"One of the carriers brought in a mobile unit, so it might be easier until it overloads. How are you doing?"

"Hot," she said and laughed.

It was good to hear her laugh even if he also heard the tension in it.

"Listen, Maggie, is Frankie down there with you."

"Yes."

Relief swept over him. Hannah would have been inconsolable if Frankie had been one of the three bodies they pulled from the debris. But his relief was short lived.

"She's hurt," Maggie said, her voice lower and quieter. "She's hurt bad. One of the support beams came down on her legs. We were able to pull her free."

"Is Frankie conscious?"

"Yes, but she's in a lot of pain, Ryder. How soon do they think they can get the door open for us?"

His eyes trailed back to the mountain of rubble that used to be the restaurant and the 18-wheeler sealing that door she was talking about. Then he looked at the sky, again. It was the middle of the afternoon, and it was getting so dark that headlights on the vehicles traveling the side roads had automatically come on.

How much could he tell her? How much *should* he tell her?

"Ryder?" she asked when he took too long. "It must be bad."

"There's a lot of stuff they have to remove before they can get to the door. How many people are down there with you?"

"Let me think." She started naming them off out loud, "Me, Frankie, Clara and Adele, Ronald, Val, a woman and her son, Beth, Max, Hank, Loverboy and Gus. How many is that?" He heard someone else answer her then she said, "Thirteen. Ronald has a chunk of glass in his shoulder. I think the bleeding's stopped."

"Anyone else hurt?"

"Cuts and scrapes."

"How about you?"

"I'm fine."

She answered too quickly like she was trying to convince herself as much as convince him.

"Listen Ryder, there's a gas leak. I think we turned off the valve down here, but someone mentioned the crews might be able to turn it off at the main."

"I'll check that out."

"And water's coming in."

"How high is it?"

"Not high. Almost to my ankle. Do you have any idea how long it'll take to get us out? Give it to me straight. I'm a big girl." Before he could answer, she added, "A big girl with claustrophobia."

Creed remembered too well what it felt like to be buried underground.

He'd gotten caught in a mudslide once. It didn't take much to conjure up that feeling of panic. Just the thought of layers of dirt on top of him could still break him out in a sweat. Someone with claustrophobia didn't need to imagine an 18-wheeler capsized on top of them, threatening not only a possible exit, but adding to the risk of caving in.

"They're bringing in some equipment to help move off the debris. But Maggie, more storms are coming, so they may need to back off for a short time." Even as he told her this, he watched some of the first responders waving at each other. They were loading up their equipment.

"How severe?"

"I don't know."

"Another tornado?"

He could hear the edge of panic in her voice.

"I haven't heard the forecast. I'm headed back to the Jeep. Jason will know."

"Ryder, I don't think we can take another hit. All the kitchen's equipment—the grill, dishwasher, walk-in refrigerator—Hank says it's all right above us."

He winced at the thought, and in his mind he added that burst open trailer and those blue barrels.

53

Frankie already felt better. So much better. At least her pain was easing. She slumped against the cool concrete wall and tried to take advantage of the short reprieve.

Maggie had found frost-burned packages of meat in the old chest freezer. The white butcher paper was stamped with the year 2013. She came back with an armful of various sizes. She'd distributed packages to the others, but said she'd saved the best cuts for Frankie.

"Rib-eye for this leg," she told Frankie as she carefully laid the wonderfully cold package on her burning leg. "And a sirloin for this leg."

But the best gift was the bottle of whiskey.

At first, she'd rolled her eyes at Maggie. But then she noticed the change on Maggie's face when she read her phone.

"What's wrong?" Frankie had asked.

"It might be a while. Ryder says the crews need to leave. More storms are coming."

"And they can't rescue us in the rain?"

When Maggie didn't answer, Frankie knew. She held out her hand for the bottle of whiskey.

That was four gulps ago. Maybe five.

She was no longer feeling the searing pain. Just a nice, warm buzz.

Maggie had found an old three-legged stool and sat beside her. Despite the cool concrete against Frankie's back, she was still drenched in sweat. Her legs were splayed out in front of her with packages of frozen meat taking away the rest of her pain.

"So you and Ryder," Frankie said, all inhibitions scattered in the dark. They were trying to conserve cell phone batteries. "Are you and Ryder, you know, doing it?"

She couldn't see Maggie's face. Only her profile, but Frankie laughed. Harder than she'd laughed in a long time. Hard enough to get the others to look up from their cell phones.

Before Maggie could answer, Frankie added, "Oh my God, I swear I can *hear* you blush."

"It's not exactly like that."

"But you have?"

"I think you've had too much medicine."

"I've always thought he was absolutely yummy," Frankie confessed. "You know Hannah had to tell him to stop bringing women to his apartment over the kennel. Her boys started seeing them leave in the early morning and they were asking questions."

"Are you saying he's a womanizer?"

"No, no. I'm saying he's a hot commodity." She swung her hand to pat Maggie's shoulder. "Surely, you've noticed—oh my God, I just called you Shirley." She giggled. And snorted. She hadn't giggled since she was a little girl. Yep, she was a little bit drunk.

"Let me rephrase that," Frankie said, trying to focus. The whiskey was really making her head spin. "Certainly, you've noticed the way women look at him when he walks into a room. And you know what the best thing is about that? He doesn't even notice the way women look at him. Usually he has a dog along, and he seems to think they're all looking at the dog."

She got quiet. Then serious. She hadn't let herself think about Gordon and his infidelity. Or Tyler. Oh my God, Tyler! How could he be dead? She shook her head.

"What is it?" Maggie asked.

"I've been running since yesterday morning. Literally, running for my life. I'm gonna be really pissed off if I die in a stupid tornado."

"You're not going to die. Not if I can help it," Maggie told her without looking over at her.

Frankie felt her eyes tearing up. She didn't want to cry, but that was one of the nicest things anyone had said to her in a long time. But then, Maggie had to go and ruin it when she added, "Hannah would kill me if I let you die."

It made Frankie laugh. She took another gulp. A small one. She didn't want the buzz to go away.

"Hannah does have that effect on people. How long have you known them?"

"A couple of years. I met Ryder and Grace at a crime scene. We needed them to help us find dead bodies. A serial killer turned an abandoned farm into his graveyard."

"Well, that is their specialty. So was it love at first sight?" Frankie giggled again, and this time Maggie took the bottle away from her.

"It wasn't anything like that. We've worked on three different cases since then, but that's the only time we see each other. I'm in Virginia. He's in Florida." Frankie saw her give a little shrug. "What are you gonna do? It is what it is."

"But you like each other. Really, really like each other, right? And you've done it?"

Maggie groaned. "Once. Only once." She confessed then wiped the mouth of the bottle and took a swig.

"What's the problem?" Frankie asked.

"For one thing, I just found out he sleeps with a lot of women, so our night together probably didn't mean as much as I thought it did."

Despite her pleasant buzz, Frankie could hear the disappointment.

"I doubt that's true. I know for a fact that he doesn't sleep with women he works with. Have you ever met their veterinarian? I asked Hannah if anything was going on between her and Ryder, and Hannah was practically indignant about it. Said he has a strict rule about that. I think the simple fact that he broke it for you means a lot."

They were quiet for a while and Frankie realized that the constant banging sound was coming from a group of men taking turns ramming the door at the top of the stairs. Everyone else seemed to keep their distance from Frankie and Maggie. They stole glances at Frankie, and she wondered if they didn't want to be reminded of how badly she was injured.

"I stink at relationships," Maggie said, her voice low and almost a whisper as if she really was making a confession. But Frankie figured it was probably the whiskey. "My dad was a firefighter. He died in a fire when I was twelve. And my mom…let's just say she wasn't a great role model in the male companionship choices she made after that. She's still fundamentally a suicidal alcoholic."

Maggie got quiet, and Frankie waited but realized that was it. Something told her it wasn't easy for this woman to share, and that was her limit.

"I guess we have something in common," Frankie told her. "My mom was suicidal, too. Third time seemed to be a charm."

"Wow, Frankie, I'm sorry. I had no idea."

"You mean it wasn't in my FBI file?" she joked. "It's okay. It happened a long time ago. I was nine. I didn't even see it. My father found her early in the morning. She slit her wrists in the bathtub. The ambulance took her away."

"My mom didn't start hurting herself until I was a teenager. I can't imagine dealing with that at nine."

"Actually, you know what the hardest part was? My dad made me go to school that day. There wasn't anyone to watch me, and he needed to meet the ambulance at the hospital. I thought mom just hurt herself again. I was too little the first time to remember. The second time she just took a bunch of pills. I thought she was sleeping."

It had been a long time since Frankie had talked about this.

"Hannah and I were best friends. She could tell something was wrong right away. Even back then she could sense things about people. She asked her grandparents if I could go home with her after school. My dad was so relieved when they called and asked him. You know, he didn't even tell me until the next day that she didn't make it. And then, I didn't find out until I was in college that she died in the ambulance. I spent years being angry with him because he hadn't let me go to the hospital to see her. To tell her goodbye. Why didn't he just tell me she was already gone?"

She could see Maggie watching her.

"I remember asking him why, and you know what he said?"

Maggie stayed quiet, listening.

"He said he didn't want me to see her like that. To remember her that way. He didn't let me go to the funeral either. For the same reason, I suppose. I mean, how bad could it be? She was my mom. I would have liked to have said goodbye."

Maggie's cell phone started dinging and both of them jumped at the sound.

54

Creed finished updating Krenshaw about his conversation with Maggie. Just as he got to the Jeep, a sheriff's deputy stopped him.

"We're moving out," the deputy said, pointing to the wall of black moving in. "Word is this storm's already produced two tornadoes. We'll come back as soon as it moves through."

"Where should we go?" Jason asked the deputy over the roof of the Jeep. He had the tailgate open and was digging through their supplies.

"Head south. That's what I've been told. This storm's tracking to the northeast. But there's a whole line popping up. Do you all have someplace safe to go? Family in the area?"

"Our hotel's about ten miles south of here."

The deputy glanced at his watch. "That might be the best place. I'd invite you to come with us, but it's not going to be any closer or safer than your hotel. I'd get moving right now. Good luck." He tapped his knuckles on the roof of the Jeep and headed to the next crew to warn them.

Utility and fire and rescue trucks were in line, maneuvering through the crowded street leaving the perimeter. Even the HAZMAT team was packed up.

"I don't like the idea of leaving Maggie," Creed told Jason.

"Yeah, I know. But we can't help her at all if we get hit."

When Creed still didn't put the Jeep in gear, Jason continued, "It wouldn't hurt for us to go back to the hotel. We can refuel. Feed the dogs. Check them over. I pulled some glass from Grace's paws."

This got Creed's attention. "Is she okay?" Why hadn't he checked her himself? What was wrong with him?

"She'll be okay. I cleaned it, field-dressed it, but I think she's done for the day."

More and more vehicles were leaving. There was a trail of taillights and another of headlights. And the sky was increasingly getting darker.

Creed shifted into gear. The truck that had been parked in front of them had already left. He made a tight U-turn and headed south. Once they were away from the jumble of rescue vehicles and equipment, he glanced in the rearview mirror. Grace's head was down, but her ears pitched forward and her eyes stayed wide open.

Creed felt an overwhelming sense of helplessness. He couldn't save Maggie and Frankie, and he had neglected Grace.

"You okay, Grace?"

Her eyes moved up to meet his in the mirror. Her ears relaxed but her head stayed down. He felt like he'd been punched in the gut. She wasn't feeling good. He was in such a hurry, he didn't notice earlier. He should never have put her in the carrier without checking her paws.

"Did you start her on antibiotics?"

"I was about to, but I figured she needed to take it with food. Right when you got back I was getting ready to pull the packs out."

They used a dehydrated mix that just needed water added. He contemplated pulling over and taking care of her, but the clouds rolling in swirled above. Behind them he could see lightning fork all the way to the ground. The rumble of thunder grew louder.

"You okay?" Jason asked keeping his voice calm, and Creed realized it was more for the benefit of the dogs than it was for Creed. He appreciated the kid's steady composure. It still surprised him how much Jason had matured in two short years.

"We get the dogs safe and taken care of, and I'll be okay."

Jason sat forward watching the sky.

"Thanks for taking care of Grace," Creed told him. "I should have checked her before we left the last site."

"No problem."

Creed took a side road that looped around the damaged area. Jason pointed out a spot they could get back on the interstate just to the south of where they'd almost gotten sucked up into the earlier storm.

It took hardly any time to get to the hotel. Every vehicle had headlights on and all the buildings around the exit were lit up as if it were evening. Trees blocked the western sky, again. It started raining hard just as Creed pulled into the parking lot. He took note that there wasn't much wind. But a quick glance up and he saw the dark layers churning.

"Let's take our gear in," Creed said. "Take Scout." He turned and reached in to scratch Grace under the chin. She was up and ready to go. "You wait here, girl. I'll come back and get you. I want to carry you in."

He left the Jeep and A/C running while they pulled their duffle bags and daypacks out. Anything attached to the bags, came out, too. Lightning spiked behind them and a boom of thunder blasted overhead. Both too close for comfort. But the rain was letting up.

Jason helped Scout down and attached his leash. The parking lot was mostly empty. The rain stopped and Creed noticed a sudden stillness. About halfway to the hotel's front door, Jason pointed to the treetops on the other side of the interstate.

"I guess those birds wouldn't be flying if the storm was close."

Creed looked over his shoulder. Then he stopped and turned to get a better look. His stomach fell.

"Those aren't birds."

"What are you talking about?"

"It's debris."

55

"I've got to get Grace!" Creed untangled straps from around his neck and threw down bags, tossing them to the pavement. "Take Scout and go. Get inside. Take everyone as far inside as you can get."

"I know the drill." Jason was picking up Creed's packs and stringing them over his shoulders.

"Leave it! Just go."

The wind was already picking up. Trees swayed. He could hear a low rumble growing on the other side of the tree line. He could feel the vibration under his feet. A dark shadow started emerging, slinking into view.

"Go, Jason. Now!"

He started running for the Jeep.

"Creed!"

He stopped and turned.

"Take this."

Jason threw a helmet at him. Creed pulled it on and snapped the chinstrap just as a gust tried to rip it off his head. He had to lean forward against the wind to run across the parking lot. Now, he could hear the roar as pieces of debris filled the air. He had to use all his weight to open the Jeep's tailgate. He dived inside then twisted around and grabbed with both hands slamming it shut behind him. He double-checked that it was tight because the storm still sounded too loud inside the vehicle.

Grace's ears were slicked back, and despite the noise he could hear her low whine.

"It's okay, girl. I'm here. You're okay. We're gonna be okay."

He laced his fingers between the back grate, and she immediately licked them.

A quick glance over his shoulder and he knew he was lying to her.

Power lines danced. Branches cracked and snapped. The sky had darkened even more. It was difficult to see inside the vehicle. The air was filled with bits of debris and dirt. There was no way he was going to make it across the parking lot and inside the hotel.

He grabbed a blanket, opened Grace's crate from the rear. For a brief second he questioned the wisdom of a crate that opened at both ends. Convenience had been a selling point. Now all he could think about was two doors that could pop open, and his jaw clamped tight. He bundled her in it, even though it could make it too warm inside. She wanted to come out and he gently held her back.

"Stay here, girl."

He stuffed a towel inside, too, cushioning her until she was snug and tight. Then he closed the crate's door, making sure it was secure despite her whimpers.

Curtains of rain poured down. Wind gust shook the Jeep. Debris pecked at the windshield. Metal pinged as hail started falling. At first just a few stones, then it sounded like golf balls assaulting the roof and hood.

"It's okay," he kept repeating to Grace, trying to keep his voice calm.

He threw a blanket over the crate then he crawled up, inserting his body between Grace's shelter and the ceiling of the Jeep. He draped his torso over the hard shell, hoping to shield and secure it and Grace. His head faced the windshield and he kept it down while his legs dangled toward the tailgate.

By now, the storm sounded like an angry beast. Creed's ears popped. He couldn't see Grace inside the crate underneath him, but he kept talking to her, hoping she was focusing on his voice and not the earsplitting noise roaring over them.

The Jeep started to rock violently. He felt like he was riding a bucking bull. Riding the wrong way.

Even with his head down he could see shadows flying by. Objects hit the windows. The Jeep was being pummeled. Branches continued to crash and snap, so constant now, it sounded like fireworks.

Something ripped above him. A loud crash and a whoosh. Suddenly, he felt the rain and the wind inside the vehicle. The sunroof had blown out. Another crash and he ducked his head as glass shattered against his helmet.

He squeezed his eyes shut and kept his head down. But the force had changed. The wind inside the Jeep tried to peel him away. He could feel the storm sucking at him, threatening to dislodge him.

Creed held on tighter. He gripped the front seat then his fingers searched for the shoulder belt. Awkwardly he wrapped it around his wrist. His mind flashed to the passenger in Baby Garner's car. He had no idea if staying with the vehicle protected or doomed him, but he new one thing for certain. He was not leaving Grace. This monster would not separate them.

The whistling rush of wind surrounded them now. The pressure was so intense Creed was sure his helmet wouldn't matter because his head was going to explode. He held on as the creature's hot breath sucked at him. It peeled his shirt off his back. Then it tried to do the same with his skin. It tugged and punched at him. His bare back felt sandblasted, poked and stung by a thousand bees.

He gritted his teeth and continued to hold on.

Grace's crate shifted. Now it pressed against his ribcage, digging in and threatening to cut off his breath.

He opened his eyes and tried to look down at it. In the darkness, lightening flashed like strobe lights, making everything look like it was moving in slow motion. Pieces of debris flew in the air. Some of it hit him now that the windshield no longer was there. The rumble was so intense he could feel the vibration all through his body. Curtains of rain started filling the inside of the Jeep.

He wanted to see in the crate beneath him. The blanket still covered it. Were the steel-grated doors still latched or had the force sucked them open? Was Grace still with him? She had to be. Would he know if she had been sucked out from under him?

His left hand was tied to the shoulder belt. He pushed his feet against the metal frame of the Jeep to better secure himself. Then, he released his right hand. He had to be sure she was okay.

As the winds pulled at him, he twisted his arm enough to allow his hand to weave under the blanket. His fingers felt the metal grate. He poked a finger in between and almost immediately was rewarded by Grace's soft tongue.

A flood of relief washed over him.

She was there! She was able to respond.

"Hold on, girl," he yelled, but he could hardly hear himself. It had to be almost over. "Just a few more minutes. Hang on, Grace!"

The storm was on top of them, snarling and clawing, poking and stabbing at his back.

It couldn't last forever. He couldn't hold on for much longer.

Just then, the vehicle jolted like hitting a speed bump at sixty-miles-per-hour. It slung Creed up against the remaining roof then dropped him hard, slamming the breath right out of him. He gasped for air, his mouth sucking in dirt and choking him more than helping.

The Jeep bounced. It skidded. Forward, backward, sideways.

Then suddenly, they were flying.

56

Southern Blessings

Maggie tried to scroll through the text messages and missed calls that were coming through now, a string of pings at a time. It should have been a relief to be connected again, but each one only made her feel more helpless.

"The mobile cell tower must be close by," she told Frankie. "I'm getting a whole bunch of messages I missed."

Frankie was feeling no pain, but she should have monitored her better. The woman was clearly drunk. Which presented a new problem. Maggie realized the alcohol could cause dehydration. Earlier she had found a case of bottled water. The expiration date was two years ago, but everyone was parched from the stifling heat. She'd handed out bottles to the others when she distributed the packages of frozen meat. She plied Frankie with water trying to compensate for her mistake.

"I really am better with dead people," Maggie said out loud before she could stop herself. She'd had two sips of the whiskey hoping it would relax her and keep her from thinking how damn hot it was. Hoping it would stop her from noticing how the ceiling and walls were closing in on her.

"I can't drink anymore water," Frankie complained. "I'll need to pee."

"And that would be a good thing. It'd mean you're hydrated."

There was movement in the dark. The woman who had been sitting with the teenaged boy was wandering over to them. She left the boy back in the dark while she weaved her way around the toppled support beam and the pile of debris that separated Maggie and Frankie from the others. She used her cell phone's flashlight and stepped carefully.

Maggie had guessed that she was maybe forty. Her shoulder long, dark hair stuck to the sides of her head. She was sweating profusely. It could have been the unflattering light, but Maggie thought the woman's eyes looked glassy and her skin pasty.

The woman waited until she was a foot away before she greeted them, and then it was only a head nod.

"I understand you're an FBI agent?"

Maggie bit back a grimace. Good 'ole Beth—"we all have secrets, Beth"—sure didn't keep that secret for long.

"My name's Maggie," she said instead of confirming or denying. "This is Frankie. What's your name?"

The woman looked thrown off by the question. "It's Stephanie. Listen, I'm not from here," she talked fast like she didn't have much time to say what she wanted. She brushed at the damp strands of hair on her forehead. "We were driving down from New York. We've been on the road for two days. We just stopped for lunch."

She glanced back at her son. He was on his own cell phone. Maggie suspected he was fourteen or fifteen. Now that they had mobile service, he looked content. From what Maggie remembered of the pair, the son had been the one leading her to safety while Stephanie had been paralyzed by her fear.

"We can't be here," the woman said, addressing Maggie as though she were a retail clerk at a return counter. "We're supposed to be in Gulf Shores, Alabama. We should have been there by now."

Maggie didn't respond. It was possible the woman was in shock and didn't realize what she was saying. Maggie waited. She wasn't sure what Stephanie from New York was expecting her to do. She heard Frankie snort an exasperated laugh. The woman noticed.

"Can't you do something?" she finally asked Maggie, still using that impatient tone. "I don't think these men know what they're doing. Is there anyone even trying to get us out of here? I don't know who to text or call. But *you* must?"

"Stephanie, there are rescue crews."

"Oh, thank God! I thought so!"

"But they've had to pull back."

"What? No!"

"Just until these next storms go through the area. It's too dangerous for them to be out in the open."

"More storms?" She shook her head like she couldn't believe it. "This is the most godforsaken part of the country I've ever been to. I can't believe this. Who lives like this? I swear I'm never coming here again."

"I tell you what, Stephanie, I'll let you know when I know more," Maggie told the woman, reminding herself that she really was better at crime scenes. The dead were never this demanding.

Instead of watching Stephanie shuffle her way back, Maggie returned to her messages.

"Did you notice she didn't once ask if I was okay?" Frankie said, her tone unusually sober.

"Yes. And I also noticed you didn't offer her any of your whiskey."

"Don't need to. She's already tripping on something. I've seen her popping pills a couple of times."

Maggie glanced at the woman, again. That could explain the glassy eyes and the unrealistic perception of her surroundings. She couldn't worry about it right now. She scrolled to the first text message from Agent Alonzo. She wanted to read his in the order he sent them.

HE'S DEFINITELY THERE.

The second one read:

STILL HASN'T LEFT.

The third:

I'M EMAILING WHAT I'VE FOUND ON CARSON FOODS. LOTS
OF GOVERNMENT SUPPORT.

And a fourth:

2 OUT OF 4 SEPARATE LAWSUIT LITIGANTS HAVE DIED
FROM "UNFORTUNATE ACCIDENTS." I'M DIGGING DEEPER.

The fifth one read:

MAGGIE, YOU OK? I JUST SAW THE DAMAGE.

And the last:

LET ME KNOW YOU'RE OK.

She tapped out a message telling him she was fine, but they were trapped underneath the restaurant.

His response was immediate:

DAMN! ANYTHING I CAN DO?

Before she could type another message she stopped. She smelled something. More gas fumes? No. It was something else. Sulfur? Smoke?

"What is it?" Frankie asked, alarmed by Maggie's expression.

"I think something might be on fire."

57

Maggie left Frankie so she could investigate. The water was getting higher. She still couldn't figure out where it was coming in. Halfway to the stairs she practically ran into Hank. In the halo of the flashlight's beam the man's eyes were bulging, even more pronounced by the sunken, dark circles under them.

"Something's on fire up above," he told her.

He said it so loud she could hear gasps around her coming from the dark.

"Fire! What are you talking about?" Stephanie was on her feet.

"And there's a tornado on the ground just ten miles south of us," Beth said without looking up at them, her head bent over her phone.

Gus came down the steps. Max was close behind him. It occurred to Maggie that she hadn't seen the man she had nicknamed Loverboy. She heard him at the top of the stairs, still pounding. She remembered now how the stairwell wasn't a straight-shot down. It was an L with a landing in between two sets of stairs.

"What were you guys doing to the door?" Maggie asked. "Did you accidently create some sparks? Remember you said there could be gas in the broken lines." That's exactly what Hank had told her earlier. "Which could mean there's gas leaks up above, too."

She tried to study Gus' face, thinking at this point Hank was too upset to read. She expected Gus to be the exact opposite. The man had been calm and composed and totally unreadable since the storm hit. But now, she could see his jaw was clenched, his hands balled up into fists.

Max was a little easier to read. The expression on his face told her he was pissed and ready to get the hell out of here. He tapped on his phone even as Maggie waited for a response.

It was Hank who answered while one side of his mouth twitched. "I told them to be careful. They could have ignited something."

"We didn't ignite anything," Max said without looking up from his phone.

"They've only made such a small hole," Hank continued. "I don't see how it could have sparked anything."

She glanced back at Gus and caught him checking his watch. Only then did she realize it was a smartwatch like Frankie wore. But he wasn't checking the time. She could glimpse a message across the square face, a miniature screen. He was receiving messages without having to use his phone. Convenience or did it allow him a level of secrecy?

It didn't matter, because now he was clearly rattled. He ripped a cell phone from his back pocket, started punching in a message. When he noticed Maggie watching, he turned his back to her and walked off into a dark corner.

Maggie pulled out her own phone and called Ryder. If the rescuers had to back off because of the approaching storm, he might still know what's going on. It rang for a long time then went to voice messaging. She asked him to call her as soon as possible.

She tucked the phone into her back pocket, no longer caring who saw the shoulder harness and gun tucked under her arm. She had tried to be discrete letting the lightweight shirttails cover it. But the shirt was drenched in sweat now, as was her T-shirt.

She hated feeling so completely helpless. As long as she took control and guided the others she could keep the claustrophobia at bay. The dim light and the dark corners only made it worse. And then for the first time she noticed something else. Her breathing was a bit labored. The air was getting thinner.

Maggie whipped her phone back out. She tapped out a message to Ryder. She sent one to Jason, too.

Then she waited.

58

Creed didn't remember blacking out. He woke with a jerk. Cold water lapped against him. His eyes blinked. The lids scraped like sandpaper. It hurt to breathe.

He tried to keep his eyes open. The world looked upside down.

He remembered Grace's crate underneath him, pressing against his ribs. Now, it was up on top of him. The floor of the Jeep had replaced the roof. It was dented in, trapping him. He couldn't move.

"Grace!" The one word took his breath away.

He tried to lift his head then dropped it back. It was too heavy to hold up. He still had his helmet on. He lifted his head a second time. He needed to see inside the crate.

His wrist was caught in the seatbelt strap and he remembered wrapping it to secure himself. Now, it handcuffed him to the frame of the vehicle restraining his movement. His other hand was free, and he twisted his arm so his fingers could feel the metal grate, the door to Grace's crate. It was still intact. He couldn't reach the other side to see if the rear grate was in place.

The water was getting higher around his neck, gurgling close to his ears. From what he could tell it was starting to fill the inside of the vehicle, seeping in through the blasted out windows.

Creed tried to move his body out from under the hard-shell enclosure. Pain stopped him. He was pinned in.

The water was cold against his skin. But it actually felt good, soothing his raw back. Was that really possible or was it simply shock?

"Grace?" His voice sounded like a croak. The emotion he heard surprised him.

If she was gone, he'd never forgive himself. She trusted him. She depended on him to keep her safe, and he let her down.

He laid his head back. It was too difficult to keep holding it up. The water climbed up towards his ears. His chest ached. He heard his own rasps. He was breathing through his mouth, and it was still difficult to get enough air.

He closed his eyes. Maybe it was too difficult to care. If he'd lost Grace...

There was motion outside of the vehicle. Boots crunched glass and sloshed through water.

"Over here," he heard someone yell.

He opened his mouth to call out only to have water trickle down his throat. He choked and spit. He arched his back and tried to shove the weight off his chest.

Nothing moved.

And this time pain exploded inside his chest. He craned his neck, keeping his face out of the water. It hurt too much. He dropped his head back down, splashing water over his face, sucking in another mouthful. He jerked up, choking and spitting.

The water had seeped all around his body. He no longer could hear what was happening outside. He closed his eyes and held his breath as his head fell back. Water lapped entirely over his face now. He was a good swimmer but he couldn't do this. Not with the weight of the vehicle crushing down on top of him. He wasn't strong enough. He couldn't breathe without panic.

His fingers still gripped the metal grate. And just then, he felt Grace's soft tongue on his fingertips.

He jerked his head back up, sputtering and choking.

"Grace!"

It took all his strength to twist and turn, but he still couldn't see her.

He was gulping for air when a shadow came over him. Someone was lifting the crate. From behind him he felt strong hands grabbing his shoulders and starting to pull him free.

"Grace," he spat out the word along with a mouthful of water. "She's inside."

"We've got her," someone told him.

A woman's voice. Familiar.

But he couldn't see anyone. Free of the confines of the demolished Jeep, the brightness hurt.

He blinked. Finally, he could see the sky, and he could feel grass against his searing back. It was like lying on a bed of needles. No more cold water to soothe the raw pain.

Out of the corner of his eye he got a glimpse of the black metal hand still holding onto his shoulder. He tilted his head back, and he could see Jason. There were two other men, but he didn't recognize them.

"Hey," he croaked.

"Hey, yourself," Jason told him, and in those two words Creed could hear the mixture of fear and relief.

"Here she is," the woman said.

Creed looked around just in time to see Dr. Avelyn deposit Grace at his side. Penelope Clemence was standing behind her. He gently pulled Grace to him. She was wet and shaking, but wagging.

"You're a sight for sore eyes," he told the veterinarian.

"I'm never sure what that means," Dr. Avelyn said. She squatted down next to him.

"It means I'm glad to see you. You too, Penelope."

"Well then, right back at you," Dr. Avelyn told him. "Truthfully Ryder, you look like hell."

He laughed, but pain stopped him cold.

Her fingers unsnapped the chinstrap, and she removed his helmet. A wave of fresh air swirled around him.

He groaned and rolled onto his side.

He was still trying to catch his breath when Jason said, "I don't think we'll be able to keep this one a secret from Hannah."

59

Birmingham, Alabama

Willis asked Mia to stay on the air while he juggled all the information coming in at a rapid-fire pace. Everyone including anchors, producers and staff was helping, taking phone calls, downloading livestream video and recording damage reports while Willis tried to map out tornadoes on the ground. At last count there were five. Paul would barely hand Mia a new set of warnings and Willis would give him more.

And in the middle of this, Beth kept calling and texting him.

Willis had asked Paul to leave one of the monitors on the live video feed the station had set up at the scene, showing the damaged restaurant. His eyes skimmed over it every time he looked from the radar screens to the other monitors sending views from their other city cams. Some of those had already been knocked out by the previous storms, but a couple of them still showed black, churning clouds filling the viewfinders.

"We have a report of a hotel being hit," Paul said as he came in the door to the weather desk. For the last half hour Paul's voice had taken on a high pitch, the sudden inflection of urgency a bit nerve-racking to Willis.

"Which tornado?"

"It's making its way up I-65. Just south of where the one hit earlier."

Willis twisted around to a radar screen and pulled up the area.

"It looks like it's following the same path," Willis said and he could feel the acid in his stomach from too much coffee.

His eyes flicked to the video feed watching over the restaurant debris. He almost missed the curl of smoke then he saw the flames.

"What's going on there?" He pointed.

"Oh yeah, the news desk had a report of arson."

"Arson?"

"Suspicious activity. There was a HAZMAT team before the storms made them leave the area. All those blue barrels."

Willis stood. The monitor was one in a row, up above and bracketed to the wall. He came in close, his head tilted up. Dozens of barrels were scattered around the site. They must have fallen out of the trailer.

"Oh my God," he whispered.

If the contents were flammable the whole place could go up in flames any second. Suddenly, he knew why Beth was texting and calling. She and the others must already smell the smoke.

He started to search for his cell phone when his eyes caught something else on the monitor. In the sky above the battered restaurant he could see a shadow slinking into view. A dark column was already emerging out of the gray mass.

60

"You might have a concussion," Dr. Avelyn was telling Creed.

"I was wearing my helmet," he countered.

It was a weak defense, especially since he knew he had blacked out for part of the journey the tornado had sent him on. He had won the battle over whether or not he should be taken to a hospital. Creed argued that the ER would be filled with storm victims needing a doctor, and he had his own personal doctor with him.

Dr. Avelyn had rolled her eyes at him. "Someday you're going to need an MD, Ryder."

But in the end, she agreed with him that an ER wait could be a long one.

Right now, he looked up from the bed. Grace was fast asleep in the pillows. He'd made sure Dr. Avelyn checked her before she started on him. Creed was lying on his stomach, and it hurt just to turn his neck. He didn't dare admit that it hurt, nor did he admit he wasn't quite certain where they were.

He knew their hotel had been damaged. Dr. Avelyn and Penelope Clemence had barely checked in before the storm hit. He vaguely remembered Jason packing up all their gear into Jason's Jeep. Creed's was obviously totaled. At some point, they had caravanned to another hotel up the road. Now, from his limited view—mostly of the rug and bed linens—he noted they'd upgraded. This was a much a nicer room.

He jerked and winced at the pain.

"Sorry," Dr. Avelyn said from above him.

She had pulled the desk chair to the edge of the bed. When that didn't work, she crawled onto the bed with him and went to work on his back. Creed had insisted they take a photo and show him. He hardly recognized it as his own. Never mind the cuts and bruises. The middle of his back was riddled with pine needles. It reminded him of a porcupine. Dozens of them were driven into his skin, all in the area where his back had been exposed after the sunroof got sucked out. Dr. Avelyn was removing them, one by one, dabbing each puncture with rubbing alcohol. He wasn't sure which hurt more—the stab of the needle or the sting of alcohol.

"How many?" he asked every once in a while to gauge her progress.

"Twenty-seven. You sure you don't want something for the pain?"

"I'm good.

"You'll need an antibiotic."

"Okay. What about Grace?" he asked.

"Already took care of her."

It wasn't the first time the veterinarian had tended to his wounds or stitched him up. He trusted her with his dogs. Why wouldn't he trust her with himself?

"She's doing really well by the way," Dr. Avelyn said. "Wrapping her up like you did cushioned her. It probably saved her life."

"What about her paws?

"Actually, they don't look bad. Jason did a good job taking out all the glass. She didn't blow any pads. But I do think she's finished for this site. She'll need to rest for a week. I'd suggest two weeks, but I know Grace."

Creed felt his muscles tense.

"Sorry. I'm digging out some glass. You want to take a break?"

"No, keep going."

"You know, I think Brodie could be on to something," she told him as she worked. And now he knew she was trying to get his mind off the pain. "She watched me chipping dogs last week. We put one in Kitten. But she wanted to know if it would work in people. I'm thinking we might need to chip you with a tracking device, so we can find you when you get buried or fly off."

"Very funny." He thought about Brodie's curiosity. "Do you know if she was thinking about herself or me?"

"I'm not sure. I explained to her that it only identifies a dog and tells us how to contact the owner. I can't remember exactly what she said, but clearly she was wondering about the tracking capabilities." She paused for a moment then asked, "Do you think she worries about being taken, again?"

"I hope not. It's interesting that she asked about it. When we found her she had a tracking device strapped and locked around her ankle. Iris Malone put it on her after Brodie tried to escape too many times."

"Wow! I didn't know that. When we talked about it she didn't seem traumatized by the thought. She was genuinely curious like she could see the benefits."

"Did you see her yesterday or today? Hannah said her nightmares are back. I can't help but wonder if it's because I'm gone."

"No, I didn't. But she needs to know that she can survive without you."

"Yeah, but my mom's visiting this weekend."

"Ah! You sure that's not why you bailed? Although, I can't imagine you choosing this over spending time with your mother."

"Have you met my mom?"

A soft tap-tap at the door interrupted them.

"Come on in," Dr. Avelyn said.

"Still not finished?" Jason asked.

Creed could see he was carrying a tray. Before he put it down Creed could smell something wonderful. Leave it to Jason to find food.

"Anything about Maggie and Frankie?" Creed asked. He shoved

himself up on his elbows so he could look at Jason better.

"Why don't we wait until Doc is finished. I brought you both something to eat. Three women in a silver SUV pulled into the hotel parking lot with all these sandwiches and stuff for all the first responders and storm victims."

"Thanks, but just tell me what you know."

Dr. Avelyn tapped him on the shoulder and gestured for Creed to lie back down.

"Okay, first of all, Maggie says they're okay," Jason said.

"But?"

"There's a fire on top of them."

"What?" This time Creed rolled over to look at Jason. Even Grace lifted her head. "Those barrels. The HAZMAT team thought they were flammable."

He was up on his feet and putting on his boots before Dr. Avelyn could stop him.

61

Southern Blessings

Maggie retreated to the other side. She needed to stay with Frankie though her instinct urged her to keep as close to the door as possible. It didn't matter. The air was getting thinner no matter what side of the room. It wasn't her imagination. She noticed Frankie struggling to breathe. There were coughs and choking from the others. Whatever slivers and gaps there had been were now being clogged.

She checked her phone. NO SERVICE AVAILABLE.

"Is anyone else getting texts or calls to go through?" she called out.

"I was," Beth answered. "My last call got dropped."

"My battery died! This is crazy. We need to get out of here." Maggie recognized Stephanie's voice.

She heard thumping and banging. The men were still trying to ram the door. A crash and boom made both her and Frankie jump.

"Thunder." The rumble vibrated the walls. "Ryder said there were more storms."

"Oh no," someone moaned, realizing the same.

Another crack of thunder. Then came a whoosh followed by a barrage of drumming.

Rain.

Maggie cocked her head, listening. It had to be rain. That was a good thing. Maybe it would put out the fire.

That's when she felt the water rushing against her legs. What had been a trickle before was now a stream. She pointed her cell phone's flashlight and followed the flow. Clara and Adele saw it before Maggie. They hurried toward her, away from their bench. The water was coming down the wall right behind them.

"Move to the other side," Maggie told them. "Hank!"

It was Gus who showed up first. "It's coming in through the wall," he said. "Can we get out through this way?"

"It's solid cinder block," Hank told him.

"But the water—"

"There's dirt on the other side," Hank insisted, but water was flowing in between the concrete blocks.

Above them Maggie thought she could hear engines roaring. Ryder had mentioned they were bringing in large equipment to help move the debris off of them.

"Here we go again," Hank yelled. "Everyone take cover."

She realized her mistake when the floorboards started shaking. It wasn't heavy equipment. It was another tornado.

62

"Can't you drive any faster?" Creed told Jason at the same time he looked back to make sure Grace and Scout were okay. Both had their heads down, but their eyes watched their owners.

Dr. Avelyn had loaned them a crate for Grace when it became obvious the little dog was not going to stay without Creed. And it was already obvious Creed wasn't going stay no matter what the good doctor said.

In the side mirror, Creed could see the sky lightening behind them, but they were heading into darkness. He hoped they were following behind the storm and not driving straight into it.

"Here's my cell phone," Jason handed it to him. "See if you can bring up some radar. I don't want another son of a bitch sneaking up on us."

They hadn't been able to find Creed's cell phone. Even the GPS watch Maggie had given him for his birthday had been stripped off him along with his shirt. He had put on a fresh T-shirt before leaving the hotel room, but wanted to rip it off, because it pressed against the pine needles still impaling his back.

He checked first to see if Maggie had answered any of Jason's text messages. The last answer had come fifteen minutes ago. Creed sent another before he brought up the weather.

"Why did they think the fire was arson?" Creed asked.

"Sheriff Krenshaw said something about seeing a guy right before. One of the television stations left a video cam on the scene, and they have a live feed."

"Why would someone do that?"

"Crazy, right? Almost like he didn't want those people to be saved."

Creed punched the radio volume up. It was a woman meteorologist now.

"Again, we have a tornado on the ground. Those of you on the south side of Montgomery, you should already be taking cover. This one looks like it's following the same path of the tornado that hit Sterling Ridge and the Southern Blessings restaurant earlier today. I know some of you have already sustained damage to your homes. Go to a neighbor's. Take shelter. Do not try to drive or outrun this. Get somewhere safe. Do it now."

Creed turned the volume down.

"It's going to hit the restaurant, again," he said, staring ahead as if expecting to see the tornado reveal itself right in front of them.

"There's nothing we can do about it," Jason told him. "These bastards keep dropping out of the sky all over the place."

"What about Brodie and Hannah?" Creed couldn't believe he'd forgotten to check on them.

"They're okay," Jason reassured him. "I talked to Hannah just a bit ago. Only thunderstorms. Lots of rain. They still had electricity. They're all watching old home movies your mom brought with her."

"They're doing what?"

"Watching old home movies."

"I didn't know we had any." For a second or two he wished he were back there watching with them.

"Is this the exit?" Jason asked.

Creed could see the snapped electrical poles and broken pine trees. They were the new landmarks in a horizon that had been scrubbed of its usual ones. He nodded.

Jason took the exit, slowed and came to a full stop at the intersection despite there no longer being a stop sign. When he turned, he slowed again. Then stopped. Creed didn't have to ask why. They were far enough away that they were safe, but close enough to see the debris spewing out of the black.

"Son of a bitch," Jason said, "Looks like it's already hitting them."

63

Maggie yelled over the thunder. She gestured and directed whoever would listen to get back against the far wall. They needed to get out from under the cracking floorboards. And they needed to do it quickly.

It sounded like the storm was picking up objects and flinging them back down. The monster clawed and bashed, almost as if it was purposely trying to finish them off.

Debris rained from the ceiling. Beams groaned overhead. Maggie didn't dare look up. She knew there was no way this basement could sustain the collapsing structure and all those heavy kitchen appliances.

Gus had found dusty old tarps. Maggie held onto the ends while he unfurled each one, trying to cover the others. Stephanie screamed while her son tried to pull her under. Clara and Adele huddled together. Beth and Val made sure Ronald and Frankie were shoved against the wall, up out of the water on the wooden benches.

Gus and Max moved the tall wooden shelving unit, tilting it, creating a teepee to absorb the brunt of the falling debris. Then both men disappeared in the direction of the stairwell; still believing it would eventually become their best path for escape. At one time, Maggie may have agreed, but now in the hazy dim light, she didn't think any place was safe.

The ceiling was being ripped apart. Just as she found a corner of the tarp and started to get under, she saw a table come tumbling down. She leaned out of the way against the cold concrete blocks, but a heavy object slammed into her arm. She grabbed at the shooting pain.

Debris pelted her. Already she could feel the wind whipping and shredding the thin canvas. And in no time, she was drenched from the down pouring rain. In that brief moment, she realized something—she could breathe again. There was a gust of air, but it came with an electrical charge. And it carried in the odd mixture of pine trees and sulfur.

More debris crashed down. The concrete walls and floor vibrated. Maggie imagined them cracking and caving in around them. She thought she heard someone scream, but it quickly got lost in the roar of the storm.

She closed her eyes and slid to her knees, ignoring the cold water gushing around her. She remembered her initial reaction coming down here and realized it was coming true. They had gone underground hoping to escape, only to be buried alive.

64

Creed gritted his teeth as Jason followed a screaming ambulance. The kid was keeping a safe distance, pulling over whenever another rescue unit with flashing lights raced around them. He was doing a good job, and yet, Creed wanted to tell him to go faster.

Not being in the driver's seat only seemed to fuel his panic. It wouldn't let go of him. His hands clasped into fists, only interrupted whenever he scrubbed one of them over his face. His pulse raced. Sweat trickled down his back. He knew he was running on adrenaline. Evidently, not enough because his chest still hurt, and he swore his head was going to explode for a second time in the same afternoon.

Creed kept checking Jason's cell phone. It had a signal. A strong signal, but there wasn't a new message from Maggie. He sent another text. He called her number hoping this time it would go through.

No such luck.

She was unreachable. His brain listed all the reasons why, and it kicked up an overwhelming sense of urgency in his gut.

"The mobile cell unit is probably flooded with calls," Jason told him, reminding him that the cell tower had been demolished in the earlier storm.

"The signal's strong."

He knew Jason was trying to stay positive, but Creed had glimpsed the white knuckles of his hand on the steering wheel. He was worried and anxious, too.

What Maggie had said earlier kept running through his mind. He could still hear the tension and fear in her voice. When he told her about more storms coming, she said she didn't think they could survive another hit.

They had been following the storm, driving into darkness. Headlights—their own and those racing to the scene—provided a limited view. There were no other lights. The electricity had blown out during the first hit. But now, the storm clouds moved on. The sky cleared, and it was still dark. Only then, did Creed realize the sun had already set.

Twilight cast shadows over the devastation making everything look worse. Soon the entire area would be pitch black. Vehicles lined the road, again, jockeying for a better position while trying to stay out of the way of rescue crews. State troopers were directing the chaos. In the glare of the headlights Creed recognized Trooper Sykes. He brought the Jeep's window down and waved to him. Sykes looked relieved to see someone he knew.

"Hello Mr. Creed. Mr. Seaver," he said as he bent down and glanced inside the Jeep. He took a second look at Creed and said, "What happened to you?"

"Got caught up in the storm, but I'm okay."

"Well you guys can relax. I don't think they'll be needing the dogs."

Creed's stomach took a nosedive. Did that mean everyone was okay, or that no one made it out? He tried to see over the hoods of vehicles in front of them.

"A couple of our friends were trapped in the basement of the restaurant," he told Sykes.

"Oh, I'm sorry. I didn't know that."

"How bad is it?"

The trooper straightened to his full height and glanced in the direction of where the restaurant used to be.

"Pretty bad."

"Mind if we go take a look?" Creed didn't like pressuring law enforcement to do him any favors. But he was already unbuckling his seatbelt and opening the door before Sykes could respond.

"Jason you mind staying with the dogs?" he asked as he closed the door

Sykes didn't argue. Instead, he looked back in at Jason and said, "If they ask you to move there's an empty lot right behind you to the east."

Creed remembered the phone and handed it back to Jason through the window.

"You sure you don't want to keep it?"

"No, that's okay." He stopped himself from saying the obvious. That Maggie and Frankie weren't texting or calling because they couldn't. One way or another, he wasn't going to leave until he found them.

"Come on," Sykes told him. "I'll take you in."

65

The storm finally stopped, though Maggie's ears were still ringing. It was dark and quiet, so very quiet…until the moans began.

She could hear the others shoving out from under the rubble. Objects skidded and banged. Someone was whimpering. Slices of white light flashed as cell phones were turned back on.

"Maggie?"

It was Frankie's voice, but she couldn't see her. Then she realized why. Only now did she feel the suffocating weight of debris on top of her. She arched her back. Pieces slid off. Something heavy still pinned her down.

Don't panic, she told herself.

Her knees were on the concrete. Water sloshed against her thighs. With the weight holding her down, she couldn't adjust herself to get her feet under her. She started to reach up. A sharp pain in her left arm stopped her. She tried again, and this time the pain shot down all the way to her fingers.

"She's over here."

Frankie was directing someone. And just then, Maggie felt the weight being peeled off of her, layer by layer. She pushed up, using her back and her right arm, helping shove off chunks. She heard and felt the objects. She still couldn't see. Little by little, her vision adjusted. The last layer was removed, and she finally stood straight. She was gasping for breath when she turned to find Hank and Ronald tossing aside a section of the floorboard. Both of them were covered in dust. Blood ran down Hank's bald head.

"You good?" he asked as he blinded her with his flashlight beam, running it over her to see for himself.

She started to answer and realized her mouth and throat felt like cotton balls were stuffed inside. She nodded, instead. Without a word, the two men moved on to the next pile of rubble where someone else was trying to crawl out.

It was almost impossible to move without slamming into something. Maggie looked up and every muscle in her body tensed when all she saw was murky black. And yet, she swore she could feel a breeze. The air felt different. How could the ceiling collapse down on top of them and not leave a gaping hole? Was it possible the storm sealed it back up with the wreckage from up above?

"Maggie, are you okay?"

In the dim light, she tried to follow Frankie's voice.

She coughed and managed to croak, "I'm okay. How are you doing?'

"Over here."

Maggie saw her waving her hand on the other side of the wooden shelf. She reached for her cell phone in the back pocket of her jeans. Her T-shirt was drenched. She'd lost her buttoned shirt, exposing her shoulder harness. A quick check made sure her revolver hadn't also been stripped away by the wind. Just lifting her left arm to adjust the holster sent a new wave of pain.

"You sure you're okay?" Frankie asked.

By now, some of the others were sending beams of light over the area. It was difficult to see around the collapsed debris. Maggie stepped carefully, trying to make her way to Frankie. The woman was still on the bench but one of her legs had slid off. She saw Frankie trying to lift the leg back up out of the water.

"Let me help you," Maggie said. Gently, she readjusted her.

Frankie was biting her lower lip, making it bleed. The pain had to be severe, still, she pointed to Maggie's forehead and said, "You're bleeding."

Maggie wiped at the sweat on her face. When she brought her fingers back, she saw blood. It didn't hurt. It was probably the cut from the first storm. She'd worry about it later.

Now that she had her bearings, she shot her cell phone's flashlight toward the stairs to see if the door had, at least, blown off. She waved the light back and forth then up and down before she realized the stairs were gone. In their place was something huge and stainless steel.

That's when she noticed a jagged hole in the ceiling. She could feel fresh air coming down from it, but there was only black on the other side. She shut her light off and tried to focus on the hole. She stared until she was convinced the dotted black was sky.

Yes, black sky with stars!

And she heard something or someone up above. Voices and engines.

Please be engines and not another storm.

She started looking for anything sturdy to help her crawl up, but quickly wondered if she could do that with only one hand.

Now, she noticed streams of lights up above.

"Is that lightning?" Frankie asked. She was searching the same spot.

From the other side of the debris pile, a woman's voice cried out, "Oh no! I think she's dead."

66

The closer they walked the more Creed thought the site looked like a giant meteor had hit the area. Trucks with generators pulled in front of them. Paramedics and firefighters were using headlights to find their way around the wreckage.

Creed remembered earlier there had been a concrete foundation along with a couple sections of teetering walls. And in the middle, right on top, the 18-wheeler had sprawled across the area, crumpled and surrounded by blue barrels tossed everywhere. Now there wasn't a sign of the truck or the trailer. And there was absolutely nothing that resembled a restaurant or even walls.

"There was a fire," Creed said to Trooper Sykes. Night had sneaked in around them, and in the stark light from the vehicles he couldn't tell whether the crater was scorched. "Did the fire do this?"

"Someone tried to set a fire. The HAZMAT team had sprayed foam on any of the spilled fuel."

"But there were barrels. Were they flammable?" Creed asked.

"That's what the arsonist must have thought."

"Vinegar and tomato sauce," someone said from behind them.

They turned to find Sheriff Krenshaw.

"In the barrels?" Sykes asked.

"Yep. Turns out those blue barrels are made of some poly-something-or-another that makes it safe to ship acidic foods. The asshole who tried to start them on fire didn't know that. Actually, I didn't know that until a few hours ago."

Creed couldn't take his eyes off the crater. Dust still filled the air. Pieces of debris floated in the streams of light.

"Have you heard anything from your friends?" Krenshaw asked.

"No. Nothing."

Creed shifted his feet, anxious to run to the edge and start pulling stuff off the piles. His jaw hurt from clamping it tight for too long. The panic churned in his stomach. Was it possible for anyone to survive that?

As if the sheriff could read his mind, he said, "They've already pulled two bodies from the wreckage. I don't know anything more than that, right now, but I thought you should know."

67

The black sedan was exactly where Rex said it would be. But where the hell was Rex?

Braxton kept to the shadows and weaved around the line of response vehicles. All of them were empty now. Sirens filled the air. Pieces of crap drifted on the breeze. His eyes felt like he had glass in them. The entire scene looked like a bomb had gone off. It reminded him of his past life. Something from El Salvador, Lebanon, Kosovo. And for a second time in as many days, he told himself that he was getting too old for this.

He opened the driver's door, reached in and popped the trunk. The blue duffle bag had been stuffed in a corner, and Braxton leaned all the way under the trunk lid to grab it. But he didn't pull it out right away. Instead, his eyes darted around. No one paid attention to him. He unzipped the bag and found what he wanted.

He needed a new strategy. One thing he'd learned all those years ago was how to change quickly, adjust and recalculate at a moment's notice. He had learned how to survive under the most impossible of circumstances.

Survival of the fittest.

The man Braxton worked for was a politician, and he had a sterile vision of what that phrase meant. The man was used to ordering others around. He hired people like Braxton to clean up his messes, so that he never got his hands dirty. He was so far removed from the carnage that the blood wasn't even real to him anymore. In his little world, he asked for something to be taken care of, and it was done. No questions. No consequences.

But after all these years, it never occurred to Braxton that his own loyalty and dedication would be paid back with betrayal. He didn't expect a gold watch, but he certainly didn't expect to be considered collateral damage.

That might be how you treat dinosaurs, but it wasn't how August Braxton was going to be treated.

68

Willis' drive down from Birmingham had been mostly a blur of urgency mixed with scattered downpours. He joined the WACL news crew outside their television van. This close, the wreckage looked so much worse than it did on the station's monitors. He couldn't take his eyes off of it.

They'd already heard that his wife was one of those trapped under the restaurant debris. Instead of exchanging looks of pity, they filled him in on what they knew so far. He appreciated that so much, he was moved speechless. His emotions were already running high. Just before he left the station, Paul told him he'd located Simon, the college storm chaser. Simon from Kansas. Someone had found his battered vehicle. He'd been taken to an area hospital, but his condition was critical.

The air was now so chilly Willis wished he had grabbed his jacket. He rolled down his shirtsleeves and accepted the take-out container of coffee, though his stomach churned with acid from a day filled with too much coffee.

"We're hearing there may be bodies," the news reporter named Chelsea told him.

"We don't know that for sure." Lawrence shot her a look over his shoulder as he raised the camera higher on its stand.

Willis had been told they were still filming, though the audio had been turned off. The station was carrying the live feed of the rescue while Mia continued with damage reports as they continued to come in.

At last count, seventeen tornadoes had been confirmed in Alabama alone, but Willis knew by the end of the night they would have reports of others. The fact that this area had been hit twice in the same day was not unusual, but it was always heartbreaking when it happened. They already knew of victims who had survived the first hit, only to die in the second. So he expected to hear it might be true at the restaurant site as well.

His eyes were glued to where the firefighters had brought two people up on a ladder they'd extended down into the hole. He couldn't stop thinking about his last conversation with Beth. He'd never heard her so frightened. What was worse was the humbling remorse in her voice. It was almost as if she thought she deserved this.

"Mr. Dean." A firefighter came around the van. He put up his hand to block Lawrence's camera and asked Willis to step aside with him.

Willis ran nervous fingers through his thinning hair. This was it. They must have found Beth. But how did they know she was his wife?

"Come with me, please," he told Willis.

Then he led him through a crowd of by-standers. He lifted the yellow perimeter tape and gestured for Willis to duck under.

"Your wife saw that you were with the news crew."

"Is she okay?"

"No broken bones. She has lots of bruises. A few cuts and scrapes. We're recommending she go to the ER. Make sure there's no internal bleeding. She insisted she wouldn't go without you."

"Really? Okay."

Willis didn't know what else to say. He was suddenly shaking, and not sure it was just the chilly air. In all his years as a kid fascinated by the weather then a storm chaser and a meteorologist, he'd never lost someone close to him. It occurred to him that he still loved his wife…very much. He wasn't ready to lose her. To a storm or to a divorce.

"You okay, Mr. Dean?"

"I'll be fine," Willis said. He pushed back his shoulders and followed the firefighter to the waiting ambulance.

69

Creed was pacing. He stayed back despite it going against his gut instinct. He wasn't law enforcement. He wasn't trained as a first responder. Usually, he did his job then moved himself and his dog out of the way so investigators could do their jobs. But this was different, and he felt completely helpless. Without his phone he couldn't even give himself the false sense of control by checking for unanswered texts.

Sheriff Krenshaw explained that they'd take digital photos of the bodies they'd found. Just the faces or what was left of them. He promised to let Creed know more as soon as he knew.

Trooper Sykes left to help secure the perimeter, and Creed could see that was becoming a challenge. A couple of television vans had parked as close as possible, setting up lights and cameras. It looked to Creed that they had reporters doing live broadcasts. A crowd of on-lookers—some of them family members—had also descended on the area. Law enforcement officers had their hands full keeping people out while escorting fire and rescue units.

All the while he kept thinking and hoping that Maggie might still be down in that hole. And what about Frankie? He knew she had been hurt.

The firefighters were bringing up another person. They had lowered a ladder and had already helped three people, two women and one teenaged boy. In the stark light of the portable floodlights each of them looked startled as they crawled out. This woman was covered in dust and dirt. As soon as she was on solid ground, someone wrapped her in a blanket and escorted her to the nearest rescue unit.

They continued to come up. Slowly. Some of them needed more assistance than others. Each time Creed saw a head emerge, his pulse raced faster. It was almost unbearable to watch. And each time, his hope would surge only to crash when he recognized it wasn't Maggie. His head still throbbed and his chest ached from his rollover. Dr. Avelyn had said he might have a concussion. When Sykes came by to check on him, Creed accepted the bottle of water the trooper offered.

He lost track of how many they had brought up. Then suddenly, the firefighters were pulling up the ladder.

That couldn't be all.

His heart was racing now. He had tried to block out the sirens and yells and calls of law enforcement and rescue crews. Suddenly, he strained to hear what they were saying. His eyes darted frantically for Krenshaw or Sykes. Before he could find either, he saw the firefighters exchanging the ladder for a stretcher. And this time, Creed felt his knees threaten to buckle underneath him.

"Hey," he heard someone behind him.

"Jason!"

"Don't worry, I left the windows partially opened and the doors locked. The dogs are good."

Only now did Creed realize the temperature had cooled. So much so, that his sweat-drenched body was chilly.

"I was listening on the radio," Jason said.

"You probably know more than I do."

"Seventeen tornadoes touched down today, just in Alabama."

Creed shot him a worried look.

"None in Florida," Jason added. Then he pointed. "Looks like they're bringing up someone strapped to a stretcher."

"This is driving me crazy."

"You're already inside the perimeter. What's stopping you from getting closer?"

He realized Jason was right. And yet, his feet stayed planted. Maybe he needed this safe distance.

"Come on," Jason told him.

The kid pulled down his cap and ventured closer.

"I think that's Frankie," Creed said, keeping up with Jason.

He could see the light shoot across her face as they carried her to a waiting ambulance. He was concentrating so hard on her that he didn't notice they'd lowered the ladder, again, for the last survivor.

"There she is," Jason said.

"You don't even know Frankie."

"No, Maggie. She just climbed out."

This time Creed didn't wait for permission. He started walking quickly before someone stopped him. His eyes stayed focused on her as if afraid she'd disappear from his sight if he glanced away for even a moment. Halfway there she noticed him, and a smile started slowly at the corner of her mouth. She did a one-shoulder shrug as if to say, "Can you believe this day!"

He broke into a jog the final yards, and the firefighter that had been escorting her, stepped to the side when he saw him coming. Creed grabbed her by the waist and his hug brought her feet off the ground. He kissed her long and hard before he released her. He heard her gasp then laugh.

"You taste like whiskey," he said, but then he saw the way her arm hung down at her side. She was holding it in place with her other hand.

"You're hurt! Are you okay? Did I just hurt you?"

"I don't think you would ever hurt me, Ryder Creed." She was still smiling even as she winced from the pain.

70

Maggie wanted Ryder to stay with her and Frankie in the ambulance, but they said there wasn't enough room. When she saw them working on Frankie, she didn't argue.

Ryder promised that he and Jason would meet them at the hospital. She traced the cuts and bruises on his face with her fingers and her eyes searched his.

"Are you okay? she asked.

"I am now," he smiled, taking her hand and kissing it then stepping back and letting them close the ambulance door.

Now here at the ER, she wished they'd let her stay with Frankie. They might have if Maggie had been better at hiding her own injury.

Ryder had texted her. He and Jason were making their way to the hospital, but the route was clogged with emergency vehicles.

She told him not to rush. To be careful. The hospital was packed. Most likely they'd be turned away to make room for storm victims and emergency healthcare personnel. A nurse had told her that the lobby was even being used as a prep and triage area.

Cell phone service was spotty. Calls wouldn't go through, so they continued to use text messages.

FRANKIE'S ALREADY IN ICU.

HOW ABOUT YOU?

THEY'RE TAKING CARE OF MY ARM RIGHT NOW.

She didn't, however, get a chance to tell Ryder how serious Frankie's condition was. The paramedic and the ER doctor tried to explain crush syndrome. Maggie thought she'd done the right thing by getting the beam off of Frankie's legs as quickly as possible. But it wasn't that simple. The impact, pressure and weight would have already damaged the muscle. When the compressive force was relieved, a cascade of events had begun with toxins from the damaged tissue's cellular components being released. This systemic release could ultimately be fatal resulting in renal failure, shutting down other organs and possibly even prompting a cardiac episode.

Maggie's undergrad included a minor detour in pre-med. But even so, down in that dark, sweltering bunker she never suspected any of this. And why would she? For a decade now, she looked after the dead, not the living.

The entire time her arm was being worked on, she was distracted by what she should have done differently. Finally, alone again as she waited between x-rays and what came next, she pulled out her cell phone and started reading through Agent Alonzo's messages. He'd linked a video from Detective Jacks in Chicago, and she debated whether she should watch or conserve her battery. Alonzo's text said:

THIS WAS TAKEN FROM A SECURITY CAMERA. NOT GREAT

BUT SHOWS GATES' ATTACKERS.

She texted him that she was out from under ground. Both her and Frankie. Then she asked:

ARE YOU STILL ABLE TO TRACK GATES' CELL PHONE?

If the men who were chasing Frankie had been watching the scene, they knew where Frankie had been taken. Her eyes darted around the small ER room looking for her weapon. They didn't make her get out of her T-shirt and don a gown, but she did have to remove her shoulder harness. Now, she suddenly felt naked without it.

Her phone dinged with Alonzo's response. Only then, did Maggie notice that it was almost midnight.

LOST IT WHEN THE STORM HIT.

She shouldn't have been surprised. It was difficult enough to have a conversation without the call getting dropped.

CALL ME WHEN YOU'RE ABLE TO. SOME INTERESTING

DEVELOPMENTS.

Why did people do that? Now all she wanted to do was call Alonzo. But first, she'd take a look at the video, if she could access it.

The connection was slow. A few seconds after the video started it stalled then began, again. Typical security footage. Grainy, but not jerky. No audio. From the angle she could watch the men approach from the opposite direction. Frankie was right. One of the men was huge. Square shoulders, no neck, a block for a head.

Both men wore jogging suits. Gates stopped to talk to them. A few seconds later, he put up his hand. The gun came up close to his forehead and Gates' head jerked back then he crumpled to the ground. A street lamp blocked part of the view. The other man cocked his head and pointed. He must have seen the earbud in Gates' ear.

The big guy kneeled to grab the phone while the other man backed away. Maggie had paid little attention to the other man, but now, she watched intently as his head swiveled casually and he started walking up the street.

She hit pause and started again. She zoomed in, zoomed out and started again. After the third time she knew she was right. She had to find Frankie and fast.

71

Frankie remembered the firefighter strapping her to the stretcher. He had gorgeous blue eyes and a calm, deep voice that made everything he said sound fascinating. She remembered the cool night air and how wonderful it felt even if it gave her goose bumps. But somewhere after her being loaded into the back of an ambulance, she lost her focus. She knew Maggie had crawled in beside her. She heard her responding to the paramedic's questions.

"How many hours? How much weight are we talking about?" the man wanted to know.

A blanket appeared, billowing up and draping over her body. An IV bag swung overhead. She hardly felt the needle, and she hated needles. A warm sensation seemed to flow through her veins almost immediately, but that's when her eyelids refused to stay open.

Now, as she tried to focus on her new surroundings she couldn't make her brain work. Machines hummed. IV lines trailed from her arm and disappeared somewhere above and behind her. She didn't have the energy to turn her head. She nodded off and jerked awake. How many times, she wasn't sure. Once or twice she thought she'd seen someone sitting in the chair over in the corner. But maybe that was a dream.

Nurses and doctors and techs came and went. Some of them had questions. Others worked around her silently. Every time the door opened she could hear—and sometimes glimpse—the chaos in the hallway. Then she drifted back to sleep.

All concept of time had gotten lost underground. Did the tornado happen a day ago? A week?

She woke bleary-eyed and feeling no pain. It took her a few seconds to notice the man standing over her. She saw the white coat and waited for his questions. He looked familiar when her eyes finally focused. His head cocked to one side while he examined her. It was the same way he'd looked at her the first time they'd met. Like he couldn't decide whether or not to be bothered with her.

"Hi Gus," she said.

Her voice was so quiet and weak she wasn't sure if he heard her, because he didn't say anything. Instead, he turned to someone behind him.

"Let's make this quick," he told a huge man with a blockhead and wide shoulders.

72

Creed didn't realize how bad he looked until he walked into the ER and a nurse said they'd take a look at him as soon as possible.

"No, I'm fine. But a couple of my friends came in by ambulance." He glanced at his wrist to check the time and remembered the tornado had taken his watch. "Maybe an hour ago. One was brought on a stretcher. The other had a broken arm."

"Sorry sir. You have any idea how many people fit that description tonight?"

He glanced around, frustrated and noticed the television in the ER waiting area. On the screen was a replay of the rescue efforts from earlier. He gestured toward the TV.

"They were part of the group trapped in the restaurant debris."

"Okay, hold on. I do remember. We transferred the rhabdomyolysis to ICU."

"The what?"

"ICU's on the second floor." And she was gone, hurrying down the hallway.

He weaved between the gurneys and wheelchairs filled with storm victims—broken, bloodied and impaled. Before he reached the elevator he realized how lucky he'd been to have only pine needles driven into his back.

"Ryder?"

In the fluorescent light, Maggie looked pale. Her hair still had chunks of drywall and pieces of glass. Her arm was in a sling. Her eyes were darting everywhere, like she was looking for someone.

"I need to find Frankie. We got separated."

"I think she's up on the second floor in ICU."

Maggie punched the elevator button even though it was already lit from Creed pressing it just a second ago. He'd seen her like this before. Though exhausted, she was in high alert. Something was wrong.

"What is it?" he asked when the door finally opened and she rushed inside.

"The men who are trying to kill her," she said in a low voice as she waited impatiently for the elevator door to close. "I know who one of them is."

73

It was the man with the scar. Frankie recognized the caveman forehead, his hawk nose and black eyes. He wore a white coat, just like Gus.

She couldn't move. Her hands grabbed for the bed rail. She wasn't strong enough to pull herself up. She didn't know what to push to call for help.

"Gus, what's…what's going on?"

Her voice was so quiet, so weak. And yet, she was exhausted from the effort.

But Gus had moved away from the bed. She couldn't see him anymore. Had he left the room?

The man with the scar scowled at her as he pushed the needle of a syringe into a small bottle. He was filling it.

"No, wait! What are you doing?"

Her heart was pounding. She tried to shove herself up, but there was no getting away from him. With the syringe ready, he looked at the intravenous port on her hand then at the IV bag up above her, searching the best place to insert it.

From somewhere inside the room there was a muffled pop-pop. The big man's head jerked. Frankie couldn't take her eyes off the needle to look for the sound.

Then she glanced up to see why he stopped. His eyes stared straight ahead. His hand dropped the syringe. He fell forward. His body thumped against the bed before he crashed to the floor.

When Frankie looked up, she saw Gus still holding the gun. She closed her eyes and braced herself for the next shot. Maybe it was the drugs. Maybe she'd wake up and find out she had hallucinated the whole thing.

"Frankie? You okay?"

"What happened?"

She opened her eyes to find Ryder and Maggie running through the door.

Gus was gone. Or maybe he'd never been there.

"He's dead," she heard Ryder say. He was kneeling next to the giant on the floor.

So it was real. But she was still alive. She looked to Maggie and met her eyes.

"It was Gus," she whispered to her.

"I know." To Ryder, she said, "Stay with her." Then Maggie took off out the door to go after him.

74

Braxton watched as she came racing out the nearest exit. He rubbed a hand over his jaw and pulled the ball cap lower. FBI agent, Maggie, had good instincts. Her head pivoted in all directions. Her eyes darted around. She came to a stop and turned a full circle taking in the chaos, searching for him. Her left arm was in a sling. She no longer wore her shoulder holster, and she didn't have her weapon. Yet here she was chasing after him.

Rescue units weaved their way out of the emergency bays and left the parking lot making way for those arriving. Injured storm victims staggered from their vehicles with the help of family or friends who were also bloodied. Braxton watched Agent Maggie's head swiveling back and forth. She was checking every face, looking around corners and hurrying up and down aisles of vehicles. At one point, she dropped to her knees to glance under a row of cars.

But she didn't consider checking the ambulance driving right by her.

He glanced at her one last time in the rearview mirror as he drove out of the hospital parking lot. He and Rex had left the sedan two blocks away. He'd be inside it and catching the interstate by the time they discovered the ambulance missing.

Now he drove the sedan to a busy drugstore parking lot. He wrapped the stolen white jacket around the Ruger SR22 pistol with the sound suppressor intact. Later he'd drop it in a river, two or three states away. It didn't matter. The gun would never be traced back to him. Besides, he had other things to take care of first, and he didn't have much time. If this was going to work at all, he needed to move quickly. Otherwise, they would hunt him down and then send someone else to eliminate Francine Russo.

Braxton and Rex had been hired to do whatever was necessary to keep secret the information that Tyler Gates and his friend, Deacon Kaye had hacked into. The only reason Braxton targeted Frankie Russo was because she may have seen the compromised emails, and she could recognize Rex.

Now, she knew his face, too.

In a day or two, Agent Maggie would probably know exactly who he was. But Braxton planned to be long gone. He'd already prepared. His go-bag was stashed inside the trunk with passports and credit cards. At three different banks across the country he had safe deposit boxes under as many different aliases stuffed with more documents and enough cash to retire anywhere he chose. And that's exactly what he planned on doing.

But first, he needed to make sure he wouldn't be killed, or worse, have a price put on his head. He'd need to play the game better than the man he worked for.

The man Braxton had worked for and killed for had crossed the line when he gave Rex the orders to set a fire on top of the restaurant ruins. The man Braxton had given his dedication and loyalty to for almost a decade had repaid that loyalty by considering Braxton collateral damage in order to make sure Russo didn't make it out alive.

And Rex...Braxton shook his head. He still couldn't believe Rex had betrayed him.

So what was the best way to stay alive now? He needed to make sure those secrets that were worth killing for, were no longer secrets.

DAY 3

Sunday, March 10

75

Maggie was on her second doughnut. It was hard to believe that only eighteen hours ago she and Frankie had met for lunch at Southern Blessings. It felt like a lifetime ago.

Around six in the morning, Jason and Ryder had left to take care of Grace and Scout. The two of them had come back with dozens of doughnuts. Ryder had pulled out two especially for her. She couldn't remember telling him that her favorite was a cake doughnut with chocolate frosting. The two men had left, again, to distribute the rest to staff and family members in the ER and ICU waiting areas.

Earlier in the wee small hours of the morning—after things had settled down, after Frankie was resting without a dead man at the foot of her bed and after Maggie's arm had finally been taken care of—Maggie and Ryder sat in one of the waiting rooms down the hall from the ICU unit. Neither could sleep. She told him about Gus and how she'd identified him from the street cam video. She told him everything she could remember that Alonzo had discovered. Then Ryder shared with her what information he had learned from Sheriff Krenshaw about the others who had been trapped with her and Frankie.

Six people were dead. The waitress who hadn't gone down into the basement was found with two other women: a kitchen staff worker and the hostess. Two unidentified men were found crushed when heavy kitchen appliances had fallen into the stairwell.

"Max and Loverboy," Maggie said. "They kept thinking that would be the only exit."

"*Loverboy?*" Ryder had asked.

"I never knew his name. There was a woman with him before the storm hit. Beth. She'll be able to identify him."

The last was one of the older women.

"Clara or Adele?" she asked, but Ryder didn't know for sure.

Together they had watched the sunrise, though their view was over one of the hospital's parking lots. Maggie couldn't believe how incredibly blue the sky was. Not a cloud in sight. The television in the corner had been muted but the weather map for the coming week showed temperatures in the upper fifties and lower sixties, and no sign of another storm. She remembered Stephanie's outrage about the weather, and Maggie had to agree: this was a bit crazy.

It was in that early morning quiet when Ryder told her he and Jason would need to leave for Florida. Since he totaled his Jeep, they were down to one vehicle.

"What happened to your Jeep?" she asked him.

"It's a long story." He smiled and shook his head. Instead of attempting to tell the story, he said, "Hannah's anxious to get up here and be with Frankie. They've been friends for a long time."

"I know," Maggie said. "I'm glad she has someone like Hannah."

Ryder explained that he and Jason would stay with Hannah's boys. He didn't need to say that he was worried about Brodie. She could see it on his face. He had made sure that Maggie was taken care of. That she was safe. But he had other obligations to the other people in his life. He wouldn't be the man she knew and cared about, if he didn't leave her to go take care of his family.

At the time, they'd been sitting side by side, and she reached over and took his hand. There would be no declarations of their emotions or feelings. There wasn't a need for words. And it didn't feel like a copout. It simply felt right.

"We really need to stop spending so much time in hospitals," she told him.

Now, Maggie found a quiet corner with an outlet for a borrowed cell phone charger. A couple of hours after her unsuccessful search for Gus, her phone's battery had finally died.

The dead guy at the foot of Frankie's bed allowed Maggie to justify 24/7 protection for Frankie. The sheriff departments for several counties were still overwhelmed with the aftermath of the storms, so Agent Alonzo managed to get agents from one of the FBI's field offices in Alabama. Two of the men had arrived at three in the morning. Maggie was impressed. She didn't think Assistant Director Kunze would approve. She was anxiously waiting to hear how Alonzo had pulled it off.

She finally had the small waiting area all to herself. It felt too empty without Ryder. She watched the flat screen TV on the wall. They had left it muted with the closed captions crawling across the bottom. The local news was talking about a special report the station would be doing tonight. It would include details from one of their storm chasers who had survived his vehicle being sucked up into the storm.

When her phone rang, she grabbed it, sitting awkwardly so she could leave it plugged in.

Instead of a greeting, Alonzo said, "Are you near a television?"

"Yes," she told him. "What's going on?"

"Turn it to one of the cable news stations."

She found the remote and channel surfed until she found one. A news anchor was talking about Carson Foods. Photos of the CEO, a couple of his executives and Senator John Quincy were lined up in the upper corner of the screen.

"Someone leaked a bunch of emails to the *New York Times*," Alonzo told her. "In the emails, Carson Foods' CEO admits to Senator Quincy that the levels of glyphosate are too high. But he tells him not to worry. He can control the reports and the test results, so their global initiative can go forward. Maggie, these leaked emails look exactly like the ones Tyler Gates and his buddy hacked into."

"But how do you know that?"

"Because I'm looking at what Gates sent to Russo's email account right now. He must have had it sent with a time delay. His email with the attached files only showed up in her email account early this morning."

"Do you think Gates sent the emails to the *Times* with a time delay, too?"

"It's possible. But from what I'm hearing, they have actual copies of the tests results and other reports that I'm not seeing in Russo's attachment. They say they have evidence that Carson Foods changed the lab results. And they have emails saying they had to change results or risk losing billions of dollars, because the company already had products waiting to ship as part of this global initiative. I think it must be someone from the inside who had access."

Maggie immediately thought of Gus. Alonzo hadn't been able to find out who he was. The only link they had was the black sedan's license plate number, and Alonzo claimed it didn't exist.

Just then, she noticed A NEWS ALERT flashed across the bottom of the television screen. A national recall was being issued for products made by Carson Foods, and the specific cereals and breakfast bars were listed, one by one. There had to be over a dozen of them. The alert claimed that it would be the largest food product recall in history.

"Word is the CEO will be announcing his resignation by the end of today," Alonzo said. "Through the grapevine, I've heard that Senator Quincy is being pressured to do the same."

Maggie realized this was the political fallout that evidently had been worth killing for. With the secret exposed, hopefully Frankie would be safe.

"There's something else, Maggie," Alonzo said. "This hasn't hit the news yet, and no one except you and me might make the connection."

"What is it?"

"Assistant Director Kunze resigned this morning."

76

Florida Panhandle

Creed hated leaving Maggie, but there was no question that he would go home and take care of things for Hannah, so she could be with her friend. Creed and Hannah had been each other's family for over seven years. He'd mow down mountains before he'd let Hannah down. And now, he felt the same way about Brodie.

By the time Jason and Creed left Montgomery, Frankie's doctor sounded more optimistic. She was starting to feel her legs. Her kidney levels were holding steady. Creed didn't fully understand all the complications of her condition, but he knew Frankie's recovery would benefit from having her friend by her side.

What Creed didn't expect was to find Hannah already gone when he got home. Jason took Grace and Scout to the fenced yard behind Hannah's house. Creed was pleased to see Grace prancing along, tail wagging. She was glad to be home and already back to telling Scout that she was the boss of him.

He was smiling to himself when he walked in the back door and found his mother in the kitchen. She had an apron on and was chopping vegetables at the center island. Lady and Hunter came to greet him then quickly returned to their spot at his mom's feet, waiting and hoping for something to drop.

"Mom?"

"Don't be mad," she glanced at him then focused on her chopping. "I'm the one who talked Hannah into leaving earlier. I wanted to be sure she'd make it to Montgomery before dark."

His mind got snagged on the fact that she thought he might get mad. At the same time, he realized why Hannah hadn't told him about his mother staying. She wouldn't want him to worry about Brodie.

"Whatever you're fixing smells good," he told her.

"It's a stew for tomorrow. We've already had dinner. Did you boys eat, yet?"

"We did."

Then she looked up, really looked at him. "Ryder, are you okay?" She put the knife down and started around the counter, stopping short of touching him but clearly concerned about the bruises and cuts on his face.

"I'm okay. Really, it looks worse than it is." He wanted to change the subject. "Where are the boys and Brodie?"

"They're watching a movie. Something animated that Hannah's already approved."

She stared at him for a bit longer then went back to her chopping board, as if all this was perfectly normal for her to be preparing meals in his kitchen. Correction, Hannah's kitchen. The two women had easily and quickly become friends, though they'd only just met last fall.

"Brodie, too?" he asked. Something felt wrong.

"Oh, I'm sorry. She was watching the movie with the boys, but she took the cat for a walk." She glanced up, again, as if she may have missed something. "Hannah said she takes the cat everywhere. But do you walk a cat?"

"Yep, she does." Still, something kicked in his gut. "I'm just anxious to see her. Maybe I'll go see if I can find her."

He left before his mother saw his alarm. He wasn't sure why he was feeling so uneasy. Since she arrived, Brodie had been free to walk anywhere she wanted on the property, and yes, sometimes she took Kitten with her. They'd warned her about bears, and she never wandered into the woods by herself. If anything, she was extra cautious.

But the nightmares had returned. She'd been stressed about their mother's visit. First, Creed had left her, and then Hannah. Her therapist had warned Creed that things could come crashing down with little warning. He had a bad feeling that Brodie might have left the house because she needed to get away.

He noticed a light on in the fieldhouse. It wasn't quite dark, yet, but the high windows didn't allow much light after the sun started to sink. As soon as he opened the door, he heard water sloshing around, and he felt the panic.

The first thing he saw was the cat sitting on the edge of the pool, watching. It took Creed a few seconds for his eyes to find Brodie in the water, clear on the other side. He saw someone beside her and immediately started kicking off his shoes. He was ready to dive in when she saw him and waved. And suddenly, he got a good look at who was swimming beside her.

The big, pewter-colored dog paddled as Brodie steered him toward the steps. Creed walked—trying hard not to run—to meet them. But Brodie was already helping Knight as he stutter-stepped up the pool steps. She came up with him, her arm wrapped firmly around him. Her arms were longer than he realized. Longer and stronger.

She grinned at Creed, proud of herself.

"Did you see how brave he is?" she asked.

He smiled and nodded.

The last two days Creed had witnessed so much death and devastation. There were so many victims picking up the scraps of their lives. But he and Grace had discovered a miracle in Baby Garner.

Hannah said it was a miracle that Maggie and Frankie had crawled out from under the ruins. They had been threatened and battered by the storms, and they had survived.

Now, as he watched Brodie toweling off Knight and making sure the dog was okay, Creed realized Jason was right. Despite fighting her own storm, Brodie was stronger than any of them believed. Strong and brave.

Of course, she was. *She was a survivor, too.*

Author's Note

Growing up in Nebraska, has given me a healthy respect for the weather. When you live in Tornado Alley the threat of tornadoes is a constant reality. I know what it feels like to take shelter from a storm; I've seen the aftermath firsthand; and once, I even outran a tornado. I don't mind admitting, that just like Hannah Washington, tornadoes scare the bejesus out of me.

We have amazing advanced technology. With a tap of a button we can send a text message across the world. Drones can give us a birds-eye view of places unreachable. DNA testing is answering questions we never thought possible. But we still can't predict exactly when and where a tornado will form.

Does that surprise you? It surprised me. I didn't realize that radar doesn't actually detect tornadoes. It only detects the "conditions" known to be present. Radar can't even confirm a tornado. Meteorologists depend on what they call "ground truth," which is exactly what it sounds like. A tornado is confirmed when a storm chaser or storm spotter has actually seen it, observed it and provided real time critical information. In fact, meteorologists admit that supercells that produce tornadoes look almost exactly like supercells that do not.

So why write about something that scares me? Tornadoes have been observed on every continent, in every American state, at every hour of the day and every month of the year. I'm guessing that means I'm far from alone in my fear. I imagine that many of you have experienced this weather phenomenon or you know someone who has. Perhaps some of you are like me and are simply fascinated as much as in total awe.

Readers often ask how I come up with my ideas. With every new book, I try to cover something different: human trafficking, the bird flu, contamination of our foods, or the everyday struggles of our veterans. I'm not interested in following the latest genre trend or duplicating current bestsellers. Most of all, I want my readers to be entertained, to connect to the characters, and come along for an adventure. And for the Ryder Creed series, I'm always looking for new ways to show off the numerous talents of scent detection dogs.

Dogs can sense storms, not only the changes in barometric pressure, but they can smell the ozone in the air from lightening and the other scents associated with approaching storms. There's even some speculation that dogs can detect earthquakes before they occur.

But for *Desperate Creed*, I wanted to concentrate on how amazing scent detection dogs are in finding victims after natural disasters when every minute counts. Some of the stories are truly miracles. I can't tell you how many true accounts I read about babies and toddlers being found after tornadoes, not just in the wreckage, but sometimes hundreds of feet from their homes—in one case almost a mile away.

If there's anything in the book that you think sounds too crazy or too unbelievable, let me assure you, all the stranger-than-fiction tornado incidents came directly from real life accounts. This was one of those times when my research exceeded what I needed. I watched videos of tornadoes and listened to victims' stories. I read several books and dozens of articles. Usually I fill two notebooks. This time I ended up with four.

So why isn't this book set in Nebraska? Two reasons. First, I needed Ryder to stay close to home for Brodie. During my research I discovered Dixie Alley and learned that Alabama was one of the top five states with the most fatalities and injuries from tornadoes. Just the sight of a tornado is frightening, so I can't imagine one wrapped in rain and hidden behind forests until the very last minute.

The second reason I didn't choose Nebraska is a bit selfish. Things I write about tend to come true. Yes, that might sound a bit silly, but while I was finishing the book an outbreak of tornadoes hit the exact location in Alabama that I had chosen, and on the exact date. Twenty-three people were killed. It unnerved me so much that I changed my setting from Lee County to Butler County. I also moved my timeline from the first weekend in March to the second. And I changed my tornado to hit the interstate instead of the small town I'd originally chosen.

Many of you who have been reading my books for years, know that I like to use real places and oftentimes, real businesses. But if you happen to be in Montgomery, Alabama, you won't find a meat-and-three named Southern Blessings even if it might seem very familiar. The restaurant is a figment of my imagination. I didn't have the heart to destroy a real café.

As for glyphosate showing up in our foods? I wish this wasn't true.

First, let me say that our farmers work hard to bring us the best and safest food supply in the world. Some of the processes and products were originally put in place to protect us as well as make production easier and faster.

The EPA insists the levels of glyphosate in our foods are safe, but at the same time, they don't deny that test samples have found the herbicide on sixty-three percent of corn samples and sixty-seven percent of soybean samples. Wheat and oats also use glyphosate as a pre-harvest drying agent, but the EPA hasn't released any of those test results. The EWG (Environmental Working Group) has done some of its own testing and has found glyphosate in a number of products from granola to pasta to cereal and breakfast bars. If you're interested in finding out more or seeing their list, you can go to this *USA Today* article: https://usat.ly/2BdHArq.

Glyphosate is the herbicide recently linked to cancer by the World Health Organization and also named in the lawsuits involving Monsanto's Round-Up.

Lastly, to all the readers who sent me messages worried that *Lost Creed* might be the end of this series with the rescue of Brodie, I hope this book assures you that there are many more stories to come. And I'm already hard at work researching *Hidden Creed*. If you enjoyed *Desperate Creed,* please tell a reader friend. That's actually the biggest compliment you can pay an author. And as always, I thank you for continuing to read my books.

Acknowledgments

I want to thank all my friends who put up with my long absences and help keep me grounded. Thanks to Sharon Car, Marlene Haney, Sharon Kator, Amee Rief, Maricela and Jose Barajas, Martin and Patti Bremmer, Leigh Ann Retelsdorf, Pat Heng, Doug and Linda Buck, Dan Macke, Erica Spindler, Dr. Elvira Rios, Luann Causey, and Christy Cotton.

Special Thanks to:

Deb Carlin and Prairie Wind Publishing for making the publication and distribution of this novel possible.

Dr. Enita Larson, for answering all my dog questions even in the middle of *"girls night out."* Also, I want to thank Dr. Larson, again, for allowing me to use her children's names for my veterinarian, Dr. Avelyn Parker.

Again, to James Rollins for an *awesome* quote.

Sandy Rockwood for lending her name to Brodie's therapist. I know you will gracefully accept the Ph.D. I just bestowed you.

All the booksellers, librarians, book clubs and book bloggers for mentioning and recommending my novels.

And huge thank you to all of my readers, VIR Club members, and Facebook friends. With so many wonderful novels available, I'm honored that you continue to choose mine. Many of you have been with me on this journey from the very beginning. Without you, I wouldn't have the opportunity to share my twisted tales.

Last, but never least, a huge thank you to my pack: Deb, Duncan, Boomer, Maggie and Huck. You guys are truly my heart and my soul.

RECOMMEND

DESPERATE CREED

FOR YOUR NEXT BOOK CLUB

READING GROUP GUIDE AVAILABLE AT

WWW.PWINDPUB.COM/READINGGROUPGUIDE